# The Woman in 3B

ELIZA LENTZSKI

Copyright © 2020 Eliza Lentzski
All rights reserved.

This is a work of fiction. All names, characters, places, and incidents are the products of the author's imagination or are used fictitiously. Any resemblance to events, locales, or real persons, living or dead, other than those in the public domain, is entirely coincidental.

No part of this book may be reproduced, re-sold, or transmitted electronically or otherwise, without written permission from the author.

ISBN: 9798649572828
Imprint: Independently published

# OTHER WORKS BY ELIZA LENTZSKI

*Don't Call Me Hero Series*

Don't Call Me Hero

Damaged Goods

Cold Blooded Lover

One Little Secret

+ + +

*Winter Jacket Series*

Winter Jacket

Winter Jacket 2: New Beginnings

Winter Jacket 3: Finding Home

Winter Jacket 4: All In

Hunter

http://www.elizalentzski.com

*Standalones*

The Woman in 3B

Sunscreen & Coconuts

The Final Rose

Bittersweet Homecoming

Fragmented

Apophis: Love Story for the End of the World

Second Chances

Date Night

Love, Lust, & Other Mistakes

Diary of a Human

+ + +

*Works as E.L. Blaisdell*

Drained: The Lucid (with Nica Curt)

## CONTENTS

| | |
|---|---|
| Chapter One | 1 |
| Chapter Two | 13 |
| Chapter Three | 25 |
| Chapter Four | 40 |
| Chapter Five | 52 |
| Chapter Six | 67 |
| Chapter Seven | 77 |
| Chapter Eight | 91 |
| Chapter Nine | 104 |
| Chapter Ten | 118 |
| Chapter Eleven | 129 |
| Chapter Twelve | 141 |
| Chapter Thirteen | 151 |
| Chapter Fourteen | 161 |
| Chapter Fifteen | 172 |
| Chapter Sixteen | 181 |
| Chapter Seventeen | 193 |
| Epilogue | 198 |

# DEDICATION

To C

# CHAPTER ONE

The giggling gave them away.

Even over the constant roar of the 747's turbofan engines, I could hear the mischievous laughter of two people who knew they were doing something that they shouldn't have been doing. It happened on at least one flight a month where a couple thought they were being original and unpredictable and spontaneous by squeezing into an airplane bathroom that was barely large enough for one body, let alone two.

I knocked briskly on the plastic bathroom door. The passengers were from my section of the plane, so it fell to me to get them back to their seats.

"Excuse me." My voice interrupted their clandestine actions. "You'll have to return to your seats. The captain has turned on the fasten seatbelt sign."

"Just a minute!" I heard a panicked, feminine voice. "I'll be right out!"

"Don't worry," I drawled, unamused. "I'll wait. Right here."

Slight turbulence bumped and shook the plane, but my legs automatically tensed and I naturally shifted my weight from one foot to the other, like balancing on a boat at sea.

I heard the sounds of shuffling and frantic whispering before the bathroom door eventually unlocked and opened. A man exited, his dress shirt untucked in the front, followed by a woman in a similar state of fashion disrepair. They both ducked their heads and averted their gaze as they passed rather than acknowledge me.

"Thank you for your compliance," I stated in a too-loud voice.

My eyes followed their walk of shame down the left aisle of the wide-body plane and back to their assigned seats. It made me feel like a disapproving school teacher, or worse—a mom. But it was my job to babysit these people until we returned safely to the ground.

Once I was satisfied that the couple was securely fastened into their respective seats again, I returned to my place in the narrow galley at the front of the plane. My friends and fellow flight attendants, Kent and Gemma, were just cleaning up after our final beverage service of the flight.

"Do they really think no one will notice?" I huffed.

Kent, a small, angular man with fine blond hair and icy blue eyes frowned and wrinkled his nose. "I think that's the point—for everyone to know."

My other friend, Gemma, leaned against the beverage cart and sighed. "I don't know," she said, twisting her thick braid. "I think it's kind of romantic—not being able to keep your hands off each other; even for a two-hour flight."

"Yeah, *real* romantic," I scoffed. "Two hundred people listening to you have sex in a phone booth."

I couldn't be too upset with the couple, however. In fact, I was probably a little jealous.

I could understand the appeal. Once the plane reached a cruising altitude, we were all seeking some kind of release.

Takeoff was a little like foreplay—if you did it right. The engines hummed and turbines twirled. You coast, you glide, you bump along the tarmac. The wing flaps flex their reach. You pick up speed, teasing, not quite meaning it. Each little false acceleration builds the anticipation.

The plane pauses on the landing strip. It snorts and spews like a muscle-corded bull about to charge a matador. A low rumbling, the plane rolls forward, tentative at first, as if afraid of its own power. The engines grow louder. You spurt forward. Another false start.

You've been grounded for too long. The frustration grows. The engines scream to be free like a braying dog, pulling against the leash that tethers it in place, keeping it from what it most desires. The light touch on the brakes reminds you of the engines' explosive potential.

You sit. The plane shudders. The sounds of the engines grows louder again until they seem to swallow up all other noises. The voices in the plane are vanquished. It's so loud, you forget all other sounds.

The force of takeoff pins you to your seat. The pressure crushes down on your body as the airplane climbs and climbs. It feels unending. Eternal. Your body folds in on itself.

And then it's over. You level out. The unbearable weight lessens. The noisy world returns.

"Don't mind her," Kent's voice interrupted my thoughts. "She's still pining over Luscious Lara."

"Am not!" I hotly protested.

My friends had accused me of being in a bad mood ever since breaking up with another flight attendant: Lara Pierson. I couldn't really call it a breakup though since it hadn't exactly been a relationship. Rather than seriously dating, it had been a thrilling month of stolen moments in-flight and fiery overnight stays on three-day flights, but it had ended nearly as suddenly as it had started.

I hadn't fallen in love with Lara, but she'd certainly been exciting. With my rigid flight schedule, I doubted I would ever repeat those same kinds of experiences unless it be with someone else on the crew. But my airline employed very few female pilots and even less queer female flight attendants. The ratio tended to favor straight women and gay men, even in the flight deck.

"I don't even *like* women, and I would have hit that," Kent proclaimed.

"We had fun," I said stiffly. "But now we're on different schedules, so it's over."

"What does working the same line have to do with it? You know people *do* date people they don't work with, right?" Gemma posed.

"When's the last time you went on a non-work date, either of you?" I flipped the question on them.

"I don't date," Kent denied.

"I know. You only hook up with married, bi-curious pilots," I said, rolling my eyes. "And what's your excuse, Gemma?"

"I'm working on myself," she said in a matter-of-fact tone. "I'm focusing on my career and dating myself."

Kent snorted. "Every time you say that I'm convinced your luggage is just sex toys and lube."

"Be nice," I admonished.

"Thank you, Alice," Gemma said, sticking out her tongue at Kent.

"Besides," I continued, "we all know that can't be true." A mischievous grin found its way to my lips. "All that KY Jelly would have to be in three-ounce bottles in a clear quart-sized bag to get through airport security."

"Hey!" Gemma's mouth dropped open in shock before snapping back and finally settling into a sour, displeased look. "I really hate you guys."

The interphone in the front galley chimed and Kent was the first to reach it. The phones were located throughout the airplane, allowing the crew to speak to each other in the various cabins, as well as to reach the flight deck and pilots when the door was shut. Because Kent was the purser—the senior flight attendant who was technically in charge of the other crew—he made all of the in-flight announcements and attended to passengers in the First Class section.

"The captain's ready to begin landing," he said upon hanging up the interphone. "Alice," he told me, "you're on Crotch Watch in the Village. And Gemma, check on the U.M. in 25C."

Gemma beamed. She loved working flights with an U.M.—an Unaccompanied Minor. She did a great job with the crumb crunchers, giving them honorary pilot wings and pumping them full of sugary treats before reaching their final destination.

"Oh, and check your lips and tips, ladies," Kent reminded us.

I'd heard the reference to our fingernails and lipstick many times before. It was a gentle reminder that despite the 12-hour days, limited sleep, and hasty meals grabbed during short layovers, we flight attendants should aim to be flawless at all times.

I walked up and down the aisles while Kent made our final arrival announcement over the speaker system. Crotch Watch, also affectionally called a groin scan, referred to the rounds that flight attendants make prior to liftoff and right before descent that ensures that all passengers' seatbelts are on and properly fastened. I worked the Village on most of my flights—a reference to the Economy section of the plane.

Passengers dangled various garbage items in the aisle for me to pick up, even though I'd already been through the cabin multiple times with a proper garbage bag. It was one of the *many* things that annoyed me about customers. Why couldn't they remember to put their carry-on luggage in the overhead compartment with the wheels out? Was it really so hard to hold on to their jacket until everyone had boarded? And why couldn't they be bothered to remove their headphones and earbuds when they ordered a drink?

I passed the couple who had tried to join the Mile High Club. They had their heads bent towards each other conspiratorially; the whispering and giggling hadn't stopped from earlier. I considered giving them a break by just continuing to walk on by, but I couldn't help myself. I stopped in the aisle and spun around to face them.

"I hope you enjoyed your flight," I grinned knowingly.

The couple looked up simultaneously at my words; both appeared a little like deer caught in headlights. I knew I was embarrassing them, but I couldn't resist teasing them, just a little.

The man was able to find his voice first: "Oh, uh, yes," he sputtered. "Yes, it was very good, thank you."

I leaned a little closer to the two and they perceptively straightened in their seats.

"A tip for the future?" I offered, lilting my voice. "Wait until the drink trolley goes by before you try that little stunt again. The flight attendants will be too busy to notice you're both gone."

+ + +

The bingo card was waiting for me in my mailbox in the flight attendant lounge. It was the end of the work day, but Kent, Gemma, and I routinely stopped one more time in the lounge to see if we'd received anything from the airline before we'd catch a shuttle that would take us to the employee parking lot.

"Purser alert," I heard Kent's quiet warning. Kent was technically a purser himself, but he also wasn't a narc.

I discretely slipped the bingo card into my purse without looking at it. The competition was an open secret, but the higher ups at the airline probably wouldn't have been happy to acknowledge its existence. I'd have to look over my seat assignment and monthly challenges later.

Every month a new bingo card was anonymously delivered to the mailbox of every flight attendant across the company who paid their twenty dollar entrance fee. Twenty-five different challenges, at various levels of difficulty, had to be accomplished and confirmed within a month's time. Some of the challenges could be fulfilled at the airport, but most occurred in-flight. At the end of the month—

like the lottery—if no one had filled out their card entirely, the pot of money continued to grow.

I didn't recognize the woman whom Kent had alerted me about. I'd been with the same airline for nearly eight years, but it wasn't unusual not to know the other flight attendants with whom I worked. You could work really intimately with your assigned crew for a three-day trip and then you might never see them again.

She was an older woman with silver hair—a senior mama—a term used by flight attendants, but not unkindly. Her kind were a rarity in my line of work. There were no longer age restrictions for flight crew, but you still needed to be strong enough to help passengers stow their carry-on luggage in the overhead compartments. She didn't greet either Kent, Gemma, or myself, but went about her business of checking her mailbox before leaving the lounge.

I waited to be sure the older woman had exited the lounge for good before I pulled the bingo card from my purse.

My eyes fell first to the number and letter printed at the top of the card. "Damn it," I mumbled.

Gemma and Kent crowded around me and the cardboard bingo card.

"What's wrong? Did you get a shitty card this month?" Kent asked.

I curled my lip. "I'm not going be able to complete the seat-specific squares. They gave me 3B."

I thought the most difficult squares were those that were seat specific. Those were the challenges that could only be accomplished through the passenger sitting in that specific seat. 3B was in the First Class section of the plane. I wasn't a rookie at my airline, but I also didn't have enough time in to be the senior flight attendant—the purser—on my flights. I typically worked the Economy section on a three-person flight crew.

Kent sighed loudly. "Fine," he huffed. "I'll let you work First Class on our flights this month. But *don't* make a habit out of this," he warned with a shake of his finger. "Seniority should count for something."

"You're such a martyr," I teased. "But thank you."

"I don't know why you waste your time. It's a total racket," Kent opined. "You might as well spend your entrance fee on scratch-off Lotto tickets. It's less work, too."

"It's harmless," I stubbornly defended. "And it keeps me entertained. I'd probably hang myself during beverage service without it."

"I think it's kind of mean," Gemma spoke up. "Spilling a drink on someone on purpose?"

"It's not like it's hot coffee, Gemma," I continued to defend myself and the game. "It's just a little innocent fun."

I didn't particularly like the idea of the bingo card either, but the financial incentives were enough to make me momentarily forget the questionable ethics of it all. The winnings would be enough to pay off my two years of ill-advised college attendance. The only thing I'd really learned in those years of extra schooling was that not everyone was cut out for college. I wished my high school guidance counselors would have told me that; it would have saved me about forty thousand dollars.

"I still don't like it," she frowned.

Gemma had a singular talent for making me feel guilty, even if I hadn't done anything wrong. She was a rule follower, unbending and disapproving. I couldn't understand why she'd become a flight attendant; she acted more like a Sunday School teacher.

"What are they having you do this month?" Gemma asked. She didn't drop her defensive posture, but the judgmental look on her round face softened.

For someone so concerned about rules and regulations, I thought Gemma secretly loved it when I first got my bingo card. She was less excited, however, when I actually began to complete the tasks.

"Some of the usual," I noted. "Bump into a passenger when there's no turbulence. Use a fake accent all flight. Wear a life preserver until someone says something." I wrinkled my nose as I read the next task. "Assist a puking passenger is the center square again."

"Stop withholding," Kent censured. "What are the naughty challenges?"

I scanned over the twenty-five bingo squares and their twenty-five unique tasks. I read aloud the red colored squares that typically indicated a more challenging task: "Get a passenger's phone number. Get a passenger to buy you a meal." I stopped when my eyes fell on the next red square.

Gemma read aloud the square on which I'd paused: "Join the Mile High Club?!"

"At least it's not seat specific," I weakly remarked, despite how my stomach churned.

"Whoever comes up with these challenges has gone way too far this time," Gemma huffed. She hugged herself and continued to look upset. "It's basically prostitution."

"It's just a game," I tried to reason with my friend. "I'd never do something I wasn't comfortable with. I'll just aim for completing one row so I make my money back. Then I'll hope for a better card next month."

"It's totally sexist," Kent piled on.

"Oh really? How so?" I posed. Kent's complaint was a new one. I was intrigued to hear his argument.

"The challenges are much easier for women to achieve," he argued. "How would a male flight attendant ever accomplish the Mile High Club task?"

"You mean how would a *straight* male flight attendant do that," I chuckled. "You get so much ass, Kent, don't even deny it. I should be the one complaining about bias. As a lesbian, *I'm* at a complete disadvantage."

"If you'd stop being so damn picky," Kent proclaimed, "you'd probably have the whole thing won by now. Lower your standards, honey," he advised. "People do it all the time for less."

I shook my head. "I'm not going to whore myself out to win at bingo."

"You're not winning bingo; you're winning money," he pointed out. "Cold. Hard. Cash."

Gemma interrupted our juvenile bickering before it could escalate. Conflict made her itch: "You guys want to do something tonight?"

"Can't," Kent clipped. "I'm having spaghetti." He wiggled the fingers on his right hand in parting. "See you grandmas tomorrow."

Kent sashayed out of the flight crew lounge, leaving Gemma and me on our own.

"Kent sure eats a lot of pasta," Gemma observed with a wistful sigh. "I wish I could have carbs."

Gemma was perpetually on the quest to lose five pounds. I thought her curves were sexy, but I could appreciate her concern. In our profession, every little extra bit on your body added to the overall claustrophobia of the galley.

I cocked an eyebrow at my friend and laughed. "You know that's not what he's talking about, right?"

"Huh?"

"He's probably hanging out with one of his married pilot friends. Spaghetti is code," I supplied. "Straight until they get wet. Straight until they get a few drinks in them."

"Oh. *Oh*," Gemma blinked rapidly as the realization set in. "That makes so much more sense."

I couldn't understand Kent's near-obsession with sleeping with married pilots. For one, they were married. How could your conscience ever forgive that kind of behavior? For the other, pilots were notoriously cocky. Confidence was attractive, but most of the pilots I'd met over the years were ego-maniacs.

*How many pilots does it take to change a light bulb?*

*Just one. He holds the bulb and the world revolves around him.*

"What are you doing tonight?" Gemma asked. "Are you having 'pasta,' too?" She highlighted the euphemism with air quotes.

I snorted at the suggestion. "Not likely. The only pasta I'm eating these days comes out of a little blue box."

+ + +

"Honey, I'm home!"

I shut my apartment door with my foot since my hands were busy with grocery bags. I only went shopping once a month, mostly for non-perishables and a gallon of milk whose expiration date I considered as a recommendation, not the end all, be all.

My apartment wasn't much, but I didn't spend too much time at home anyway. At least I actually had a home though. I knew some people who had crashpads around the country instead of renting a proper apartment. Crashpads could be a house or an apartment with bunkbeds in each room. For a couple hundred bucks a month you could have a place to stay if you weren't keen on the commuting life.

I had lucked out that the city in which I lived—Romulus—was a central hub for my airline. Despite its name, Detroit Metropolitan Wayne County Airport was actually located in Romulus, Michigan—a small city about twenty miles west of downtown Detroit. The airport was the busiest in the state and one of the largest airports in the country. My own airline operated over one hundred gates in two different terminals.

I knew a few others whose home airport was also Detroit Metro, but they commuted to a different city in a different state to go home. They always seemed overtired and overstressed. Commuting took a lot of planning and your schedule could be ruined with a simple weather delay.

Even without commuting, our work hours were long. In a month, I typically spent between 65 to 90 hours in the air with another 50 hours of preparing planes for flight, completing reports, and other grounded tasks.

I dropped off the bags on the short countertop island that functioned as both a food prep area and my dining table. I left the bags on the counter for the moment.

"You hungry, Honey?"

I didn't expect a verbal response, but my pet turtle enthusiastically splashed in her tank. I'd had Honey—a red-eared slider—for close to a decade. My job kept me from owning more traditional pets unless I paid to have them kenneled or hired a pet sitter. That was money I didn't have. Honey was the perfect compromise. She didn't require much maintenance beyond occasional feedings and cleaning her aquarium. Plus, she had loads more personality than a fish.

I dropped a handful of floating food pellets into her tank and watched her hunt down each piece of food with erratic precision. She was clumsy—smashing her open mouth against the clear glass walls—but persistent. No piece of food went undevoured.

"How was your day?" I asked. I leaned close to the aquarium glass and watched her zip across the water's surface. I tapped lightly against the glass, but she was in hunting mode and paid little attention to me. "Get some good sunbathing done today? Take a dip in your pool? Must be nice; I was in recycled air all day while you're on a permanent vacation."

With Honey fed, I started the task of feeding myself. I didn't have occasion for eating at home too often. The airline paid for most of my food since I was on the clock during most meal times. I cooked a little though; my life would have turned into too much of a sad cliché if I relied on frozen microwavable dinners and cereal.

My conversation with Gemma had inspired me to make Italian that night—homemade meatballs on top of thick-noodled spaghetti, swimming in a rich marinara sauce. I'd just settled down at the kitchen island to tuck into my meal and a glass of red wine, when my phone rang and my sister's name and number popped up on the screen.

My sister Dawn was a few years older than me. While I hadn't made it through college and had boomeranged back into my parents' basement, Dawn had achieved practically everything she had set out to do. I was a single, gay, college dropout who lived in an 700-square foot apartment in Romulus, Michigan while she was married with kids and lived in a big house in the affluent Detroit suburbs.

"Are you coming to Peter's swim meet on Saturday?" she asked when I answered the phone.

"I'm on call on Saturday," I shared, "so probably not."

Although we had days off that scheduling couldn't touch—called Golden Days—on some off days of the week we had to be flexible. An on-call day might eventually turn into an actual day off, but if someone called in sick or had a last-minute personal emergency, we had to make ourselves available and get to our home base airport to fill in.

"But you missed his last swim meet, too!" she protested.

"He's five," I deadpanned. "How much of a competition is it really?"

"That's not the point and you know it," she sternly chastised. "You're missing out on family time."

"I'm not doing it on purpose," I insisted. "It's just not going to work out this time."

"It *never* works out," she grumbled.

My voice pitched up. "Because your kids insist on doing stuff on the days that I'm working!"

"Can't you switch with someone?" she demanded. "Or pretend to come down with a cold?"

I tugged at my hair in frustration. "You know it doesn't work that way," I growled into my phone. "I can't flake on my work. I've got responsibilities."

"I don't know why you can't just skip," she openly complained. "It's not like you're curing cancer."

"I know. I'm just a flight attendant," I bit out as my frustration mounted. "Nothing special or important about that."

"You know I didn't mean it like that, Alice."

"I've gotta go," I said, my voice suddenly flat. Even a brief conversation with my older sister had drained me of all energy. "My dinner's getting cold."

I ended the call without waiting for my sister's goodbye. I knew she would only continue to text me the rest of the night, waffling between apologetic and passive aggressive, so I turned off my phone entirely.

I swirled my fork aggressively through my spaghetti noodles and took a bite. I'd lost my appetite, but I had to eat. And my already thin pocketbook wouldn't forgive me for letting good food go to waste.

## CHAPTER TWO

In the mornings when I first arrived at the airport, I checked my mailbox in the flight attendant lounge to see if I had received anything. Then, like a regular passenger, I consulted the airport screens to find the gate where my airplane was located. If I had time before my first flight of the day, I liked to grab coffee and a pastry from one of the terminal's cafes.

I enjoyed my job partly because of the routine. Each day was different, depending on the destination and the number of flights I worked, but there was also a predictable rhythm to each flight. The passengers arrive and we help them to their seats and with their bags. We close the boarding door and walk through the cabin, getting ready for taxi. While in taxi we make a departure announcement and walk through the cabin again. Once the plane is ready, we buckle into our respective jump-seats for takeoff.

When the plane reaches 10,000 feet, we prepare for beverage service. After serving snacks and drinks, we pick up cups and other trash. Thirty minutes out from our final destination, the purser makes the initial approach announcement and we clean and prepare the cabin for arrival. A catering form is filled out for anything the next flight will need. We check our landing lips before landing—apply a fresh layer of lipstick and lacquer before the big passenger buh-byes.

I liked the routine, but sometimes it could feel like that movie *Groundhog's Day* with the day restarting every morning. The only thing that differed was the passengers, but even they started to look alike after a while.

Luckily I had my hostile older sister to keep things interesting. I hadn't turned my cellphone back on from the previous evening until I was seated at a café table with a coffee and blueberry muffin. My sister hadn't left any voicemails, but she'd composed a string of text messages all echoing the same sentiment: I was being a crappy sister and aunt.

I loved my niece and nephew, June, age 7, and Peter, age 5. And I honestly wasn't ignoring my family or making up excuses to not see them. But that was the nature of my job. It allowed for little flexibility or last-minute changes unless I wanted my paycheck to take a hit. Technically, I could fly as little or as much as I wanted to, within reason, but the debt collectors weren't going to be forgiving if I defaulted on my student loans because I'd attended a ballet recital or t-ball game instead of working.

My sister perpetually nagged me about how much I worked and how little I saw them, but she didn't have tens of thousands of dollars in student debt. She didn't even *have* to work anymore; she'd lucked out by marrying an anesthesiologist. Because of her, I felt a metaphorical cloud hovering over my day before it had even really begun.

"What's wrong, Sunshine?" My friend, Gemma, slipped into the empty chair across the table where we sat most mornings when our flight schedules overlapped.

I darkened the screen on my cellphone and tucked it back into my work bag. "Nothing. Family stuff. It's fine."

Gemma pursed her lips and nodded; she made no additional comment. She knew which topics I tended to be tight-lipped about, and family was definitely one of them. "I was thinking about your bingo card last night."

I tore my muffin in half and popped a piece into my mouth. "You need to find more hobbies."

Gemma ignored my jab. "What about Lara?"

My right eyeball twitched at the mention of my ex-whatever-she-was. I took a moment and swallowed the food in my mouth. "What about her?"

"The Mile High Club square doesn't say anything about it being with a *passenger*. Maybe you could complete the task with someone from the *flight crew*," she proposed. "And since you already know that Lara likes you, and you like her …" Gemma trailed off.

"We're not working any of the same lines this month," I reminded my friend. "We won't be on a plane together."

"Couldn't you switch with someone for one flight?"

I stared into the murky depths of my black coffee. "I don't know, Gemma. That feels a little icky. I don't want to use Lara like that just to cross off a bingo square."

"But isn't that what you're doing to the passengers?" she pointed out, her voice free of any malice. "Using them to win a game?"

"Yeah, but that's different," I tried to reason. "Spilling a drink on someone is totally different than having sex with someone."

Gemma pressed her lips together and looked unconvinced.

"You know I'm only doing this to get out of debt," I reasoned.

I really should have gone to a more reasonably-priced state school instead of insisting on attending a private college like the one Dawn had graduated from. I wasn't competitive by nature, but something about Dawn brought out a desire to be better—to beat her at all costs. Despite my grumblings about how much she annoyed me, I loved my sister; but she always managed to make me feel inadequate in comparison.

"I know," Gemma allowed, "but isn't there another way to do that?"

"Fake my own death and move to a tropical island?" I flippantly proposed.

Gemma wrinkled her upturned nose. "Not funny."

The tabletop rocked and wobbled when a third chair was dragged to our vicinity. My friend Kent eased himself into his chair.

"Morning," he grumbled.

I took in his slightly disheveled hair and the visible circles beneath his normally vibrant eyes. Even the collar of his uniform shirt looked a little less starched than usual.

"Morning," I returned. "Bad spaghetti last night?"

"What?" Kent asked. It looked like it pained him to form even the one-worded question.

"You look like crap," I observed. "What happened?"

Kent reached across the table for the remaining pieces of my blueberry muffin, but I slapped his hand away. "Get your own, dude," I complained.

"But I need to keep up my strength," he practically whined. "That boy sucked me dry. I'm going to be ejaculating dust for days."

Gemma covered her ears with her hands. "Oh gross. Too much information."

I sat up a little straighter in my chair. "Okay, new topic," I chirped. "You're letting me work First Class today, right?"

Kent stroked the visible stubble on his chin. "Maybe. What do I get in return?"

I slid my muffin plate over to his side of the table and grinned, hopefully.

"Sloppy seconds of your muffin?" He wasn't too wrecked to let the euphemism go to waste. Kent's lips twisted to a sardonic smile. "Sorry, honey. You're not my type."

"We need to get going," Gemma abruptly announced.

I didn't know if it was actually time to go to our gate or if she just sensed that Kent and I were about to get into another one of our juvenile fights. I considered Kent a friend, but if we hadn't been jammed together in a flying metal tube for multiple hours at a time, I didn't know if I'd normally seek out his comradery. He was a nice enough guy and a seemingly loyal friend, but his extracurricular activities with married pilots turned me off.

We bussed our table, gathered our wheeled luggage, and set off for our assigned gate. One of the favorite parts of my day was the brisk walk to my morning flight. Kent, Gemma, and I walked side-by-side down the long terminal. We walked with purpose, not quite frantic, but not at a leisurely stroll either. My heels clicked on the solid flooring and my wheeled luggage glided silently behind me.

I walked with my head held high, acutely aware of the admiring stare of passengers and other airport personnel. It made me feel like the cool kid in school—something I had never actually experienced while in school. I hadn't been popular, but I also hadn't been unpopular. I'd simply been present. There. My sister Dawn had been the one with the large group of friends who'd ruled the school hallways. But as a flight attendant, this was my turf. I fit in. I belonged.

Our plane was at the gate, but the captain and his or her co-pilot had yet to show up. Gemma, Kent, and I took a seat in the boarding area with the passengers while I discreetly inspected my monthly bingo card. In addition to ignoring Dawn's texts, I'd spent the previous evening mapping out my plan of attack for bingo. I'd been competing in the underground game long enough that I knew which tasks were easily accomplished and which would take a little more leg work.

Some of the challenges could even be completed simultaneously. I could whip out a fake Southern accent while wearing a deflated life preserver without most passengers ever batting an eye. Everyone was typically too consumed by whatever electronic device was in their hand to pay us flight attendants much attention. We became an extension of the airplane itself.

Some of the bingo squares that the organizers had deemed more challenging were actually pretty straight-forward if you were creative and thought outside the box. For example, I was often tasked with getting a passenger's phone number. One might think this would involve excessive batting of eyelashes, unbuttoning an extra button on your uniform shirt, or laughing at sketchy men's unoriginal jokes, but I'd discovered a far less demeaning way to get what I needed.

The most important part of every flight was the moment passengers got on the plane. I would position myself in one of the exit rows and carefully inspect each passenger as they boarded and stashed their carry-ons in the overhead compartment. It was probably akin to a con-artist looking for their next mark, but I tried to not think too critically about it. For the phone number task, the obvious passenger was an ego-maniac. The self-important slick guy in the over-priced suit who continued to wear his sunglasses on the plane. The Bluetooth device in his ear was also a dead giveaway. He always ended up being a little too handsy and called female flight attendants 'honey' or 'sweetheart.'

I looked for a totally different kind of guy though—middle-aged, Midwest dads. But it wasn't just a dad flying solo in his flat-front khakis; he had to be with his wife and kids. Families in matching outfits, especially sports-themed gear that indicated where they lived, was my specialty. When they struggled to get everything into the overhead compartments, I would swoop in to save the day. An innocent comment about their hometown and how I'd never been but had always wanted to go would inevitably result in copious chatter.

"Oh, you *have* to visit," they'd gush as they struggled with their safety belts.

They'd eagerly offer up all of their favorite restaurants and non-touristy places to go. But I couldn't *possibly* remember all of those details, so they should probably just text me all of that valuable insider information. And *ta-da*—I had their phone number. One more bingo square checked off.

"Fresh meat," Kent quietly announced.

I looked away from my bingo card and toward the gate counter to see two young men in pilot uniforms looking over the passenger log printouts. I didn't recognize either of them from previous flights, but I also didn't actively work up a rapport with the flight deck crew. It was probably unfair of me to dismiss an entire group of people based only on their occupation of choice, but I didn't particularly like pilots.

*How can you tell if someone is a pilot?*

*He'll tell you.*

Kent sighed in disappointment. "I don't see any wedding rings. Gemma, girl, they're all yours."

Gemma looked up briefly from her paperback novel, but apparently not interested in either of the two men, returned her attention to her book. She read more than anyone I'd ever met, always staying abreast of the newest, top-selling fiction to show up in the airport bookstores.

"So, Kent," I said, resuming our earlier conversation. "First Class?"

Kent had slipped on sunglasses and was slumped in his chair. He waved his hand in the air like a monarch dealing with an annoying peasant. "It's all yours," he allowed.

"Yes!" I quietly cheered.

Kent and I only shared flights one day a week that month—Wednesdays from Detroit to Philadelphia to New York LaGuardia and back to Detroit—so I would have to accomplish most of my seat-specific challenges on those days. Gemma and I were tag-teaming a regional jet on Thursdays, which gave me a second opportunity.

I doubted that any other pursers with whom I would be working that month would be as accommodating as Kent to let me work First Class in their place. I normally didn't mind working in the Village though. In my experience, passengers tended to be more high maintenance and self-entitled the smaller their row numbers.

Economy class were my people—especially the poor, single riders who got stuck in the middle seat.

Once the gate agent gave us the go-ahead, Kent, Gemma, and I gathered our wheeled luggage and other belongings and boarded our morning flight. Meeting up with the other crew members for pre-flight checks included making sure all emergency equipment is present and operational. We go through the cabin to make sure it's clean, and we check the galleys to make sure drinks and snack numbers are appropriate for the flight. After that, we give the okay to the gate attendants in the terminal that the plane is ready for boarding.

Kent and Gemma staggered themselves in the middle sections of the plane while I positioned myself in the front galley. It allowed me the opportunity to greet our first passengers while simultaneously getting ready for pre-flight beverage service. My airline provided an extra round of beverage service to passengers seated in First Class. While the rest of the plane boarded, our premier passengers received a complimentary glass of water at the same time that I recorded their first beverage request.

I easily balanced in one hand a tray of short plastic glasses, each filled to the top with bottled water. I'd waited tables in my hometown during summers when I was in high school. Going to college was supposed to be my ticket out of there—my escape to make sure I didn't have to go back to waitressing in my small town. College had been a bust, however, and now I was basically a waitress in the sky. But at least I got to travel, even if I typically didn't get to see much of the country beyond the insides of different airports and hotel rooms.

I had decided to conquer a relatively simple, seat-specific bingo-card challenge that morning: to make it appear as though you've accidentally dropped a beverage on a passenger's lap. I started from the back of my section and worked my way towards the front of the plane. Since I had been assigned the seat 3B on my bingo card, it made better strategic sense to spill on that passenger when I was near the end of my water service instead of the beginning. I would have less eyes on me. And if I dumped water on this person at the beginning of the flight, they still had the entire trip to Philadelphia to clean themselves up.

I bent slightly at the knee as I delivered each glass of water. Few passengers acknowledged me as I routinely pressed the plastic cup into their hands. They were already hooked into their noise-canceling headphones or were finishing up last-minute phone calls, emails, and texts. First Class passengers were typically commuters, traveling for business, rather than honeymooners who'd splurged on their once-in-a-lifetime tickets. Flying for these passengers was old hat, routine, like what riding the subway during morning rush hour was for some people. I was part of the scenery, like a piece of the airplane. Aisle seat. Oval window. Landing gear. Flight attendant.

My tray was nearly empty by the time I approached seat 3B. I kept my eyes on the seatback, keeping my target in sight. I couldn't see much beyond the top of a woman's head. She was compact; nothing else spilled beyond the perimeter of her assigned seat. I bent at the knee to drop myself closer to the passenger's level. The woman's attention was concentrated on a tablet she held in her left hand, away from the aisle.

I noticed her lower body first. Her heels were higher than mine, but she also didn't have to be on her feet all day, or so I assumed. My attention raked next over the slender, naked ankle. Dark grey dress pants. No noticeable wrinkles or creases although the material appeared to be linen. I thought it was a bold choice considering how poorly the fabric withstood traveling, but at least after I poured water into her lap, it would dry more quickly than denim or wool.

My gaze traveled farther up. A cream-colored shell beneath a dark grey blazer. The shell was unbuttoned enough to see a hint of collarbone. A thin string of pearls hung around her neck. Her head was tilted down and to the left, just slightly. The downward angle had caused her long, dark hair to fall forward, forming a curtain around her face and blocking her features from my view. Her hair was nearly black and incredibly glossy, like an actress from a shampoo commercial, with visible caramel highlights streaked throughout.

"Water?" I benignly offered.

A slim wrist snapped up to meet the pro-offered water glass. Thin gold bracelets jangled together with the movement.

I stretched my arm in her direction. My fingers lightly flexed around the flimsy plastic cup in my hand. Her long, delicate fingers stretched in the air to barely touch the bottom of the glass. All I needed to do was let the cup slip from my grip and I'd be on my way to completing that month's bingo card.

I had just made my decision to let go, when the woman in seat 3B turned her head to appraise me.

Her hazel eyes locked with mine. The color of her irises looked almost gold. She wore natural-tone lipstick on a full, wide mouth. My gaze swept over her meticulously sculpted eyebrows. Her high cheek bones. Her flawless copper skin. Her heart-shaped face and how her thick, dark hair tumbled in glossy waves past her round shoulders. It was like if a person had been photoshopped.

"Thank you," she murmured.

Hers was the first acknowledgment I'd received from a passenger since starting the preliminary beverage service.

Gemma's censuring words from breakfast resurfaced in the back of my mind. I had always justified that it was only water; but I started to consider the inconvenience, the annoyance, and even the embarrassment that a seemingly insignificant cup of water might cause. What if this woman was on her way to a big job interview and had nothing to change into? Or maybe she was meeting her significant other's family for the first time and wanted to make a good—not soggy—first impression. The flight might have been long enough to cosmetically fix the damage, but what I was about to do could potentially ruin this woman's entire day.

I couldn't do it.

My conscience said one thing, but my hand had other plans. The glass had already begun to slip. My fingers tensed and clenched around the cup before it could drop any farther. But in my panic to stop the glass's fall, I over-corrected. My entire right arm twitched and jerked up, just enough to change the water's momentum. And instead of the plastic cup and its contents dropping onto the beautiful woman's lap, I splashed the entire glass of water across my chest. The water wasn't particularly cold, but I hissed in surprise at the sudden dampness that soaked into my white blouse and bra.

The woman's golden eyes widened in surprise. "Are you okay?"

"Sorry," I grit out between clenched teeth.

The fabric of my button-up shirt stuck uncomfortably against my chest. I grabbed another plastic cup from my tray—which I mercifully hadn't tipped over during my spastic flailing—and handed it to the woman in 3B.

Her plush lips tilted down in sympathy and she returned the cocktail napkin I had handed her with the water glass. The cheap paper napkin would be useless in soaking up the liquid that had saturated the front of my blouse, but it was a kind gesture nonetheless.

I accepted the returned napkin with a pained smile frozen on my features and finished the remainder of my beverage service to the rest of the First Class cabin. When my tray was finally empty, I rushed back to the rear galley with my arms covering my chest. Thankfully I had an extra uniform shirt in my carry-on luggage even though that day's schedule didn't have me staying anywhere overnight. It hadn't been the first time I'd spilled on myself during a flight, and my airline required we look neat and professional at all times.

"What happened to you?" Kent eyeballed me.

"Karma," I grumbled. I wiped uselessly at the front of my saturated shirt. "I don't suppose either of you has an extra bra?"

Kent and Gemma slowly, almost comically, shook their heads.

"Do you want me to make an announcement to the rest of the plane? I'm sure we could wrangle up an extra bra or two," Kent offered with a teasing smile.

"You're a big help," I rolled my eyes.

There was just enough time for me to change shirts in the onboard bathroom before takeoff. Luckily our plane was newer; an automated video went through the pre-flight safety procedures so I didn't have to stand in the aisle in my see-through shirt and show passengers how to buckle their seatbelts. Unluckily, I hadn't packed an extra bra. I tried to soak up as much water from the padded cups with paper towels in the claustrophobic airplane bathroom, but I could already anticipate the symmetric wet spots that would eventually appear on my clean uniform shirt.

I suffered through the rest of the flight with a cold, wet bra sticking to my chest. The plane couldn't have landed soon enough with me practically shoving the final passengers from the plane. I hustled to the closest women's bathroom in the Philadelphia terminal and heaved a sigh of relief that there wasn't a long line outside.

I slipped into a vacant stall and peeled off my still-damp bra. I was amazed at the amount of water the slightly padded cups had retained; it was like a modern engineering miracle. I rung out the padding as much as I could and used handfuls of rapidly disintegrating toilet paper to dry off my naked back and chest.

I put my uniform shirt back on, but my bra remained in my hands. The women's bathroom wasn't empty, but I didn't have time to be embarrassed. My next flight would be leaving in two hours, and I couldn't go the rest of the day with a wet bra. The bathroom hand dryers would have to become my bra dryer.

I exited my bathroom stall and slinked to the nearest hand dryer. The mounted machine roared to life when I held the twin cups of my bra underneath its silver spout. I shook the bra around as if the movement might precipitate the process. I tried to ignore the curious stares of passengers and airport employees as I openly used a hand dryer to blow dry my beige bra.

"Wow," I heard a feminine voice over the noise of the blower. "You really got yourself."

I looked away from my hurried task to see the passenger from my flight who had been the original target of my glass of water—the woman from seat 3B. She stepped out of a bathroom stall, heels clicking on the tile floor, and thoroughly washed her hands. She appraised herself in the horizontal mirror that hung above the multiple bathroom sinks as she lathered up her hands. I watched her reflection with interest, my task momentarily forgotten.

The automatic faucet turned off and she shook out her hands over the sink. There were several vacant hand dryers scattered around the public bathroom, but she walked towards the machine I'd been recently monopolizing. I instinctively stepped back to give her free use of the dryer, equal parts mesmerized and robotic. Her lips quirked up in a small smile of thanks.

I watched her olive-complexioned hands move beneath the warm air. Her fingers were long and graceful, with manicured but short nails. She wore several gold bands on various fingers. I knew from experience that women who traveled extensively for their jobs sometimes wore fake wedding bands to ward off unwanted attention. Their male counterparts often did the opposite and conveniently forgot their ring at home.

My brain desperately churned to come up with something clever to say, but I only managed to stand awkwardly close with my still-damp bra clutched in both hands.

The dryer shut off, and I became acutely aware of how quiet it was in the bathroom. I also still wasn't wearing a bra.

"I hope the rest of your day goes better," the woman said with a quick wave of her hand.

I stared after her exiting form.

"Thanks. You, too," I dumbly returned.

## CHAPTER THREE

On Thursdays that month I was scheduled to fly back and forth between Detroit Metro and Chicago O'Hare on a small, regional jet. Because of the short time between wheels up to wheels down, there was no official beverage service; I was only responsible for safety demonstrations and in-flight announcements. These brief back-and-forth flights created a monotonous, mindless day where you could easily lose track of what city you were in, so I was happy to be scheduled with my friend Gemma.

After finishing the safety demonstration, Gemma and I strapped into our respective jump-seats at the rear of the plane for takeoff. The landing gear was barely off the ground when an older man, balding, with baggy khakis and a button-up dress shirt, stood up from his seat. The seatbelt sign was still illuminated, but more often than not, passengers regarded that instruction as a suggestion instead of a rule.

I watched the man open the overhead compartment door and then struggle to retrieve a duffle bag. The overhead space on the regional jet was smaller than what was typical on our standard planes. The man had obviously forced the duffle bag to make it fit and now he couldn't pull his bag out. Technically, we weren't required to help passengers with their carry-on luggage, but I couldn't in good conscience watch the older man struggle mightily with his bag. He could hurt himself or any of the passengers seated in his proximity.

I could sense that Gemma was watching the passenger as well. I patted the top of her thigh. "I've got it," I told her.

I unbuckled my safety harness and left my jump-seat. We were still ascending, so the airplane shook from slight turbulence. I used the headrests to keep me steady as I traveled down the center aisle of the narrow-body plane. By the time I reached the elderly man in the fourth row, he had nearly worked his bag free from its overhead container.

"Sir, we haven't reached a safe cruising altitude yet," I gently told him. "You'll have to return to your seat until the captain turns off the seatbelt sign."

"I just wanted to get my book," he seemed to apologize.

Our flight was so short, we would probably be back on the ground in Chicago before he ever had a chance to open the book's front cover. He looked so earnest, however, I didn't have the heart to deny him.

I waited patiently in the center aisle while the older man rummaged through his bag until he found his paperback novel. He zipped the duffle closed again and moved to return it to the overhead container.

"I'll get that for you," I offered.

Even though it was in my job description to assist passengers, I sometimes hesitated before offering physical assistance to senior citizens, especially men. The passengers I met on my flights tended to be proud and sometimes took offense when offered help from someone who was younger and female. This man, however, was more than satisfied to let me put his bag back for him so he could return to his seat and dig into his newly-acquired novel.

The ceiling was low on the regional jet and so were the overhead compartments. I didn't even have to stand on my tiptoes to shove the man's duffle bag back into the overhead compartment. I had just slammed the hinged compartment door closed when I felt something graze my backside. I might have thought it an accidental touch until I felt a more aggressive hand firmly grab my right ass cheek.

I squeaked at the unwelcomed sensation and aggressively spun on my heel to confront my overly handsy assailant. I wasn't necessarily used to being fondled on planes, but—sadly—it also wasn't a rare occurrence.

A forty-something man with thinning dark hair smiled innocently at me from his Business Class seat. "Sorry. That turbulence is a bitch."

I would have broken the hand of any man who touched me outside of work. Instead of making a fuss, however, I only forced a smile to my lips. We would be landing soon and then I'd never have to see this person again.

My phony smile slipped off of my features when I turned on my heel again. I marched down the center aisle to where Gemma waited in the rear galley. She'd unlatched herself from her jump-seat and stood at a slight angle, wedged in the limited area we were afforded on the smaller plane.

"That was nice of you to help that man," she approved.

"Yeah, until someone else helped themselves to my ass," I grumbled.

Gemma's grey-blue eyes widened. "What?"

"Someone grabbed my ass."

"No! Do you know who?" she demanded.

"The *gentleman* in 3B," I gritted out.

"3B?" she echoed. "Isn't that your bingo seat?"

I shrugged. "I decided that you're right. The bingo game is mean and dumb. I'm not going to do it anymore."

Gemma twitched where she stood, almost like she hadn't heard me. "Do they think that's acceptable behavior? Would they act this way if we were on the ground? Do they think they can treat us however they want just because they paid a little extra for their seat?"

I watched my friend struggle with her emotions. Her nostrils flared, and I could hear the heaviness of her breath.

"Don't Hulk out on me, girl," I tried to joke. "Your veins are starting to show."

Gemma was a sensitive soul. I'd once seen her burst into tears because she'd found a dead ladybug on one of our flights. Her emotions ran both ways though—from tears to quick anger. I'd heard this particular rant before. Ugly, obnoxious passengers who showed no consideration for others tended to make my sweet friend snap.

She shut her eyes and shook her head from side to side as if trying to reset her emotions. When her eyes re-opened, a peculiar smile had taken residency on her pink, painted lips. She pulled a small, plastic tray from a compartment in the galley and—almost mechanically—set clear plastic cups on top of the tray.

"What are you doing?" I questioned.

She grabbed a large plastic water bottle from another compartment and began to fill each of the empty glasses.

"Business Class looks like they might be getting thirsty," she clipped.

My eyes grew in wonder. *"No."*

Gemma ignored me and marched down the center aisle, her weapons activated and fully loaded. I watched helplessly from the rear galley, both fearing and eagerly anticipating what she might do next. She paused at a few passenger rows and dropped off single glasses of water, but her eyes remained trained on the front of the plane, like stalking her prey.

When she finally made it to the front of the plane, several water glasses remained on the flimsy plastic tray. She stopped at the third row and bent slightly over the man sitting in the aisle seat. I was too far away to hear their conversation and the plane's engines were too loud, but I could see the saccharine smile on her painted lips.

My breath caught in my throat when she grasped one of the cups and offered it to the passenger. The handoff was clumsy and inelegant, and the plastic cup slipped from Gemma's fingers and fell onto the man's lap. Her body snapped to attention and a manicured hand went over her mouth in mock horror and surprise. It was a familiar act; I'd performed the same routine many times.

Gemma rushed back down the aisle. The false apology on her features morphed into a smug smile halfway down the plane.

"I can't believe you just did that!" I said when she returned to the rear galley.

"Where's your bingo card?" she demanded.

"Oh, uh, in my bag," I stumbled, still stunned at what I'd witnessed.

"Get it," she commanded. She grabbed a handful of cocktail napkins, presumably for the man in 3B while I retrieved the bingo card from my purse.

She held out her hand expectedly. "You need confirmation for seat specific tasks, right?"

I nodded. "Yeah, but…" I didn't finish my sentence. The serious look on her face told me it wouldn't matter to her if I pointed out that *she* had been the one to accomplish the task, not me.

Gemma snatched the card from my outstretched hand and scribbled her flight ID number and initials on one of the open squares.

"There," she said with finality. "You have my blessing. Let's win this thing."

+ + +

Over the next few days, with Gemma's blessing, I accomplished several more of the bingo card challenges. I'd spoken in a fake Southern accent while obtaining the phone number of a family of four on their way to Disney World. I'd worn a deflated life preserver around my neck on a short flight from LaGuardia to Boston's Logan Airport. I'd bumped into passengers in-flight while blaming it on non-existence turbulence. I'd checked off one box after another in less than a week's time.

By the time Wednesday rolled around again—the day of the week I worked First Class for my friend Kent—I was feeling confident. I'd made amazing progress only one week into the competition. My mind was on the remaining bingo squares while I handed out glasses of water and recorded our Business Class passengers' drink requests. I paused at each row, my eyes not really focused on anything, as I went through the pre-flight routine.

No one had puked on-board for me to assist just yet, but that was bound to happen within the month. The toilet paper gag required I walk the length of the airplane with toilet paper stuck to the bottom of my shoe. I could do that on a Thursday flight to Chicago since it was the smallest plane I worked that month. I still needed to get a passenger to buy me a meal, but similar to the phone number challenge, there were out-of-the-box strategies to achieve that task. And there was still the issue of the Mile High Club, but I really didn't see that happening; it would be impressive enough to check off all the other boxes. I wondered if there was a cash prize for that.

I was nearly finished with water service and my serving tray was almost empty by the time I reached the front of the plane.

"Can I get you something to drink besides water?" I asked the next passenger.

"Oh! It's you!" I heard a woman exclaim.

My eyes dropped to the seated passenger. Dark hair with caramel highlights. Bronzed skin. Hazel eyes. An impeccably tailored suit. I typically didn't take stock of the people who filled the airplane seats unless I was honed in on a specific passenger for the purpose of completing another bingo challenge. I served drinks and snacks to hundreds of people every day. Eventually their faces became indistinguishable from each other. But I remembered her—not only because she was strikingly beautiful, but because I'd embarrassed myself so epically in front of her the week before.

A tight smile found its way to my lips. "Welcome back," I stiffly greeted.

The woman in 3B seemed to scramble in her seat. "Just a second," she said as she fumbled around. "I didn't bring a rain jacket with me."

Despite her exotic looks, her voice was absent of any accent. I'd naively assumed from the color of her skin, the luster of her dark hair, and the thickness of her lips that there would be the shadow of an accent lightly tugging at her words. But she spoke with a clear and unaffected voice—the sign of a true Michigander.

Despite my embarrassment, her exaggerated antics made me chuckle.

"Can I get you something besides water?" I repeated my earlier question.

"I'm almost afraid to ask," she said.

"I promise I'm not normally that clumsy," I assured her. "I was having an off day."

Her golden-colored eyes narrowed in contemplation. "Are you *sure* you won't spill it on anyone else?" she pressed. "Because I would really love a cranberry juice with a splash of seltzer water if you have it."

I arched an eyebrow. "Oh, you *really* want to ruin someone's day," I teased. "Might as well go all the way and order a Bloody Mary."

She tapped at her lips in thought. The motion drew my attention to her plump lips and her nude nail polish. "Mmm. Tempting," she hummed. "But I'm technically at work, so I guess I should behave."

"Oh, what's the fun in that?" I grinned.

I couldn't explain from where my flirtatious attitude was coming. I typically only turned on the charm when there was a bingo card square in the balance. She was a beautiful woman, however, so perhaps I simply couldn't help myself.

She waggled a finger at me. "You're a bad influence, I can tell."

I grinned wider, not really having a clever response for her. "Cranberry with a splash of seltzer, coming right up," I promised.

The safety video was about to play, so I jammed myself in the rear galley and began to prep the drink orders for First Class. I was only a few minutes into making drinks when Gemma appeared.

"You're awfully chipper," my friend observed.

I continued to crack open soda cans and fill plastic cups with ice cubes. "Am I?"

"You're humming like Snow White at work or something."

"Is it a crime to be in a good mood or enjoy my work?" I defended myself.

Gemma smirked. "No. But normally it's *me* getting teased for enjoying what I do."

"Am I usually a grump?" I asked.

"You're not a grump. Professional," she decided on. "You're always professional."

"So, I'm a grump," I laughed.

The third member of our flight crew—Kent—rushed to the rear of the plane. There wasn't really room in the back galley for all three of us, but we made it work.

"I'm taking First Class back," Kent announced.

I paused in my drink construction. "What? Why?"

"Didn't you see who's seated in 2A?" he asked.

I tried to jog my brain. Second row, window seat. 2A. I would have served them after I'd taken drink orders from the woman in 3B. I was drawing a blank. Had I even finished beverage service? Or had I rushed straight back to the rear galley to make a cranberry, splash of seltzer? I couldn't remember.

"Uh …" I struggled.

"Oh, you wouldn't even know her," Kent huffed. "She's only like the most famous makeup tutorial person on the internet."

"Is she really?" Gemma gushed. She craned her neck and stood on her tiptoes as if to get a better view, but we were over thirty rows away from the front of the plane and could only see the backs of passengers' heads.

I blinked a few times. "Is that a thing? Getting famous for doing your makeup?"

Kent laid a sympathetic hand on my shoulder. "Oh, honey. Next you'll be telling me you've never heard of TikTok."

"Be nice. Alice is having a good day," Gemma protested.

"Which drink is hers?" Kent asked.

"Who?" I asked.

He rolled his eyes. "Makeup Tutorial in 2A."

"Oh. Right. Uh …" I looked at the slip of paper on which I'd written down my section's drink orders.

Apparently I was moving too slowly for Kent. He snatched the piece of paper from my hand. "Don't worry about it. I'll deliver drinks to First Class."

I stared down at my serving tray; the glasses of water were now replaced with specific drink requests from specific seat assignments. The cranberry, splash of seltzer for the woman in 3B was in the center of the tray. First Class was technically Kent's section, and I didn't have any seat-specific challenges I could accomplish that flight. It didn't make sense for me to put up a fight over wanting to bring a passenger a glass of cranberry juice.

"Okay," I reluctantly agreed. "But take my phone. I need a picture of this so-called celebrity. It's another square on my bingo card."

I worked the rest of the flight with Gemma in Economy. I was mildly disappointed not to have had the opportunity to serve drinks to the woman in 3B, if only to prove to her that I wouldn't spill her drink on me again. But at least with the photograph of the phony internet celebrity, I'd gotten another elusive bingo square completed on the trip.

We landed in Philadelphia, and after the last passenger had deboarded and we'd tidied up the plane for the next flight crew, I headed to the food court in the central terminal. Most crews were stuck together at the hip during their layovers, but I managed to separate myself from the herd so I could have some alone time and quiet my mind. Both Kent and Gemma knew my preference, so they didn't tag along. I would see them soon enough on the next leg of our trip.

Philadelphia International Airport wasn't a hub for my airline, but I'd flown to the airport enough to know what my food options were in each terminal. After nearly eight years on the job, I'd flown through most major airports in the continental United States. I loaded my plastic tray with leaf lettuce and other vegetables from a kiosk that specialized in overpriced salad.

I wasn't a vegetarian and I didn't even really like salad, but since I spent most of my mealtimes in-flight or in a terminal, it could have been fast food for every meal. The narrow airplane aisles and confined rear galleys kept me from overindulging, however. If I gained too much weight that also meant buying a new set of uniforms. It was easier and less expensive overall to stick to salad instead of fast food value meals.

I handed my debit card to the young man behind the cash register.

"You're all set." He shook his hand and refused to take my debit card. "There's no charge."

I slowly returned my debit card to my wallet. "Is it like National Free Salad Day or something?" I asked.

"No. That woman paid for the next five meals."

"Who?"

I turned my head to see who the young man was referencing. I looked just in time to see a vaguely familiar woman standing in the busy food court—the passenger from First Class on whom I'd decided not to spill water—the striking woman from seat 3B. My brain reflexively rolled to my bingo card. One of the challenges that month was to have a passenger buy you a meal. I typically satisfied that task by loudly pretending to not be able to find my debit card while in line for coffee between flights, but this worked just as well.

"Can I get a receipt?" I requested.

A number of the challenges required documentation as proof, especially for some of the more difficult tasks. The salad shop employee already looked bored by our interaction, but he printed off the paper receipt and handed it to me.

I stood with my tray of food, scanning the food court for an empty table. The moments between receiving my food and finding someplace to sit were nerve wracking, like being a new student at a new school and trying to find a welcoming place to sit.

"Dang it," I mumbled under my breath.

I couldn't find an open table. Every place I looked was already occupied. I considered taking my food to the airline's lounge and eating there, but my eyes fell to a small table in the center of the chaos. I recognized her. The woman who had unintentionally bought my meal. The woman from seat 3B.

My feet started moving in her direction before my brain could catch up. She didn't notice my approach. Her eyes were down, focused on the screen of her phone.

"Excuse me," I said.

She looked up from her phone at the sound of my voice.

"Do you mind if I sit here?" I asked, motioning to the vacant chair at her table for two. "There doesn't seem to be anywhere else to sit."

I watched her do a quick scan of the tables in the surrounding area as if to confirm the truth in my words. Finally, she grabbed her oversized leather bag off of the vacant seat across from her to make room for me.

"Thank you," I said, tucking myself behind the small table. "I've never seen it this busy before."

She hummed, but didn't really engage or make eye contact.

"I suppose I should thank you for the meal, too," I added.

She looked up at that. Her dark eyelashes were impossibly long; each time she shut her eyes, I marveled that she was able to open her eyes again without her eyelashes becoming entangled.

"The worker at the salad place said you paid for the next five meals?" I clarified.

"Oh, that. It's nothing. Just a superstition of mine. I see it as an offering to the Flight Gods," she explained. "They get me to Philadelphia, I give them thanks in return."

"That's an awfully kind superstition," I observed.

She shrugged again. She'd been so chatty, almost flirtatious, on the plane earlier; her reluctance to speak now felt like a little like rejection. I briefly considered apologizing for not personally delivering her cranberry juice, splash of seltzer, but that would have required a lot more explanation about switching duties and internet celebrities and bingo cards than I was comfortable with sharing.

"Do you fly a lot?" I asked instead.

She nodded while she chewed her food. I'd caught her mid-bite. "Probably almost as often as you."

"What do you do?"

"I'm an HR consultant."

"And what does an HR consultant do?" I asked, hoping it wasn't a dumb question.

"Well, you know what HR does, right?"

"Hiring, firing … making sure I get paid?" I listed off.

She nodded. "That and more. Payroll and personnel is a big part of the job, but HR also deals with things like sexual harassment complaints and job discrimination. As an HR consultant, I get brought into companies to help their own Human Resource division."

"Help them do what?" I asked.

"A few things. If it's a new company—a tech start-up, for example—I might come in to help them write policies and procedures and make sure they're complying with U.S. labor laws. Larger, more established companies might call in a consultant to help mediate an employee grievance. Usually though, I help employers update their company's infrastructure to make sure they're being as efficient as they can."

"Efficient," I repeated. "Like firing people."

She nodded, unashamed. "Yes, that's part of the job. When a company is too chicken shit to do their own dirty work, sometimes I get called in to do it for them."

"That's got to be hard," I observed.

"I try not to think about it too much," she said in earnest. "That may come off as callous, but they were going to get fired anyway. Better it be by me who actually has training than some bumbling middle-manager type."

I made a humming noise. "I suppose I wouldn't mind being fired by you."

It sounded a little flirty, but I hadn't really meant it like that.

"I'm Anissa, by the way," she introduced herself.

"Alice," I returned.

She reached across the table and shook my hand. Her grip was firm, but her skin was unbelievably soft. I wondered what kind of moisturizer she used.

"Do airlines still have all those crazy regulations about what you have to wear and how you need to fix your hair?" she asked.

"I've heard from some veterans that it's relaxed a lot over the years, but we still have a lot of rules—probably more than most kinds of jobs," I confirmed.

Many of the realities of my job necessitated certain things, regardless of airline policy. Because we spent so much time in small spaces, you really had to be a certain height and weight. It was probably a good idea if you knew how to swim, too, just in case our flight became a cruise. But other requirements were far more subjective and cosmetic in nature. Makeup, but not too much. No visible tattoos. Only one pair of earrings, and they had to be in your ears. A hairstyle no more than three inches in fullness—nothing too extreme in volume. A pleasing complexion—no acne or facial scars.

The woman in 3B—Anissa—stabbed at her salad. "Did you know that flight attendants were the first group of employees to use the Equal Employment Opportunity Commission to file grievances against their employer? In the 1960s and 1970s, flight attendants were typically let go after they got married, were pregnant, or had their thirtieth birthday. Among other things, Title IV of the Civil Rights Act of 1964 prohibits sex-based discrimination."

"Wow," I marveled. "That's an impressive bit of trivia."

"It's part of my job," she deflected. "I'm sure you have all kinds of airplane trivia or insider knowledge that the typical flyer doesn't know."

"Don't drink the water," I mumbled around my next bite of salad.

"Huh?"

"On the airplane, don't get water unless you see a flight attendant pour it from a plastic bottle. The water taps on the planes are notoriously dirty—they hardly ever get cleaned."

"Is that why you spilled my water on yourself?" She leaned forward in her plastic chair. Her generous lips ticked up in a teasing smile. "Were you trying to save me from dirty water?"

"No," I defended, "that was me being a klutz."

A broad smile, almost mischievous, spread across her lovely face. "Your airline is like Sea World; they should put signs on the front seats that warn 'You May Get Wet.'"

I snorted and continued to stab at my salad. "Been thinking about that line for long?"

"I just used up all of my best material," she laughed as she settled back in her seat. "I'll have to come up with something new for you next week."

"I can't wait," I said, rolling my eyes.

In truth, I probably wouldn't be able to wait. I could easily see myself looking forward to every Wednesday if only to have the opportunity to briefly interact with this stunning woman.

I looked at my watch—a nervous habit, not one out of boredom.

Anissa noticed. "Do you have another flight soon?" she asked.

"I've got some time," I decided.

My layover in Philadelphia was only two hours—long enough to get a meal, but not long enough to get into trouble. It wasn't economical for the airline or the crew member to have a layover much longer than that. The airline was actually contractually required to provide us with a hotel room for layovers longer than four hours.

"Do you actually get to see the places you travel to or is it just the insides of airports all the time?" she asked.

"Mostly the latter," I confirmed. "But that's only because I try to pick lines that don't have days-long layovers."

"How does that work?" she asked, looking interested. "Are you flying all the time? Are you away from home often?"

"It depends; I have a new schedule each month. Once the flight schedules are made we get to bid on the schedule we like the most. People with the most seniority get first pick. When you first start out you're a reserve flight attendant and you're basically on call all the time. But now I'm on the line, which means I have a pretty regular schedule, although we still have to be flexible. Delayed and canceled flights impact us as well."

Anissa hummed in thought. "I never thought about that."

"Where are you flying to next?" I assumed Philadelphia wasn't her final destination since she was hanging out in the airport food court.

"Miami. The one in Florida—not Ohio."

"There isn't a direct flight to Miami out of Detroit?" I wondered.

"There is," she confirmed, "but it's a cheaper flight with this layover, and my employer is notoriously tight-fisted when it comes to my travel budget. It sucks up all of my free time, but at least it's only for the duration of my current job."

"How long is that?"

"Only a couple of months."

"That still sounds like a headache," I sympathized.

She shrugged noncommittally. "My dad always says you can endure anything for a year."

"Funny. My parents said the same thing to me about college," I mused.

"This is probably rude of me to say," Anissa qualified, "but I didn't realize you needed a college degree to be a flight attendant."

I shook my head. "You don't. It's actually only a six-week class and then we're certified."

My airline had provided the six-weeks of formal training for me to earn the FAA's Certificate of Demonstrated Proficiency. Students are required to achieve a 90 percent or higher to pass each exam. The final exam included a mock flight where we had to pretend to perform our regular duties and then handle an in-flight emergency. My final test had included a simulated water landing not long after beverage service.

Anissa cocked an interested eyebrow. "Six-weeks? That seems really fast."

"Nervous about flying now?" I teased. In reality, we were continually retested and recertified while on the job.

"As long as you can help me inflate my lifejacket, I think I'll be okay," she laughed back. "Speaking of which …" she murmured, more to herself than to me. She retrieved her leather bag from the ground and spent a moment searching its contents. She eventually fished out a small plastic bottle, removed its cap, and popped a small pill into her mouth.

I watched her wash down the white pill with a sip from her bottled water. Our eyes connected when she returned the plastic bottle to her bag; I realized I'd been rudely staring.

"Dramamine," she explained. "I get terrible motion sickness on planes."

"And yet you have to fly for your job?" I wondered aloud. "That sounds less than ideal."

"Not much I can do about it until they invent teleportation."

"And then I'd be out of a job," I laughed.

"Good point," she chuckled.

Anissa returned to eating her lunch. Our back-and-forth conversation had left little opportunity for either of us to really eat. Her lips wrapped around the leafy greens dangling from the tines of her plastic fork. I found myself staring intensely at her mouth while she ate. Her mouth was drawn wide with full lips and white, even teeth. She wore no lipstick; her lips were naturally the color of dusty pink rose petals. There was a slight divot in the center of her lower lip that she touched with the tip of her tongue every so often.

Anissa set down her fork. "Hold still," she instructed, her face suddenly becoming serious.

"What? Is there something on my face?" I became horrified at the thought that part of my meal might have been clinging to my face this whole time.

"No. It's your wings."

The words still made no sense until Anissa was leaning across the table and narrowing the space between us. My body stiffened at the unexpected proximity. Her outstretched hand traveled the rest of the distance and my breath caught in my throat when her fingers lightly touched my uniform, close to the top of my right breast.

My flight crew pin had become twisted with the silver wings vertical instead of horizontal. It was the kind of detail Kent would have scolded me about on our next flight. Anissa turned the pin in place and returned the wings to their correct position.

I let out the breath I'd been holding when she settled back in her chair.

"Don't worry. I wasn't trying to cop a feel," she smirked.

I anxiously tucked hair behind my ears and felt everything burn red. "Or at least buy me dinner first," I tried to joke.

"I thought I'd already done that," she smartly returned.

## CHAPTER FOUR

I frowned at my cellphone screen while traveling down the jet bridge to my first flight of the morning. My cellphone had been busy all morning with passive aggressive texts from my sister, Dawn.

*I thought you'd like to know that June is graduating from Daisies to Brownies tomorrow. Not that you have time for milestones like that.*

*We're planning a vacation with the kids soon. Tell me your flight schedule so maybe we can arrange to see you at the airport since you're too busy to see us away from work.*

*Your niece and nephew are starting to forget what you look like.*

Fridays were actually a Friday for me that month, meaning I didn't have scheduled flights on Saturdays or Sundays, but I was still on call. I couldn't promise my sister that I'd be at the next youth soccer game or chess tournament or bake sale without hurting someone's feelings when I inevitably got called in to work.

"Morning," a voice called to me from inside the plane.

I paused just short of the aircraft's door when I spotted the one person I hadn't expected to see. Lara Pierson, the flight attendant with whom I'd enjoyed a brief fling the previous month, stood in the front galley of the Airbus A220.

I lingered in the entryway with my wheeled luggage lagging behind. "Am I on the right flight?"

Unlike myself, Lara didn't appear surprised to see me. "Boomerang to Philadelphia and then to Boston, right?"

I nodded.

"Then you're on the right plane," she smiled mildly.

I shook my head, still unclear what she was doing on my plane. "But this isn't your line," I observed.

On Fridays that month I'd been working with two other flight attendants, a middle-aged woman named Cheri, and Derek, one of the only straight men I knew at the airline. I didn't want to be rude, but I wasn't supposed to see her that month. It was the whole reason we'd ended whatever it was we'd started.

"I swapped with Cheri," she explained. Her smile flattened. "Don't worry though; it's just for today." She began to stab at a container of ice cubes that had fused themselves together. "Then you won't have to see me again."

"No, no. That's not it," I insisted in a rush. "I was only surprised to see you, that's all."

Lara didn't verbally acknowledge my words; instead, she continued to aggressively stab at the stubborn block of ice. Derek wasn't on board yet, and Lara continued to ignore me, so after storing my carry-on luggage in the rear of the plane, I started my portion of the pre-flight routine.

I observed Lara out of the corner of my eye while I made sure the evacuation slide was properly pressurized. She had abandoned the ice cubes in the front galley and had taken an aisle seat in First Class. Her three-inch high heels occupied the empty seat beside her. I never went over a two-inch heel myself, preferring function over fashion, while Lara tended to push the boundaries of our uniform regulations. She could also wear the hell out of a pencil skirt. I tended to feel like a shapeless potato in my skirt and button-up uniform shirt, but Lara's small waist, long legs, and shapely backside seemed especially built for the outfit.

Watching her work the pads of her thumbs into her nyloned arches reminded me of our brief time together. She'd complained about her feet hurting often enough that I'd finally worked up the courage and had offered to rub them for her. I didn't have a foot fetish, but I'd definitely had a crush. Rubbing her feet between flights had eventually matured to something much more intimate. I wondered what she would have said now if I'd made the same offer.

"Sorry I'm late!"

My eyes snapped away from Lara and her stocking feet to see the third member of our flight crew—Derek—stumble onto the plane.

Derek looked ready to launch into a myriad of excuses for why he'd been delayed that morning, but he too noticed the substitution to our typical flight crew.

"Where's Cheri?" he vocalized.

I answered before Lara could get more annoyed. "This is Lara. Cheri swapped lines with her. It's just for today."

The curveball had no reason to trip up Derek as it had me. He flashed Lara a megawatt smile. "Glad to meet you, Lara."

The flight to Philadelphia was as routine as they came, which gave my brain plenty of opportunities to wander. Derek and I worked the Economy section together. He was a nice guy with a quick laugh and good sense of humor, but he had no chance of holding my interest. I found myself getting distracted, with my attention drifting too often to the front of the plane where Lara was working.

Cheri was typically the purser on our Friday flights. I would have taken over the position in her absence since Derek was pretty new to the airline, but Lara had seniority over me. I hadn't even considered asking her to switch assignments so I could complete another seat-specific task in First Class. Lara had never approved of the bingo game, and I would only end up owing her. It might have been kind of thrilling to be in her debt, but we were over—not that we'd even really started.

Working separate sections of the plane should have eased the tension between us since we weren't trying to maneuver around each other in a cramped space. There were no opportunities to innocently brush against the other person. No chance for witty banter or flirtations. And yet, I couldn't deny the almost electric charge I experienced the few times I caught Lara looking in my direction. I tried to ignore my own lusty and confusing emotions and focus instead on completing beverage service, but unresolved questions cluttered my mind.

Had she known I would be on this flight? And if so, why had she agreed to switch with Cheri if she knew with whom she'd be working? Was she regretting how we'd ended things?

Disappointingly, I also considered my bingo card. Gemma had been the one to suggest I might be able to complete the Mile High Club challenge with Lara, and even though I'd originally rejected the proposal, the longer I stared at Lara, the more reasonable the suggestion became. We'd already slept together; would it really matter if we had sex one more time and it just so happened to be mid-flight?

Thankfully we had a quick turnaround between our arrival in Philadelphia and our next flight to Boston. We didn't have a plane change, but we had just enough time between arrival and departure to quickly pick up trash in the seat pockets and to inventory supplies before our Boston-bound passengers would be boarding.

Because Derek was the newest member of the flight team, and therefore was low man on the totem pole, he had the honor of picking up the bathroom areas while Lara and I divided up cleaning the rest of the plane. I was going to suggest we start at opposite ends of the plane and meet in the middle, but she had other ideas.

"Want to do sides?" she suggested. "I'll take the seats left of the aisle if you go right?"

We'd similarly separated clean-up duties for the flights we'd worked together before. Neither strategy was more efficient than the other, but my proposal would have continued to separate us.

I shrugged. "Sure."

Lara held the garbage bag for both of us while we cleaned the cabin on our respective sides of the plane. She seemed content not to manufacture small-talk, so I followed her lead. We worked in silence until she discovered something particularly disgusting that a passenger had left behind in their rear seat pocket.

"Oh, that's nasty," she practically gagged. She made a face and dangled a dirty diaper away from her body.

I couldn't help my own laughter. The tension had been building over our three-hour flight, and I needed some kind of release. It wasn't all that funny, but my initial chuckles morphed into a guttural guffaw that had me holding my sides.

I didn't laugh alone, however; after her initial disgust, Lara joined in on the almost-manic giggling. She lay her hand on my forearm and doubled over. I was too distracted by my efforts to reign in my own laughter to dwell on the fact that she was touching me, but the action didn't go entirely unnoticed.

After a moment, Lara righted herself and wiped under her eyes. Her cheeks were damp, but her mascara was unaffected.

"Oh God, I must be a mess," she worried.

"You look perfect." The words had escaped my traitorous mouth before I could stop them.

"Thanks," she said with a soft smile.

"You're welcome," I felt compelled to return.

The moment—a truce, perhaps—was interrupted by a quiet buzz. A chirping noise followed as a reminder that I hadn't silenced my phone. Lara pulled out her cellphone from the pocket of her dark blue uniform blazer as it chimed almost simultaneously.

I heard Lara's frustrated sigh before I could check my own phone: "Our flight's been delayed."

---

The weather had been clear when we'd left Detroit, but while we'd been in the air, a thick fog had settled across the East Coast. The text from the airline said we were delayed by at least two hours. If I'd been working with anyone else, I would have suggested we grab dinner together. But I couldn't picture myself sitting across a table from Lara and pretending like nothing had ever happened between us—like I didn't know what she looked like beneath her navy blue uniform. I knew the length of her fingernails and the red trails she'd left on my back. I remembered how her thighs twitched when I sucked on her clit. I knew the noises she made when she came undone.

I had to get away.

The Philadelphia food court was busier than usual that afternoon. No flights were coming in or out because of the fog, so everyone was in the same holding pattern. I scanned the food court's offerings. Chinese. Burgers. Salad. Burritos. Giant pretzels. My stomach all but growled when my eyes landed on a specific kiosk. I'd always had a particular weakness for cheap food court pizza.

I found an empty table, which was only vacant because the previous patrons hadn't bothered to throw away their food wrappers, used napkins, and half-finished sodas. I grumbled all the way to the nearby trash can. As if it wasn't annoying enough to pick up after passengers in-flight, I was still doing it while grounded.

I dabbed at the outer layer of cheese and pepperoni grease with a handful of napkins. The grease-soaked paper was an over-the-top reminder that I shouldn't have been eating that kind of food, but between having to see Lara again and being stuck in the Philadelphia airport for at least the next two hours, I deserved this small indulgence.

The single slice of pepperoni pizza was comically large. The crust wasn't structurally stable, and I had to hold it in both hands to steer it towards my open mouth.

My teeth had only made first contact when I heard the vaguely familiar voice: "Is this seat taken?"

My eyes cast up from my pizza slice to see Anissa—the woman from 3B on my Wednesday flights. My glance went first to her face and then to the sensible salad on her cafeteria-style plastic tray.

My teeth sank the rest of the way into my first bite. As I tried to pull away, hot cheese made contact with the roof of my mouth. A startled, gurgling noise tumbled up my throat. Half of the toppings and the thick layer of melted mozzarella cheese slid off the tomato-sauced crust. I clumsily dropped the sloppy pizza back onto its paper plate. The stubborn cheese pull continued to connect my mouth to my meal. I had to use my fingers to break the thick string of cheese.

Anissa cocked an eyebrow. "You okay?"

I hastily gulped down the piping hot bite without chewing. The molten lava cheese burned all the way down my throat. "Yeah," I gasped.

Anissa continued to stand with her food tray in hands. "There doesn't seem to be any other free tables."

I realized she was waiting on me.

"Shit. Yeah. Sorry." I grabbed at the handfuls of grease-stained napkins that littered the small table to make room for her. Anissa waited patiently while I consolidated my mess. "Sorry. Sorry," I continued to apologize.

"You're fine," she assured.

I hopped to my feet as she sat down.

She frowned at my action. "You're not leaving, are you? You hardly touched your food."

"Give me your tray," I said, holding a hand out to her. "It'll give us more room."

"I can do that," she insisted.

"I'm already up."

She relinquished her plastic tray without further protest. I brought her tray to the trash can and took the opportunity to also throw away my mountain of wasted napkins.

Anissa had already started to eat her salad by the time I returned to the table. I felt a little out of breath as I sat down. I'd done nothing physical to warrant the quickened pulse or the flushed skin, but I suspected Anissa's unexpected presence had produced the reaction.

"Hi," I said.

Anissa smiled. "Hi, Alice."

I was privately pleased that she'd remembered my name.

"That pizza looked dangerous," she remarked. "I thought I was going to have to call airport security to save you."

My cheeks warmed. "Yeah. I guess I should have stuck to a safe salad."

She hummed in agreement, but didn't continue to tease me. I watched her use a plastic knife and fork to cut her salad toppings into smaller, more manageable bites—something I probably should have done with my pizza if I hadn't wanted to look like a buffoon.

I took the opportunity to inspect my tablemate while her attention was on her salad. Her charcoal grey suit was tailored to her slim silhouette. The three-quarter lengthened suit jacket left her wrists exposed. The leather band of her rose gold watch matched the hue of her slightly darker pants.

"I don't suppose you have any insider knowledge on when flights will start leaving again?" she asked.

I shook my head. "Sorry. I know just as much as you."

"So much for getting home in time," she sighed.

I was tempted to ask her what she needed to get home in time for, but I didn't want to come across as nosy.

Anissa was quiet as she ate her salad. The action of her plastic fork delivering bits of green leaf lettuce and cucumber slices drew my attention to my two favorite body parts—her mouth and hands. I loved feminine hands. Delicate wrist bones. Slender fingers. Her lips looked pillowy soft, like I could fall into them and never emerge. Her eye makeup was meticulous. I envied her skill with mascara and eyeshadow. Whenever I tried to be more liberal with eye makeup I ended up looking like the undead.

"Your eyebrows are unreal." I spoke aloud without meaning to.

I tended to mute myself around seemingly straight women. I worried about coming across as flirty without meaning it; I didn't want to be like an obnoxious man who couldn't take a hint. But women complimented each other all the time, I tried to reassure myself. Shade of lipstick. Killer heels. Perfectly sculpted eyebrows. And this woman had them all.

Anissa arched one of the aforementioned eyebrows. "Thank you. Good genes I guess."

I forced myself to look away and picked at my mutilated slice of pepperoni pizza with no intention of actually eating it.

Anissa sighed and threw her plastic fork into her salad bowl. She'd eaten about as much of her salad as I had of my pizza.

"I'm about to drop," she announced. "I've got to find a quiet corner to sleep off this wasted Dramamine." She grabbed her salad container and stood abruptly. "Thanks for sharing your space."

I looked up after her. "Sure thing. Have a good flight home."

She gave me a tight smile. "If I ever make it."

+ + +

My phone continued to give me bad news. Our original two-hour delay turned into three. The weather continued to worsen on the East Coast as a particularly stubborn storm hovered directly over our location and refused to budge. When my phone alerted me that the three-hour delay was now in question, I went in search of more complete answers.

I didn't know the gate agent who stood at the computer by our boarding gate to Boston.

"Hey," I greeted with a smile. "Do you have any updates on our flight?" I kept my tone light and conversational, knowing how many disgruntled customers she would have dealt with that day.

I didn't envy the work our gate agents did. They were the ones who had to deal with irritated customers whose flights had been delayed or canceled because of reasons out of their control. They had to smile while getting hollered at about lost luggage or missed connecting flights. I only had to serve free drinks and remind passengers to get off their phones before takeoff.

The woman made a face. "The fog's too thick, the lightning strikes are too frequent, and the wind gusts might as well be a hurricane. Nothing's coming in or out tonight."

"Nothing?" My voice cracked. "We're grounded?"

"I'm afraid so; every remaining flight's been canceled. I'm working on rebooking passengers on tomorrow's flights right now."

Her eyes dropped back down to her computer screen and her fingers continued to type away at the plastic keyboard.

I lifted myself up on my toes and leaned against the gate desk. "Er, so, uh, what do I do now?"

She didn't look back up. Her attention remained on the computer monitor. "We're trying to arrange overnight hotel stays for everyone, but it's a bit of a zoo. Everyone's been affected by the weather, not just our airline. We're asking everyone to be patient right now."

I nodded grimly. "It's better than sleeping at the airport, I suppose."

"Keep your phone close," she told me. "The airline will be texting details about where to catch your hotel shuttle."

"Okay. Thanks. Good luck!"

The woman weakly waved back in return.

I found a relatively quiet corner of the airport and plugged my phone into the wall. I could have set up shop in my airline's lounge, but I was still doing my best to avoid Lara. We were both stranded in Philadelphia for the night, and I didn't wholly trust myself with the situation.

I didn't have to wait long until my phone chirped with an incoming text from the airline. It laid out the details about where and when I was supposed to catch a ride to my hotel. I grabbed my wheelie bag and exited the terminal to find a cluster of people already gathered in the same location where my phone had also directed me. Everyone huddled beneath the terminal's overhanging roof, trying to avoid the sheets of rain that traveled with each dramatic gust of wind.

I spied other uniformed employees amongst the largely passenger-heavy crowd, but didn't immediately recognize anyone. My heart lodged in my throat, however, when I spied Lara. Her facial features rested in a slight frown as she stared down at her phone's illuminated screen.

Like me, she still wore her work uniform. But unlike me, she didn't have a jacket. Even though it was technically summer, the wind and rainstorm had brought along cooler temperatures. Lara had popped the collar of her flight attendant blazer, but it provided a poor barrier from the elements. I'd learned my lesson on previous delays and canceled flights to be prepared for just about everything. I never flew anywhere without a jacket, change of clothes, pajamas, and toiletries.

My wheeled luggage clattered on the sidewalk as I approached. There was no use pretending like I hadn't noticed her. I announced my presence with a generic statement. "Crummy luck, huh?"

The displaced look on Lara's face flipped to a smile when she saw me. "Oh, hey. I wondered what had happened to you."

I hated how a simple smile from her could produce butterflies that bounced in my stomach. We hadn't exactly dated, and we hadn't even been fooling around for very long. I had told my friends that our parting of ways had been mutual, but that had been a lie to save face and avoid their good-intentioned sympathy. At the end of the month, when we were no longer on the same line, it had been Lara who had suggested we end our dalliances. I simply hadn't put up a fight—too proud and too stubborn to be vulnerable and admit that I'd really liked the time we'd spent together.

Lara blew into her hands and her narrow shoulders convulsed in a shiver. "Jesus, it's cold," she complained.

I thought about giving her my jacket, but I didn't have an extra one for myself. I didn't want to come off as desperate for her approval, although I suspected that's from where the self-sacrificing impulse had come.

"Do you want my scarf?" I offered instead.

"I'm fine," she resisted.

"You just said you were cold," I pointed out.

"I said the *weather* was cold. Not me." Despite her words, I noticed how she continually tugged at the collar of her uniform jacket.

I arched an eyebrow, calling her bluff.

"Okay, okay," she relented. "I would *love* to use your scarf."

My lips twisted in a wry smile as I untied my silk scarf and surrendered it to her. "Was that so hard?"

Lara rewarded my chivalry with another broad smile. "Thank you," she said softly. "I should have known that this would happen the one time I didn't over-pack."

"Oh, so we have *you* to thank for this?" I couldn't help tease.

Lara's dark eyes crinkled when she laughed. Damn those butterflies. She bumped her hip into mine. "Be nice," she chided.

My reflex was to continue teasing her, maybe even make a suggestive comment about 'being nice' to her, but I couldn't fall down that rabbit hole with her. I smiled, but didn't show my teeth.

I squinted into the high beams of an approaching vehicle. A white 11-passenger conversion van veered toward the curb where our group stood. The shuttle's brakes squeaked as it came to a jerking stop.

Lara grabbed onto my arm and leaned against me, a motion both familiar and intimate. I could feel the press of her fingers through the thin material of my jacket. "God, I hope this is for us."

I eyeballed the vehicle, unsure if I was supposed to feel relieved or frightened.

The driver—a short, squat man with tan skin and dark eyes—jumped out of the vehicle. He rattled off our flight number to confirm that he was our ride before opening the van's rear doors to collect our bags. I noticed then that not many people in our group besides Lara and myself actually had luggage. Most had probably checked their belongings before going through TSA. Even though no more flights were leaving that night, it was airline policy to retain passengers' luggage—something having to do with security.

Lara continued to hold onto my arm while the driver loaded our luggage into the back of the dilapidated van. "They're really rolling out the red carpet for us," she cracked.

"Everybody's flights were canceled," I reminded her. "The airline probably commandeered every vehicle with wheels."

I heard her breathy sigh. "You're right. I suppose I should be thankful we've got a place to go. Speaking of which," she said, dropping my arm, "thanks for the rental." Her fingers went to her neck to remove the borrowed scarf.

I held out my hand, but instead of her dropping the scarf into my palm, she proceeded to lasso me with the silk accessory. The motion forced our bodies closer; I could practically feel the heat of her body penetrate my clothes.

She stood before me, a serious look crossing her features, as she tried to re-tie the scarf to its original knot. I felt my insides clench from our continued closeness. The combination of the silk sliding against my bare skin, her cool fingers brushing against my neck, and the lingering scent of her perfume compelled me to close my eyes.

I could only take so much torture. I suppressed a shudder and laid my hands on top of hers. "I've got it," I said quietly.

Lara gave up the effort and her hands dropped back to her sides. Her dark eyes shifted back and forth as she continued to regard me. I couldn't tell what she was thinking. Remorse? Regret? Or was I overthinking our interactions altogether?

"Ladies," the van's driver called out, "are you coming with us or not?"

My cheeks burned when I realized that Lara and I were the only ones still left on the curb. Everyone else was waiting inside the van.

"Yeah," I choked out. "Sorry."

## CHAPTER FIVE

Lara and I pressed into the vacant space remaining in the van while the driver slammed the sliding metal door behind us. Seating was limited—much less than what could comfortably accommodate two more grown adults. Lara sat down on the bench seating while I took whatever was leftover. Half of my backside hung off the seat's edge. There were too many bodies in the vehicle and not enough seatbelts to go around.

"Want to sit on my lap?" Lara offered.

I could have argued that she was smaller than me and therefore should sit on *my* lap, but I braced myself against the interior van wall instead. "It'll be fine," I said through gritted teeth. "It'll only be for a little while."

The driver turned around in the front seat to address us: "Sorry, girls. We've got about a twenty-minute drive ahead of us," he drawled in a heavy Philadelphia accent. "Everything's all booked up in the immediate vicinity, so you'll be staying at a hotel the next town over."

A slight, disgruntled murmur percolated around me, but I kept my personal discomfort to myself.

The airport shuttle bumped and rattled down a dark county highway. Every jerk and jostle caused my body to tense even more in my contortionist pose. The van's wipers worked furiously to contend with the relentless rain while the vehicle shuddered with each sideways gust of wind. All of the other passengers were silent like me, probably hoping and praying to whatever gods were listening that we'd make it safely to the off-site hotel.

My arms were practically pinned at my sides, but I managed to wiggle my cellphone out of my jacket pocket. I pulled up my most recent text message thread with Gemma to give her an update.

*Grounded in Philly for the night*, I told her.

*Oh no!* came her reply. *I saw the East Coast got slammed with weather.*

*Lara's here*, I texted.

I flicked my eyes in my co-worker's direction. It was probably ill-advised to be texting about the person sitting next to me, especially with our bodies practically crushed together, but she was similarly preoccupied with her own text conversation.

The interior of the van was dark, but nearly everyone had their phone out, casting an eerie glow around the vehicle. Lara's illuminated screen lit up the delicate contours of her face. Her mouth dipped in serious contemplation over whatever she was reading. It was the same look she'd made when she'd attempted to re-tie my scarf. She'd never been overly touchy-feely during our pseudo-relationship, which made her recent constant contact all the more confusing.

*I thought you didn't have flights together this month?* Gemma's next text read. *Isn't that why you decided to break up?*

I should have told my friends the truth about it not being a mutual separation, but I was too deep in the lie to change my story.

*She apparently switched flights with Cheri today,* I replied.

*OMG. This is so romantic! It's like Fate thrust you two together!*

I could practically hear Gemma's high-pitched squeal through the electronic words. Only her comical reaction kept me from seriously considering her words.

*There will be no thrusting*, I decided.

*Do you need me to check on Honey?*

I smiled, touched that she'd remembered my pet turtle. *No. She'll be fine for the night. I'll let you know if I'm stranded here another day though.*

*Stranded with Lara Pierson*, Gemma continued, *That wouldn't be so bad, would it?*

I looked again in Lara's direction. No. That wouldn't be so bad. But it didn't have a future, and that was the problem.

*I know you want to play matchmaker,* I wrote my friend, *but that's never going to happen. And that's okay. I don't have time for anything more serious than a fling.*

*But you're not even flinging!* Gemma's next text protested.

I put my phone away rather than respond to Gemma's most recent text. She had a point, but I didn't want to admit that she was right. I didn't necessarily *want* to be single; it wasn't like I *enjoyed* coming home to an empty apartment at night, but with my ever-changing work schedule, what other options did I have?

The airport van eventually slowed and turned into the parking lot of a roadside hotel. The neon sign out front boasted of a free continental breakfast and HBO. The van's sliding door jerked open, and I tumbled out first, eager to stretch my legs and back. My job was to travel in confined spaces, but even I had my limits.

I took a moment to inspect our surroundings. We seemed to be in the middle of nowhere—no gas stations or fast food restaurants in sight. We were far from the light pollution from the airport and Philadelphia, but no stars were visible on that cloudy night. The rain had mostly stopped, but periodic gusts of wind still threatened to carry away anything not tied down.

The few of us with luggage waited for our baggage to be unloaded from the back of the van before we filed into the hotel lobby. I was surprised to find even more people waiting inside the reception area. The hotel didn't strike me as a popular tourist destination, but it hadn't occurred to me until then that multiple flights had been canceled and that more than the people from my van needed someplace to stay.

"Can I get everyone's attention?" A tall, middle-aged man at the front of the hotel lobby waved his hands over his head and waited for the anxious chatter to subside. "I know you're all tired from a long day, so we're going to make this as painless as possible. Your airline is taking care of your accommodations tonight, so we really don't need to go through a formal check-in process. Just line up over here," he instructed, "and I'll give you a key. We've got plenty of space, so don't worry about us running out of rooms."

I pulled my suitcase behind me and fell into line with the others. Lara took up space in the queue beside me. All of this was highly unusual, but I suspected the hotel staff wanted to get each van of newcomers settled as swiftly as possible. The line of about thirty or so passengers moved forward as the hotel proprietor freely handed out plastic keycards like they were Halloween candy.

"We could share a room?" Lara chimed in as we shuffled closer to the front of the line. "Maybe save the airline some money?"

Her words and her smile were innocent—altruistic, even. And it would give the hotel staff another room in case more passengers came trickling in. But I didn't trust myself not to fall back into bed with this woman who'd already twisted my heart once before.

"I snore," I blurted out.

Lara's features pinched. "I don't remember you ever snoring?"

"It's, uh, it's a new development." I scrambled under the weight of the lie. "I wouldn't want to ruin your night."

I didn't stick around long enough for her to react. I grabbed my room key from the hotel manager and quickly scampered off in the direction of my assigned room.

Stale cigarette smoke hit my nostrils upon opening the door to my room. I pulled my wheeled luggage past the threshold and promptly locked the deadlock and engaged the sliding chain the moment the door shut behind me. Typically, I checked out my room with the door propped open—if someone was already in my room I had an easier escape—but I couldn't risk Lara knowing what room I'd disappeared to.

I fumbled in the dark to find a light toggle, but was only underwhelmed when the room eventually illuminated. Two double beds. A small, flat-screen TV on a chest with three drawers. Matching nightstands for each of the beds. The mustard-yellow lampshades that covered the bedside lamps were straight out of the Seventies. The rust-orange carpet was thin and dingy; I immediately decided my bare feet would not be touching it.

When I stayed overnight on a two- or three-day trip, the airline didn't exactly go all out and put us up in four-star hotels, but my current residence was little better than a roadside motel. Only the fact that room doors opened into a hallway and not a parking lot, kept the M- out of my lodging's category.

I hadn't had time to use the bathroom or even change my clothes when I heard a knock at my door. I sighed into the empty room. Lara Pierson seemed determined to break my resolve.

I began the task of unfastening the multiple locks of my hotel door. "Lara," I called through the barrier, "don't tell me they ran out of rooms."

When I yanked the door open, my protest died on my lips. I had assumed my colleague and one-time fling had followed me to my room. I certainly wasn't expecting to see Anissa—the woman from seat 3B. I hadn't noticed her in the group outside of the airport or in the van to the hotel—not that I'd been looking for her. She must have been shuttled to the off-site location with a different group.

She wore the same outfit she'd been wearing at the airport, only a little more wrinkled and creased than before. Since last I'd seen her, she'd pulled her long, dark locks into a high ponytail. The loose waves spilled down the back of her neck like an iridescent waterfall.

Anissa cocked a dark eyebrow in amusement. "Expecting someone?"

"No, uh, just someone I work with." I scanned the empty hallway as if expecting to see Lara lurking in the shadows. "What are you doing here?" Apparently subtly was not one of my strengths.

"My flight back to Detroit was canceled. *All* the flights were canceled," she needlessly reminded me.

She hadn't exactly answered my question. She had explained her presence at the hotel, but not at my door.

"What, uh …" I nearly asked how she had found me, but I managed to remember my manners. As long as I was in my uniform, I was technically still on-the-clock for the airline. "Can I help you with something?"

"Right. Sorry." She shook her head with a quiet chuckle. "I saw you with your luggage in the lobby earlier, but you took off before I could talk to you. I don't suppose you have an extra set of pajamas?" Her voice lilted up hopefully. "I checked my suitcase when I left Miami, and the airline wouldn't give it back after my flight was canceled. All I have is my work bag and what I bought earlier from the duty-free store."

She held up a clear plastic bag that I hadn't noticed before. Amber-colored liquid sloshed around in a liter-sized glass bottle.

"I really don't want to sleep in the clothes I've been wearing all day," she continued to explain, "and there's no way I'm sleeping naked. I've seen too many TV exposés about how dirty hotel beds are." She shuddered where she stood, but not from the cold.

I unconsciously licked my lips. My tired brain had juvenilely honed in on one word in her entire soliloquy. Naked. I bet her bra and underwear matched. She seemed the type to coordinate those things. I wondered what color they were.

I realized I'd been silent for an unwarranted amount of time. I shook my head hard and banished improper thoughts. "Uh, yeah. Sorry. Come in. I should have something."

"Thank you," she breathed in relief. "You're really saving me."

I stood back a few feet, making room in the doorway for her to enter. "Why did you check your bag? Aren't you, like, a professional traveler?"

"I know, I know," she said, making a face. "I should be living out of carry-on luggage, but I really hate having to squeeze all of my liquids into three-ounce bottles in a Ziploc bag. This," she said, flipping at her thick, glossy ponytail, "doesn't happen by itself."

I was pretty confident she would still be beautiful, unwashed and unstyled, but she hadn't asked for my opinion.

I opened my suitcase on one of the beds and searched its contents. I didn't exactly have a lot of options since I hadn't been planning on staying overnight. My wheeled bag had a few essentials for this kind of situation, however. I pulled out a t-shirt and a pair of cotton sleep shorts. The top was an old t-shirt I'd received for running in a charity 5K race. I had once entertained the goal of running a marathon, but my constantly changing work schedule precluded me from the strict training routine necessary for that kind of endeavor. It eliminated me from most areas that required persistence, routine, and consistency—like a long-term relationship.

"These should fit," I decided before forfeiting the clothes to her.

Anissa gratefully accepted the outfit, hugging the clothes against her chest. "Thank you, again, Alice. This is really kind."

"It's nothing," I dismissed out of hand.

"Can I repay you with a drink?" she offered. She motioned to the glass bottle in her duty-free bag. "It's a pretty nice bourbon." She paused, but didn't give me time to consider. "Unless your friend Lara's coming over later."

"She's not," I was quick to deny. "A drink would be great."

A ghost of a knowing smile fluttered on her mouth. "Do you mind if I change first?" she asked, still hugging my change of clothes against her body. "I can't wait to get out of my clothes."

Her word choice had me stuttering. "No, g-go right ahead."

She flashed me a quick smile, full of bright, white teeth. "I'll be right back."

I had expected her to return to her own rented room to change, but instead of watching her exit, she entered my bathroom and shut the door behind her.

I sat down on the edge of one of the double beds—the bed my still-open suitcase rested upon—and tried to catch my breath. The last hour had come at me like a runaway train. The canceled flight and detour to the out-of-the-way, run-down hotel. Lara's unexpected flirtations and poorly masked attempts to sleep with me again. The beautiful woman from 3B showing up at my door to borrow my pajamas.

I eyeballed the bathroom and tried not to think about the gorgeous woman getting naked behind the closed door. No one likes to sleep in the clothes they've worn all day, and I could appreciate her not wanting her skin to actually touch the blankets on the bed, but I also couldn't imagine a scenario where I would be so bold as to track down a near-stranger and ask for her pajamas.

The bathroom door creaked open and Anissa stepped out. I hopped to my feet as she exited, as if she'd caught me doing something I shouldn't have been doing—as if I wasn't supposed to be sitting down on my own bed.

"They fit!" she triumphantly announced.

I took her declaration as permission to check out the outfit for myself. Anissa and I were about the same height, but with different builds. We had comparable upper bodies—narrow shoulders, thin arms, and modest breasts—but her lower curves were more developed than mine. She filled out my cotton pajama shorts like I never could.

"Thank you again, Alice. I feel like a new woman." She was excessively grateful. "Still interested in a drink?"

"Sure," I bobbed my head.

"Do you want to change into your pajamas, too?" she asked. "Get more comfortable?"

"Oh, uh," I stammered, suddenly embarrassed. "I, uh, I gave you mine."

She cocked her head to the side and blinked. "What?"

"You said you needed pajamas, so I gave you pajamas," I lamely explained.

Her eyes narrowed in confusion. "Are you in the habit of giving the shirt off your back to strangers?"

"You're not exactly a stranger," I weakly protested.

"I can't take your one pair of pajamas, Alice," she resisted. "What will you sleep in?"

"The clothes I've got on. I've got a clean uniform in my bag for tomorrow. It'll be fine."

"Are you sure?" she continued to hesitate.

"We're a full-service airline," I awkwardly joked. "Just be sure to fill out a comment card when you reach your final destination."

She tucked her lower lip into her mouth in a look of uncertainty. "If you're sure."

"I'm completely sure," I insisted. I wanted to run away from the situation, but all I had was the bathroom for my exit. "Why don't you pour those drinks you were talking about?" I proposed, inching my way closer to the bathroom. "I'm just going to freshen up in the bathroom. I'll be right back."

I didn't give her the opportunity to protest further or try to return my shirt and shorts. I shut the bathroom door behind me, leaned against the back of the door, and sighed.

The bathroom was small, no larger than the toilet, pedestal sink, and a stand-up shower. The overhead light buzzed, but at least there were no visible dead insects trapped within the dome lighting. I didn't have pajamas to change into anymore, but I tried to get more comfortable by removing my navy blazer and the silk scarf that still smelled like Lara's perfume.

The light, lingering scent made me think again about her offer to share a room. I didn't know if I was making the right choice in ignoring her or at least in avoiding intimate opportunities with her. I was healthy, young, and unattached. Why shouldn't I let myself have some fun? If only impersonal trysts actually sounded appealing to me.

I rolled up the sleeves of my button-up blouse and splashed some cool water against my face. I inspected myself in the mirror above the sink. My mascara and eyeliner had all but smudged off, but at least I didn't look like an exhausted racoon. I pulled my hair free from the elastic band that had held it back in a low ponytail. Releasing my hair from its prison relieved some of the tension that had been pulling at my temples, but I could still feel the phantom beginnings of a headache. I needed to go to sleep or at least shut off my brain.

I exited the bathroom to find Anissa making herself at home. In my short absence, she had started to tear the comforter off one of the double beds, stripping it down to the white sheets beneath.

"What are you doing?" I asked.

Anissa didn't pause to consider my question. She continued to tear the bed apart, undeterred. "Have you ever used a blacklight in a hotel room?"

I wrinkled my nose, knowing exactly to what she was referring. "No, thanks. I prefer to be ignorant about the amount of body fluids in the places I stay."

I noticed the outfit she'd been wearing earlier had been folded into a neat pile and sat on the bureau upon which the television also rested. My throat tightened when I spotted a flash of pale yellow lace that belonged to either her bra or underwear. I blamed my brain's obsession with her undergarments on my exhaustion from the long day.

"Are you a bourbon drinker?" she asked. She'd completed her dismantling of my bed and transitioned next to the drinks I had been promised. She turned over two clear glasses that sat on a serving tray by the complimentary ice bucket. Her back was to me, but I could hear the sound of liquid filling glass.

"Not really," I admitted. "Hard liquor isn't my first choice."

She turned back toward me with a short, clear glass filled about halfway. "It is tonight," she grinned with a playful wink. She offered me the glass and I felt like I had no other option but to accept it.

She poured herself a drink as well, her glass filled a little more than the one she'd given me.

"What should we toast to?" she asked. She raised her glass in the air.

I shrugged in indecision; I wasn't feeling particularly clever.

"How about—to the kindness of strangers?" she suggested. Her nose crinkled when she smiled; actually, her smile reached her whole face. Deep dimples in either cheek. Elevated cheekbones. Squinted eyes. Even her eyebrows seemed to get in on the action.

I was too caught up in admiring her beautiful features to notice her traveling glass. Our drinks lightly collided, but I clenched my fingers around my glass just in time to avoid it slipping from my hand. I couldn't imagine the kind of klutz she'd think of me if I had managed to spill another drink.

Anissa lifted her glass to her mouth. Her lipstick was gone, but her lips remained a pleasant dusky rose color. I watched her lips part ever slightly and the tip of her tongue press against the edge of the heavy glass. The muscles in her throat undulated as she took an aggressive first sip.

I continued to regard the woman in my hotel room while I took a more tentative sip. The alcohol burned nearly the moment it passed my lips and hit my tongue. I at least was able to suppress a choking cough, however, so I didn't appear to be a total amateur.

Anissa topped off her drink before taking residency in the bed she had so recently stripped. Her braless breasts gently moved beneath her borrowed t-shirt as she positioned herself at the head of the bed. She sat with her legs folded, which caused the cotton sleep shorts to ride up her tan thighs.

She patted at the empty space beside her. "Take a load off, Alice," she coaxed. "You're not on the clock anymore."

Technically I was still in my uniform and still representing my airline until I returned to Detroit. But there was no harm in having one drink, I reasoned, even if it was with a Business Class passenger, and even if she was wearing my pajamas. Too bad there wasn't a bingo card square for that.

She'd offered the space beside her, but this wasn't a sleepover party—or at least I didn't think it was supposed to be. I didn't want to appear too eager to sit close to her, but I also didn't want to make it weird by not sitting next to her, like I thought she had cooties. I was going to be awkward in my tight pencil skirt no matter where I sat, so I took up the place beside her.

The glass tumbler, filled halfway with its amber liquid, looked at home in Anissa's curved hand. She balanced the glass on her bare knee while the light touch of her fingers kept it from tipping over. There was something super enticing about a woman who drank bourbon—like she'd forced her way into the Old Boy's Club of booze, cigars, and impulsive purchases. I was more into wine or beer myself.

"Does this kind of stuff happen regularly?" she asked.

I knew she meant the canceled flight and hotel detour, but I was tempted to tell her that no, gorgeous women whom I'd only recently met had never borrowed my pajamas before or drank bourbon on my hotel bed.

Instead, I shook my head and took another burning sip from my glass. The alcohol warmed me from the inside like a cozy blanket.

"For as long as I've been doing this," I said, "I can probably count on one hand the number of times I've gotten stuck because of canceled flights."

"How long have you been a flight attendant?" she asked.

"Almost eight years."

"Do you like it?"

"I do," I nodded. I cupped my glass in both hands. "I get to travel the world, see interesting places, meet interesting people."

"That sounds suspiciously like the company line," she smirked.

"Okay, well, how about you? Do you like being an HR consultant?" I turned the question around on her.

"I'm impressed you remembered," she said, raising her eyebrows.

I shrugged, not wanting to make it a big deal that I'd memorized the details of her life.

"My job is decidedly dull," she said, "and I have no social life because I'm on the road so much. But I don't really know what else I'd be doing if not this."

I nodded knowingly. While I wouldn't have described my job as dull, it certainly monopolized my time, especially when I took on extra flights to continue chipping away at my unnecessary student debt.

"What were you majoring in at college?" she asked.

I felt a small, but private victory that I wasn't the only one who'd remembered the details from our brief food court conversation.

"I have no idea," I admitted. "Which is probably why it didn't turn out so well. I took a little of this, a little of that. I stuck it out for two years before I realized college wasn't for me."

"And not even an Associate's Degree to show for your work?"

"Nah. Just a bunch of student debt." I tried to keep the bitterness out of my tone. "They should really tell people that college isn't for everyone. It would have saved me about forty grand."

I normally wasn't so open about my massive debt, especially with someone I didn't really know, but conversation came easy with her.

Anissa winced at the admission. "I can relate. I never thought I'd pay off my MBA. But I chiseled away at it, little by little."

"I'm trying to do that with my student loans," I confirmed, "but after my car payment and rent, there's not a lot left over. Luckily I don't have time for much of a social life outside of work. I try to get the two or three flights-a-day lines each month. We really only get paid when we're in the air, so longer flights are the best ones. I pick up extra flights on my days off to make a little extra cash, but we're generally limited to 12-hour days."

"Twelve hours?" she echoed. "That's a long day."

"It's not all in-flight though. Like right now," I noted, "this is technically considered part of my work day."

"You're getting paid to drink my good booze?"

"Not too shabby, right?"

"Want some more?" she offered.

"Sure." I had no place to be.

Anissa leaned across me to grab the bottle of bourbon from one of the bedside tables. She continued to lean to one side as she topped off my glass, which provided me an unobstructed view down the neck of her t-shirt. I quickly averted my eyes when I realized I could see the tops of her naked breasts, straight down to her bellybutton.

"Tell me the craziest thing that's ever happened on a flight," she commanded.

"The craziest?" I was too flustered, worried she'd caught my stare, to give her an immediate answer.

"Yeah, like, the Mile High Club. Is that a real thing or is it only in the movies?"

"People trying to have sex in an airplane bathroom is actually a lot more common than you'd think," I remarked.

"Really?"

"Mmhm," I hummed as I took a quick sip. "People try to get away with all kinds of things when we're in the air. Guys watch porn on flights all the time—totally don't even hide it. Or you get those couples who ask for blankets so they can fool around under them."

"Wow. I had no idea," Anissa blinked. "Have you done anything like that? Are you a member of the club?"

Her tone and features were so nonchalant, it was as though she'd asked if I flossed regularly instead of if I'd ever had sex on a plane.

"Uh, no. Definitely not."

Anissa shifted on the mattress, sitting up straighter. "Definitely not? Why is that a definite no?"

I took another drink of my bourbon to give myself more time to formulate an answer. I half contemplated telling her about the monthly bingo card, but it was supposed to be a company secret. "I can't wrap my head around having sex in a port-a-potty," I settled on.

She stuck out an adorable, yet juicy lower lip. "Not even once?"

"When I'm on a plane I'm typically working, and it wouldn't be responsible for me to ditch the people in my crew like that, plus there's so many people on a plane," I began to ramble, "and I'd be selfish to monopolize one of the bathrooms when so many people would probably be waiting." I could feel myself squirming.

"Okay, okay," she laughed. She knocked her shoulder against mine. "I'll stop harassing you about it."

"Have *you* done anything wild and crazy while on the job?" I asked, not wanting to feel like a rigid prude.

"I borrowed a girl's pajamas and drank whiskey with her in bed," she grinned cheekily.

Her response made me laugh. "Okay, fair enough."

I couldn't help noticing that at some point in our conversation, her shoulder had continued to press against mine. It was a friendly gesture, but it was electrifying. I lost all other feeling in my body except for the warm, solid press of her arm touching mine.

"Want some more?" she asked. Her voice was deep and round. The syllables covered my brain in a warm, velvety blanket.

I'd become too focused on the warmth radiating from her body for her question to register. In my silence, she again filled our glasses before they could ever empty. It was probably the most dangerous way of consuming alcohol. If she continued to top off my glass, I would have no idea how much bourbon I'd actually had.

As she poured, some of the liquid splashed onto the top of her hand. She brought her hand up to her mouth and licked away the few clinging drops. Her tongue was quick, but everything seemed to slow down with the action. My eyes were drawn to her broad mouth, her generous lips, and to her smooth skin. It had been an innocent movement to avoid spilling alcohol on the bed, but my mind was busy with anything but innocent thoughts.

I remembered her cute, shallow bellybutton. How much whiskey could I drink off of her abdomen? I pressed my thighs together, hopeful she wouldn't notice. I could feel the heat radiating from my core like an overworked campfire, and this woman was gasoline.

"So."

Anissa set her glass on the bedside table and licked her lips.

"So," I repeated back.

"So, are we going to fuck now or later?"

My eyes widened and my mouth fell open. "What?"

Anissa raised up on her knees in bed. "Am I supposed to pretend you haven't been ogling my ass and tits all night?"

My eyes opened even wider. "I-I ..."

Anissa put her hands on her hips and waited for a real response. The expectant posture only succeeded in thrusting her breasts higher and farther out. Without my brain's permission, my eyes dropped to her chest. I could just make out the shape of her dark nipples through the thin t-shirt material.

"See? You're doing it right now," she practically gloated.

I slapped my hands over my eyes, no longer trusting myself to not gawk at her body. I had probably looked like a hungry, cartoon wolf eyeballing a sheep all night.

"What's wrong, Alice?"

I loved how my name sounded coming off her tongue. I could only imagine how much better it would sound when I was literally making her cum from my tongue.

Jesus.

I peeked through my fingers, but I didn't drop them from my face. Anissa's eyebrows had risen so high on her forehead that they threatened to disappear into her hairline.

"Well?" she demanded.

I finally lowered my hands. "I-I should probably get some sleep." I swallowed with difficulty. "I think your bourbon's starting to go to my head."

I didn't mention that I thought she herself might be a little drunk.

She blinked a few times. "Wow," she exclaimed. "This is a first. Kicked out of someone's bed."

"I'm not kicking you out," I insisted. "But we both have an early morning, so we should probably just..." I mentally flailed for reasons why what she had proposed wouldn't be a good idea.

Anissa popped up from the bed like a hot popcorn kernel. "I get it. No hard feelings. I'll just take my booze and go." She spun on her heels to face me. "Do you want your pajamas back?"

"What? No." The thought hadn't even crossed my mind.

Her hands went to the elastic band of the sleep shorts, which she slowly rolled down until her tan hipbones were visible. "Are you sure?" she seemed to purr. Her tone was thick and syrupy—setting a trap for unsuspecting flight attendants who might tumble into her web.

I turned on my heels before I could see anymore. "Jesus, woman!" I squeaked.

I slammed my eyes shut when I realized I could still see her half-dressed reflection in the mirror on the opposite wall. I was sure she was trying to give me a heart attack. She was far too attractive to be playing with my neglected libido.

I heard her soft laugh. "You're no fun, Alice."

I couldn't come up with an appropriate comeback, so I remained with my eyes shut and my back turned to her.

I only opened my eyes when I heard the soft click of the hotel room door opening and closing. I pried one eye open and, determining it was safe to look again, opened my other eye.

I scanned the room. Anissa was gone, along with all traces that she'd ever been there. She'd collected her bottle of alcohol, the translucent duty-free bag, and the tidy pile of clothing she'd worn that day. With the exception of the residual burning in my throat from drinking her bourbon and my lack of pajamas, I might have believed she'd never come over at all.

Her attraction to me was a surprise, but not the casualness with which she had approached sex. I encountered those kinds of individuals all the time in my line of work. When you spent most of your nights at hotels instead of the place you considered home, the temptation for casual hookups and infidelity was intense.

Sleeping with someone you'd just met in the hotel lobby bar was no more unusual than finding a partner on a dating app. Late nights out at restaurants and bars, idle time in hotel rooms, and in-room mini fridges tended to be a recipe for impromptu hook ups. I probably wouldn't have slept with Lara so readily if not for the circumstances.

I flopped back onto the stripped-down bed. The sheets were still warm where Anissa had been sitting.

I certainly wasn't a fan of one-night stands, but maybe a random night with a beautiful stranger would have been just the thing to successfully knock Lara Pierson out of my brain. I rolled over and buried my face into a pillow.

Fuck, I was an idiot.

## CHAPTER SIX

I woke up not quite remembering where I'd spent the previous night. The bed was unfamiliar as were the shadowy silhouettes of furniture around the room. It wasn't a new feeling. My work schedule often had me spending the night in strange hotels. I breathed out into the room as I slowly became more awake and aware of my surroundings. I groaned as I sat up; I didn't exactly have a hangover, but the ghost of a headache pulsed in the front of my brain. Knowing that she'd drank more than me, I couldn't help but wonder how Anissa was feeling that morning.

I eased my reluctant body out of bed and pulled back the curtains. More grey skies. I hoped that the weather had cleared enough that flights would be returning to normal. I was still getting paid my *per diem*, but if I didn't work my usual flights, I didn't make my usual paycheck. And any disruption in my schedule could be disastrous for my budget.

A trip to the bathroom and a quick look at my reflection was a reminder that I'd slept overnight in my uniform. I leaned against the bathroom sink and sighed. I couldn't rationalize why I'd forfeited my only pair of pajamas to someone who was practically a stranger. It wouldn't have been the end of the world if she'd had to sleep in the clothes she'd worn that day. I could only chalk up my unnecessary generosity to extreme customer service.

I entertained a brief thought about checking on Anissa to see if she needed toothpaste or other toiletries, but I was embarrassed about how the evening had abruptly ended. I also realized I didn't know which room number was hers. Instead, I showered and got ready for the day as best as I could with the limited supplies I routinely kept in my overnight bag for situations like this one. I felt better and more like myself once I'd showered and had changed into a clean uniform. I re-packed my suitcase, double-checked the room to make sure I wasn't forgetting anything, and headed for the front lobby.

The front of the hotel was a buzz of activity. I imagined most folks staying at the budget-friendly hotel had been, like myself, stranded at the airport overnight. Rescheduled morning flights had everyone up and ready to go, awaiting the airport shuttles that would bring us back to the Philadelphia airport.

The airport vans hadn't arrived yet, and the promising scent of coffee had me exploring the lobby area for something to eat. I normally would have waited for breakfast at the airport since my airline paid for my meals, but I doubted I would find time to track down food before I was expected at my gate. Flight crews had to report to their respective gates at least an hour before the flight was scheduled to depart. I probably wouldn't be working the flight back to Detroit—the original flight had been canceled, meaning we'd all be squeezed onto flights that had already been ticketed and staffed for that day—but there was still a slight chance I would be working my ride back to Detroit.

I found a small breakfast nook just off the main reception area. The floor plan was filled with small tables and chairs. A modest offering of continental breakfast foods, coffee, and assorted juices populated a long, low table against the far wall. The morning news played without volume on a small TV in another corner of the room. That day's newspaper had been cannibalized with separate sections of the paper scattered around the small room. I scanned the breakfast offerings on the long table, but found them lacking. The free continental breakfast was little more than granola bars and old pastries, probably procured from a vending machine.

I poured myself a cup of coffee and pocketed a granola bar for later. I scanned the room for familiar faces, looking for the other members of my flight crew, when my eyes fell on a woman sitting by herself at a corner table. The oversized sunglasses that she wore inside told me exactly how she was feeling that morning. Her hair was wet from the shower and she wore the same suit she'd been wearing the day before, only more wrinkled and creased from continued use.

I didn't announce my arrival, but discretely slipped a travel packet of aspirin onto the small table where she sat. Anissa looked up and winced, either from a lingering headache or from memories of our previous night together. She didn't say anything, but her hand curled around the pain medicine's individualized packaging.

I heard her sigh before she motioned to the empty seat across the table from her. The other tables in the room were already occupied, so I accepted her nonverbal invitation and sat down.

"Rough morning?" I tried gently.

In lieu of answering, she tore open the foil packaging and gulped down two pills with her orange juice. She removed her sunglasses and tossed them on the table.

"I'm sorry about last night," she opened. She pinched the bridge of her nose. "It was very inappropriate of me."

"It was," I concurred.

"I suppose I got my signals mixed up," she said. "I'm sorry for putting you in an uncomfortable position."

"It, uh—it's not that I wasn't interested. I'm, uh…" I couldn't admit to her that I'd been intimidated to go to bed with her. I scrambled for a different excuse. "I-I'm on my period, so, I, uh, I couldn't….You know…"

"Fuck," she finished for me.

Her blunt language had me ducking my head. "Yeah."

I pretended to be interested in a blemish on the surface of the table. I ran my thumbnail along a shallow groove that had been chipped from the imitation wood. When I looked back up, Anissa was still staring at me. Her eyes had narrowed in contemplation as if trying to decide if I was telling the truth.

She spoke after what felt like a very long time: "Another time, perhaps."

Her reaction was confusing. Was she suggesting a raincheck on sex? I didn't know how to respond to her words, but luckily I didn't have to. My attention was temporarily diverted when I spotted Lara getting coffee from the makeshift breakfast buffet.

"Shit," I swore without meaning to. I slumped down in my seat, half tempted to bolt out of the room entirely.

Anissa sat up a little straighter in her chair and craned her neck as she scanned the room. "Who are you hiding from?"

"No one." I picked up a brochure that had been on the table and pretended to be interested in its contents. "Lara."

"Ah—the infamous Lara," she clucked. She continued to unabashedly stare in Lara's direction. Her boldness made me squirm in my seat, sure she was going to get us caught. "Do you not like her or something?"

"No. Nothing like that," I mumbled. "I probably like her *too* much."

"Ahhh," she hummed as if she understood, although I had no idea if she actually did. "She's pretty," she observed.

"She is," I agreed. "We kind of dated, but then she moved on."

I didn't know why I felt compelled to share intimate details with a near-stranger. I didn't have the bourbon to blame anymore.

I allowed my attention to drift back to the breakfast buffet. Like me, Lara was in her airline uniform. It was a different combination than the day before—a short-sleeved blouse tucked into skinny trousers. My eyes traveled down her long legs to her high heels.

"In my line of work, we discourage fraternizing with co-workers." Anissa's voice pulled my attention back to the table. "It can get messy. And we in HR don't care very much for messes."

I slumped down lower in my chair. "Thanks for the tip," I drawled sardonically. "Got any more professional advice?"

"Yeah. Don't get drunk on a work night."

"You have to work today?" I asked, amazed.

She nodded and gulped down more of her orange juice. "My boss emailed me this morning to see if I could fill in for a colleague since I'm already on the road. He'll have to pay me time and a half since it's technically my day off, but at least it'll be a productive trip."

"Maybe after this you can convince him to only book direct flights," I proposed. "If you hadn't had a layover, you would be home in bed right now."

"Sure, but then I never would have gotten kicked out of a charming flight attendant's hotel room."

"I didn't kick you out!" I huffed in exasperation.

Anissa grinned broadly, her hangover seemingly forgotten for the moment. "You're too much fun to tease, Alice."

It wasn't much longer until an airport employee entered the breakfast area to announce that the shuttle for all airline personnel had arrived.

"I guess that's me," I said, standing up. I was partly relieved to have an excuse to leave, but another, bigger, part of me wanted to stay at that breakfast table. "I hope your head feels better. And don't forget to take your Dramamine."

Anissa's eyes narrowed slightly. "You remembered that, too?"

That I'd remembered so many details about her after only a few brief interactions was irrationally embarrassing.

"We pride ourselves on customer service," I lamely excused. "Don't forget to fill out that comment card."

Her eyes narrowed in further contemplation, but thankfully she didn't call out my obvious lie.

The grey skies from earlier had burned off and the morning sun was practically blinding compared to the thick fog that had kept us grounded the previous night. The sky was blue and cloudless; it would be a beautiful day in the air. Multiple shuttle vans were lined up in front of the hotel lobby to take us back to the Philadelphia airport. I loaded my suitcase, one pair of pajamas lighter, into the back of one of the vans.

"Did you have a good night?"

I squinted into the glare of the morning sun to see Lara and her roller bag approach.

"Mmhm," I confirmed. With anyone else I might have shared the details of my bizarre evening. But Lara herself had been part of that weirdness.

"What are you doing when we get back?" she asked.

Her question was vague, but I assumed she meant when we got back to the Detroit airport. We wouldn't be resuming our original flight to Boston. Since that trip had been canceled, the passengers for that flight would have been reassigned to other regularly scheduled flights. Lara, Derek, and I would probably be deadheading on a return trip to Detroit. Deadheading referred to when an airline employee flied as a passenger as part of their job, typically in uniform. We weren't still on the clock and wouldn't be expected to work the flight, but we also weren't on vacation either.

"I'm on call," I said. "But I'll probably check out the Trade Board when we get back. Maybe I can pick up a few flights today."

Lara frowned. "Even after yesterday's hassle?"

I shrugged noncommittally, and didn't go into additional details. Since we hadn't flown to Boston and then back to Detroit, my paycheck would be two flights lighter.

"You should really give Cheri hell for asking you to switch flights." I changed the subject to avoid talking about my financial situation. "You shouldn't even be here right now."

Lara gave me a peculiar smile. "You assume she was the one who asked," she cryptically replied.

+ + +

I didn't have any more seat-specific bingo challenges to complete, but I didn't tell either Kent or Gemma that so I could continue to work the First Class cabin on our Wednesday flights. I also hadn't told them that I'd been propositioned by a Business Class passenger over the weekend. It was the kind of juicy gossip that would have kept them preoccupied for the rest of the month, and I didn't want their entertainment to be at my expense.

I held the customary tray of complimentary water for the First Class passengers while the rest of the plane boarded. Anissa was already buckled into seat 3B.

"I think it might rain today," I announced with a mischievous tone. "The forecast is calling for cloudy with a chance of showers."

Anissa looked up from her tablet at my words. Unlike the majority of my other passengers, I noticed she never wore earbuds or headphones. I understood the appeal of noise-canceling technology, but it made my job a thousand times harder.

A slight look of panic crossed her features when she saw me and the full tray of water glasses. She clutched her armrest with her free hand like the plane was going to crash. "Oh no. This isn't some kind of payback for last Friday, is it? Tsunami warning?"

I laughed—a genuine laugh, not the hollow, empty laugh that came with customer service. "Just bringing you your complimentary drink, Miss. We value your continued loyalty."

Instead of the standard glass of water, I handed her a glass that bubbled. "Cranberry, splash of seltzer."

"You remembered." She chuckled and shook her head. "This airline's customer service is unparalleled." Her caramel-colored eyes locked their focus on me. "Or maybe it's just a particular flight attendant."

I could feel the apples of my cheeks warm. "I figured you'd say no to whiskey," I deflected.

I watched the tip of her pink tongue sneak out from her parted mouth to wet her full, lower lip. "There you go being a bad influence again, Alice."

The movement of her mouth and the low burr of her voice caused an involuntary reaction beneath my bra and in between my thighs. God, why hadn't I had sex with this woman when I'd had the chance? Who in their right mind turned down that?

"Oh! That reminds me. I've got something for you." Anissa unbuckled her safety belt and stood up. She opened the overhead storage bin above her seat and unzipped the main zipper of an oversized leather purse. While she retrieved something from her bag, my eyes inadvertently slid down to her backside.

The linen suit she wore was beautiful, just like the woman who wore it. I marveled first that the pants weren't already creased from sitting, but soon found myself admiring more than the resilience of the cotton fabric. The fitted material hugged her lower curves and hit at just the right places. A thin leather belt cinched at her waist. The t-shirt beneath her light jacket was probably more expensive than my fanciest shirt.

Anissa turned around and my eyes snapped up to her face. I worried she'd caught me staring, but if she had she didn't call me out for ogling her. Again.

"I washed them," she said.

I blinked. "Washed what?"

"Your pajamas?" She held out a neatly folded stack of familiar-looking clothes.

"Oh, right."

I cast my eyes around the general area, hoping no one was watching our exchange. But no one ever noticed me, and especially not the passengers in First Class. Despite this knowledge, I felt the heat of embarrassment slip over my cheeks. It wasn't like she was returning my underwear, but the intimacy and familiarity made me blush.

I was still holding onto a tray full of complementary water, so I awkwardly lifted my elbow like a bird's wing. Anissa understood the nonverbal cue and tucked my folded shirt and shorts between my torso and my arm.

I was used to people being in my personal bubble, especially on airplanes, but her close proximity had me holding my body tense.

"Thanks," I choked out.

"No, thank *you*, Alice," she genuinely returned.

I turned on my heel to return to the rear galley where my carry-on luggage was stowed. But I spun back around in the aisle when a ridiculous request popped into my brain.

Anissa was still standing in the center aisle.

"Can I buy you dinner? Friday? In Philadelphia?" I proposed.

She arched a perfect eyebrow. "I might upset the Flight Gods if I break from tradition."

"Maybe they'll allow it just this once," I reasoned with what I hoped was a charming smile. "Besides, they seemed to ignore your food tribunal last week."

I watched her generous lips part. The tip of her tongue darted out to wet the center of her lower lip. Her perfect, bee-stung lips did unfair things to my overly-active imagination.

*Why the hell had I said no to her?*

"I'm sorry. I can't."

My eyebrows knit together. "You can't?" I echoed. "Already have a hot dinner date?" I tried to joke.

She chewed on her lower lip. "I'm sorry, Alice. I just can't."

I nodded stiffly and swallowed the lump in my throat with some difficulty. I tried not to let her rejection get to me. It had been an impulsive request on my part, and we were both technically at work. It was probably an inappropriate ask, anyway. I turned back around on my heels, my ego moderately bruised.

I spent the rest of the flight hiding out in the rear galley. I didn't say anything, so neither Kent nor Gemma suspected that anything was wrong; we typically all crammed in the rear of the aircraft, so nothing appeared out of the ordinary. Our plane landed in Philadelphia and the passengers gathered their belongings to exit the plane. I reapplied my lipstick before the landing gear touched down, plastered a smile to my lips, and said my one million goodbyes.

We had a different plane and gate for the next leg of our trip, but before we could deplane, we had to clean up the plane's interior and take stock of the beverage and snack inventory. I started at the front of the plane, picking up plastic cups, napkins, and food wrappers.

Tidying the plane, getting it ready for the next flight crew, was probably the least favorite part of my job description. It made me feel like a bitter mom who had repeatedly reminded her kids to clean up after themselves, only to be ignored. We walked up and down the aisles with trash bags all throughout the flight, and yet inevitably I still ended up collecting a mountain of trash after the plane landed.

I nearly bypassed seat 3B, knowing Anissa was good about throwing away her trash before arrival, but something made me stop. The immediate area was clean of debris, but I peeked inside the rear seat pocket. I reached inside the slim opening and pulled out a silver iPad.

I looked around the plane to see if anyone was looking in my direction. Both Kent and Gemma had their heads down as they went about picking up their sections of the plane. I unobtrusively slipped the electronic device into my workbag. I had no intention of keeping the tablet for myself, but an impulsive plan had started to assemble in my thoughts.

+ + +

Even though we didn't spend our layovers together, I knew I would find Kent at the Cinnabon in Concourse C. He avoided carbohydrates like the plague, but he liked the scent of the sticky, sugary treat. Predictably, I found him sitting on a bench within sniffing distance of the fast food kiosk.

I plopped down in the empty space beside my friend. "Do you still talk to that guy from ticketing?"

Kent looked up from the on-going text conversation splashed across his phone screen. "There was never really any *talking* involved. Maybe some grunting and cursing."

"You're like a poet," I remarked, rolling my eyes. "Would he be able to get me a passenger's home address?"

Kent's features perked up with interest. I knew this was new territory for him; I rarely did or said anything of significance, according to him.

"Why, pray tell, do you need me to break company rules?" he asked.

"A passenger left their tablet on the plane. I want to return it."

"You know we have a Lost & Found for that," he pointed out.

"I know. But I don't want her to freak out when she can't find it. She might not even realize she left it on the flight."

Kent's manscaped eyebrows rose. "*She,* eh? Does someone have a little crush?"

"No," I immediately rejected. "I just want the address so I can mail it back."

"Such a little do-gooder," Kent sighed, already sounding exhausted with me. "You're in luck. I've been meaning to reconnect with Steve. You've given me a legitimate reason to call him beyond missing the things he can do with his tongue."

I appreciated Kent's willingness to help me, but I couldn't keep my remarks to myself. "You should really be writing this down. Seriously, Kent. You're like a Poet Laureate."

## CHAPTER SEVEN

It had taken some convincing to procure Anissa's home address. Kent's 'friend,' wasn't so enthused to be breaking company policy for me, but eventually he'd done what Kent had asked. I already owed Kent for letting me work First Class on the flights we staffed together, and now I would have to find a way to pay him back for this favor. My debt to him was piling up like the interest on my student loans. I'd had to wait until my next day off, a Saturday, to drive out to the suburban address Kent's friend had found for one Anissa Khoury.

"This can't be right."

I slowed my car to a slow crawl, mindful of the children who played in the streets, zig-zagging in and out of highly manicured lawns. Automatic sprinkler systems watered the lush green grass and dribbled onto the concrete sidewalk and blacktop streets.

Dearborn, Michigan was an affluent Detroit neighborhood, not too far—only a dozen miles—from the airport. Nationally it was known for its disproportionately high Arab American population, along with being automobile giant Henry Ford's hometown. The city remained the Ford Motor Company's World headquarters.

Bloated mansions, nearly indistinguishable from each other, towered above the landscape on either side of the street. It was a wealthy neighborhood, but not quite at a price point that afforded privacy. The rows and rows of houses looked into neighbors' windows and backyards.

*Why would she live here?* I'd assumed her to be single and living in an apartment complex, like myself.

I had realized, too late, that the address Kent's friend had looked up might not even be Anissa's home address. Because she traveled for work, all of her billing information might have been the listing for the consulting company for which she worked.

I double-checked the address before parking and getting out of my car. My reliable and economical sedan was typically the nicest and newest car in the airport employee parking lot, but it looked like a jalopy parked on the curb of the affluent subdivision amongst all the Mercedes, BMWs, and Jaguars.

The air was filled with the sounds of leaf blowers and lawn mowers, not the constant air traffic that surrounded my apartment building. My apartment's location made for an easy commute to work, but I rarely spent time on my balcony because of the constant buzz of planes taking off and landing.

A newly poured cement slab directed me up to the front door. The blinds and curtains in all of the windows of the two-story home were drawn, denying me a glimpse of the house's interior. I had gone to the address Kent had procured for me, but each step toward the oversized home heightened my doubts that this was where Anissa actually lived.

I reached the front porch—a narrow composite wood landing—and nearly lost my nerve. A mailbox slot was built into the front door. The opening was large enough that I could have shoved the tablet through the door and run away, but I still didn't know if Anissa actually lived here.

My throat progressively tightened the longer I stood on the front stoop. This was such a dumb idea. Before I could psyche myself out, I jabbed my index finger against the glowing doorbell. Its loud, rich tone echoed through the house.

I heard a muffled voice on the other side of the heavy front door. "Coming!"

It might have been Anissa's voice, but I couldn't be sure.

I'd nearly made up my mind to scamper back to my car and return her tablet on Wednesday when the lawn mowers and leaf blowers collectively paused long enough for me to hear the distinct sound of children's laughter. The houses were close together and the tall privacy fences around each property's backyard made it hard to decipher from where the squeals and laughter was coming.

I heard a high-pitched voice ring out—"Cannonball!"—followed by the sound of a body plunging into a pool.

I froze on the front stoop. The voice had come from the direction of Anissa's backyard. Was I at the right house, or did Anissa have a family?

The anxiety that had resided in my gut transformed to quiet indignation. I had heard about these situations through my friend Kent, but I'd never actually experienced it myself. I knew about pilots and other flight attendants who had "arrangements" with other crew members away from their regular life. The potential to live a double life presented itself when one traveled extensively for work and was often on the road and away from home. When Anissa was in the air or at a hotel, she could be one version of herself—single, flirtatious, promiscuous. And in Dearborn, Michigan she could be a soccer mom—devoted wife, president of the PTA.

We hadn't done anything untoward in that Philadelphia hotel room, but if not for my cowardice, we could have. How many others had been in my position? How many others hadn't turned her away?

The front door swung open.

I took only a moment to register the familiar face before unleashing my frustration: "You have kids?" I hissed. My hands were balled into tight fists at my sides in barely contained anger. "Does this mean you have a husband, too?"

If I hadn't been a coil of hot anger, I would have felt sorry for her. I'd ambushed her, showing up unexpectedly at her front door, not completely unlike what she'd done to me in Philadelphia.

Anissa took a few steps outside and closed the front door behind her. "Alice? What are you doing here?"

My gaze took in her swimwear coverup. The patterned, brightly colored material looked like a kimono or short robe that was open in the front. My eyes quickly traveled to her tan, bare legs, down to her flip-flops and manicured toenails. Her long, dark hair was pulled back in a messy bun. Mirrored sunglasses were perched on her forehead. She modestly pulled close the front of the coverup.

She'd ignored my questions, so I ignored hers.

"I *heard* them, Anissa. There's children in your backyard."

"Yeah. My nieces and nephews," she explained. "I don't have kids. No husband either."

I didn't believe her. "But this house!" I flailed my arms at my sides. "It's *enormous*!"

"I live here alone," she insisted. "I like my space. It's why I always purchase seats 3A and 3B together."

Her revelation made me pause. I thought back to my Wednesday flights. Had anyone been sitting in the seat beside her? I couldn't recall; I'd been so distracted by her, there might as well have been no one else on the entire flight.

I realized I'd been staring, probably slack-jawed.

She crossed her arms across her chest. "Now why don't you explain what you're doing out here?"

Her voice was alarmingly calm despite my unsolicited visit.

"You-you forgot this in your seatback pocket."

I produced the tablet that had been my flimsy excuse to drive to her home.

The sharpness to her features softened. "You could have given it to me on Wednesday."

"I thought you might be worried you'd lost it."

She shook her head. "You didn't need to come all this way. You could have called. You somehow found my home address. Couldn't you have found my phone number, too?"

My eyes dropped to the curb, and I chewed on my lower lip. I wanted to tell her the truth—that I'd wanted to see her. But the truth felt too forward, too insane.

"Well, since you're here, you might as well stay for the barbeque."

Her words had me returning my eyes to her level. "Oh, I don't want to interrupt your family time."

"Nonsense. You're here. And there's plenty of food. Come in, Alice."

Despite my earlier words of hesitance, I followed her inside. A blast of air conditioned air greeted me as I entered her home.

A carpeted staircase in the entryway led to the second floor. An office space separated from the rest of the house by French doors was on my left. A formal dining room was set up on my right. I spied a large rectangular dining table surrounded by at least eight high-backed chairs.

The front foyer was open and spacious, but a chaotic pile of little shoes cluttered the space around the door.

"My nieces and nephews like to leave their stuff everywhere," she explained, noticing where my eyes had lingered.

Anissa continued to walk deeper into her home and I felt compelled to follow. The sounds of shrieking children grew louder the farther inside we went.

The front half of the house consisted of tidy, defined rooms; the back half opened up into one large, lofted space that included both the kitchen and a sunken living room. A large flat-screen television hung above the mantle of a gas fireplace. The vaulted ceilings had to be at least twenty feet high. Twin ceiling fans rotated the refrigerated air.

"You have a beautiful home," I remarked.

Her house was more than nice—it was excessive, especially if she was telling the truth and was the only one who lived there.

"Thank you," she threw over her shoulder. "My parents and siblings all live in identical houses down the street. I'm the only one with a pool though, so it tends to become party central in the summer."

She dropped off her tablet on the granite kitchen island before continuing towards the rear of the house. She slid open the kitchen slider that led to an impressive backyard. A tall privacy fence wrapped around the perimeter of the yard. The in-ground pool was the center attraction. The light blue water bobbed as a gaggle of children laughed and screamed while the adults looked on from the dry safety of the concrete patio. I did a quick scan, but didn't really observe numbers or ages or gender.

"Everyone, this is Alice," Anissa introduced. "Alice, this is everyone."

I heard a few hellos and welcomes, but I didn't know from where they came. I gave a wilted wave in return.

Anissa didn't elaborate on how we knew each other, and for that I was grateful. What would she have even said?

*"Hey, everyone, this is that weird flight attendant I was telling you about."*

Anissa turned to me. "Would you like to borrow a bathing suit?"

"I've already imposed too much," I resisted.

An eyebrow arched at my hesitance. "Still on your period?" she questioned. Her skeptical tone indicated she suspected I'd been lying in Philadelphia.

"No."

"Then come on."

Anissa grabbed my arm, and I had no choice but to follow her. She tugged me back inside her refrigerated home and pulled the slider closed behind us. I still couldn't tell if she was happy or annoyed to see me, but she'd insisted that I stay a little longer, so it couldn't have been too bad.

We made the trek back through her house to the staircase in the front foyer. She gripped her fingers first around my wrist, but then her fingers slid through mine as we marched upstairs. I took no notice of décor or room layout; my attention was entirely concentrated on the heat of her hand and the softness of her skin. It made me wonder what she felt like in other places.

She pulled me into a room at the top of the staircase. A king-sized bed took centerstage yet there was still ample space for various clothing bureaus and a free-standing full-length mirror. Anissa dropped my hand and walked directly for one of the wardrobes. I remained in the doorway, still feeling like an uninvited intruder.

"Is this your room?" I asked. The bedroom was so large, my voice practically echoed.

Anissa opened the top drawer of a dresser. She glanced briefly over her shoulder to observe me. "Yes. And before you ask, I don't share it with a husband."

"How about a wife?" I countered.

Her smile was more like a smirk. "Maybe someday."

I rocked back on my heels and waited in silence. Luckily I didn't have to wallow in my awkwardness for long. Anissa shut the top drawer and turned to me.

"This should fit."

I didn't much trust the crinkle around her eyes or her upturned mouth, but I accepted the proffered swimsuit.

I held up the separate pieces of the pastel yellow bathing suit in front of me. "This is supposed to go on my body?"

"That's the idea."

"It's not even enough material for a pirate patch!" I protested.

"I guess you should have come more prepared."

I opened my mouth to point out that I hadn't intended on crashing her family's pool party, but I decided against the complaint. I'd only wanted to see her again; if I had to wear a teeny-tiny bikini to do so, then that was just the price of admission.

Thank God I'd recently shaved.

"I'll see you down there," she sing-songed in her departure. She shut the bedroom door behind her, leaving me on my own.

I held up the pale yellow bikini that probably looked dynamic in contrast to her bronzed skin tone. On me, I was sure, it would only look washed out.

"Fuck," I swore into the empty room.

A few moments later, after I'd stripped out of my clothes and wiggled into the bikini, I cracked open Anissa's bedroom door and stuck out only my head.

"Anissa?" I called out.

I realized it was the first time I'd said her name out loud. I couldn't deny how good the syllables felt rolling around on my tongue.

I paused and waited for a reply that never came.

I opened the bedroom door the rest of the way and took a tentative step into the hallway. The plush carpet felt cozy against my bare feet, but that was about my only comfortable body part. I was even more self-aware of my partial nakedness, dressed in Anissa's flimsy excuse for a bikini, in the silent, air conditioned home.

None of the clothes I'd worn over were a suitable coverup, so I searched for a linen closet amongst the closed upstairs doors. It felt presumptuous to be peeking behind each closed door, but my desire to find a towel to wrap around my body was greater than my respect for Anissa's privacy.

I breathed a thankful sigh when I finally found the linen closet. A stack of neatly folded bath towels sat amongst surplus toilet paper and sundry toiletries. I grabbed the top towel and quickly wrapped it around my midsection like a sarong.

I still hadn't heard any noises from downstairs, so I tentatively descended the carpeted stairs.

I tried calling for my elusive hostess again when I reached the ground level: "Anissa?"

Still nothing.

I cautiously tread my way to the back of the house. I tiptoed, barefoot and careful, along hardwood floors. My heart felt permanently lodged in my throat and my blood pressure was elevated. It was akin to walking through a haunted house, unsure of my steps and anticipating that someone might pop out from an adjacent room or from behind a piece of furniture.

The muted sounds of a pool party filtered into the kitchen through the back sliding door. I peered through a window above the kitchen sink to observe the activities beyond the pane of glass. I had been overwhelmed the initial time Anissa had pulled me outside to introduce me to her family, but now I had a moment to breathe and take stock of the poolside activities.

Five children—two boys and three girls—ranging in various ages, although all under twelve, splashed around in the in-ground pool. The chlorine pool was large, taking over the entire backyard with the exception of a poured concrete patio where the rest of Anissa's extended family resided.

I spied Anissa herself on a lounger beside the pool. She'd removed her coverup and lay in a black one-piece bathing suit. The bottom portion was cut high up her bronze thighs, and the front material plunged in a low v-cut down the center of her chest. The suit looked impractical for swimming, but I didn't expect her to dive into the water anytime soon.

Two similarly-aged women flanked Anissa's lounger in lounge chairs of their own. Each wore a bathing suit—one a patterned bikini and the other a more conservative one-piece. They might have all been sisters or cousins or of no relation whatsoever.

A few feet from the lounge chairs, a single man sweat over a propane grill. Smoke curled in the shimmery air above the hot, open flames. The man looked to be in his early forties. He wore navy blue shorts and a short-sleeved, tropical-themed shirt open in the front.

Away from the pool, the grill, and the sunbathing goddesses, an older couple sat at a circular table beneath the protection of a canvas patio umbrella. I assumed the man and woman to be Anissa's parents, but so far my assumptions about this woman hadn't served me well.

I still had absolutely no confidence, but I knew I couldn't hide out in Anissa's kitchen forever. I sucked in a calming breath and reached for the handle of the sliding glass door.

I felt the attention of a dozen eyeballs as I opened the sliding door and stepped onto the sun-warmed concrete. Anissa rose from her lounge chair in one, fluid motion. I hovered close to the sliding door, as if ready to scamper back inside.

"Glad you decided to join us," she smiled serenely. "I was worried you'd changed your mind."

"You gave me a bikini but you're in a one piece?" I hissed in protest. I self-consciously covered my bare midsection with my arm.

"They're *my* bathing suits. Shouldn't I get to decide which one I want to wear?" she reasoned. She shifted her oversized sunglasses farther down her nose to look at me. "Besides, you fill out the top of that bikini much better than I ever could."

Her openly appreciative stare was more bewildering than anything. On a typical day, I considered myself to be pretty ordinary. Standing beside Anissa, I felt positively plain. There was nothing special about me whereas she seemed to ooze sensuality. There were a lot of words I would use to describe myself—none of which overlapped with this woman. Wholesome. Pleasant. Agreeable. Fresh-faced. Friendly.

"Are you hungry?" she asked. "You should grab yourself a plate. My brother, Sam, always grills way too much."

The patio table was covered in various trays and containers of food. Hot dogs on grilled buns. Cheeseburgers. Thick slices of seedless watermelon. Cole slaw. Some kind of pasta salad.

"Impressive," I remarked. "This is quite the all-American spread."

"Were you expecting something else? Maybe hummus and falafel?" Anissa demanded. Her caramel-colored eyes took on a sharp look. "My great-grandparents came to Michigan in 1910 to find work in the auto industry. How about yours?"

I hadn't meant to offend, but I'd spoken without really thinking. My cheeks grew hot. "Yeah, around that same time, too," I stammered. "My great-grandparents settled in Hamtramck."

"You're Polish?" she questioned.

Hamtramck was just beyond Detroit's city boundaries. It had originally been the center of Polish-American life, but in recent decades, the town had attracted new immigrants from Yemen and Bangladesh.

I nodded. "Alice Kaminski," I told her my full name. "It doesn't get more Polish than that. Hence my ignorance."

The hard edges of her features softened. "I'm sorry," she breathed out. "I shouldn't have jumped on you. But when you're from Dearborn, you get sick and tired of being called a terrorist."

"Don't apologize," I said. "I spoke without thinking."

Anissa shook her head. "I've heard much worse. You're harmless."

"And you're gorgeous," I replied without thinking.

"You're forgiven," she laughed.

I made myself a plate of food, even though I wasn't very hungry. I'd already insulted Anissa once; I didn't want to do more damage by refusing to eat. There were extra seats at the shaded table where her parents sat or the loungers near the two women who might have been her sisters. I would be forced to make polite small-talk in either situation, so I sat down by the pool's edge instead with my paper plate on my lap.

Anissa had entered the pool and played a game of Marco Polo with her nieces and nephews. They hovered in a circle around her, keeping a careful distance from their aunt, who was currently "It." Periodically, Anissa submerged underwater before popping up in a different place, much to her nieces' and nephews' delight.

I hadn't grown up with a pool—in-ground pools weren't very practical in Michigan, where we only experienced three months of warm weather—but I knew the game's rules. With your eyes closed, you had to find and tag someone else who would then become "It." When you yelled "Marco," the other players had to respond with "Polo." Because your eyes were closed, the sound of the other players' voices was the only way you could really hone in on tagging someone else to be "It."

I finished eating and set my empty plate to the side. I contemplated my next move while Anissa continued to splash around with her nieces and nephews. The sun was hot and the air smelled like chlorine from the pool and grilled meat. I could hear the local radio station calling that afternoon's Tiger's baseball game coming from an adjacent yard. It was a nice day for a pool party, but my body refused to relax; I wasn't an invited guest, and I barely knew the party's host.

It reminded me of house parties I'd attended as a freshman in college. We weren't old enough to go to the bars, so practically every weekend night my roommate and some other girls from my dorm floor floated around the neighborhoods surrounding campus, looking for house parties. Free beer was always in the back kitchen and no one stopped to ask us if we knew anyone at the party. We were young and pretty. Those qualifications were all the identification required.

One of the women from the loungers got up from her chair and settled next to me at the pool's edge. She dangled her feet over the concrete edge and let her heels sink into the chlorinated water. I smiled in her general direction, but didn't officially address her.

"Alice, right?" she asked.

I nodded.

"I'm Amy," she introduced herself. "I'm married to Anissa's brother, Sam. He's the one with the tongs."

"Your husband is a grill master," I remarked. "My cheeseburger was cooked to perfection."

The woman—Amy—didn't directly reply to my compliment. "Do you work with Anissa?" she asked.

I could tell she was trying to parse out how we knew each other, and why I'd crashed their family get-together.

"No. I'm a flight attendant," I said, absently moving my feet in the water. "Anissa has been on a few of my flights."

Amy's features pinched in confusion, but she was polite enough not to ask any follow-up questions. I could understand her confusion, however; I myself couldn't really understand what I was doing here—sitting poolside in one of Anissa's bathing suits—while her family looked on.

"Woo, it's hot," I breathed. I waved my hand near my face like a fan. "I'm gonna go in," I said, jerking my thumb in the direction of the water. "It was nice to meet you."

"Nice to meet you, too," Amy said with a nod.

I slid into the pool, careful not to splash the other woman. I quietly hissed when the colder water hit my exposed abdomen. The day was actually mild compared to how hot it typically got in the summer, but going in the pool was a convenient excuse to get away. I swam a few feet before glancing back at Amy. She continued to stare in my direction, but the mirrored lens on her sunglasses made it difficult to interpret her expression.

I half swam, half bounced on my tiptoes towards Anissa and her nieces and nephews. She was still "It." Every time she emerged from underwater, popping up like a submerged cork, her nieces and nephews shrieked with glee.

I stood still while one of her nieces doggy-paddled toward me. Of the five children in the pool, she looked to be the youngest, maybe five or six years old, but I wasn't very good at identifying kids' ages. I'd once offered pilot's wings to a boy who ended up being twelve and was therefore too cool for that kind of baby stuff.

Anissa's niece wasn't a strong swimmer; I heard her gasps and grunts as she barely stayed afloat. I let my arm float on top of the water, and even though I was a stranger, she immediately clung to the proffered limb like a buoy in the ocean.

My mouth opened in silent surprise when she grabbed onto my shoulder and crawled around to my back. She clung onto me like a human backpack and used me as a shield between herself and Anissa. I played along, bobbing in the water, keeping our distance from Anissa, but close enough to still be included in the game. Each time I floated too close for the little girl's comfort, she squealed and dug her nails into the tops of my shoulders.

Anissa popped up from the water a few feet away. "Marco!" she yelled.

"Polo!" her niece hollered close to my ear. The volume made me involuntarily wince.

Anissa, with her eyes still closed, shot towards the sound of the voice. Her hands seized onto my upper arms. "Gotcha!" she triumphantly exclaimed.

Her niece shrieked in my ear. She escaped, using my back as a spring board, as she launched herself to a different part of the pool.

Anissa's eyes popped open, and her hands remained wrapped around my thin biceps. My arms were probably my favorite body part. I was pretty scrawny everywhere else, but lifting luggage into overhead compartments had left me with toned biceps and triceps.

Anissa's cheeks were slightly flushed and her mouth was open from heavy breathing. Her cleavage heaved up and down beneath her bathing suit covering. Hair stuck to the sides of her face and her mascara had started to run beneath her eyes, but I thought she looked as beautiful as ever.

"You got me," I murmured.

"Hey," she breathed. She dropped my arms and ran her hand over her face to wipe away the excess pool water. "I didn't know you were playing."

"I didn't have much choice," I softly laughed. "Your niece kind of recruited me."

She grinned, showing off her dimples. "Second-guessing coming over yet?"

"Maybe a little," I sheepishly replied. "I definitely feel out of place. I didn't mean to barge in on your family time."

"It's no big deal. The more the merrier." Anissa floated perceptively closer. "Are you done being angry with me?"

"Angry?"

"When you first got here," she reminded me. "You yelled at me about having a husband and kids."

"I didn't yell at you," I demurred.

"You were mad at me though. Why?"

"I, uh, I guess I got mad that maybe you lived a double life. I work with some people who do that." I absently flicked at the top of the water. "They act single when they're on the job when they actually have a spouse and a houseful of kids."

She cocked her head as she inspected me. "Why would that make you angry?"

I self-consciously lowered my voice even though no one would be able to hear us over the radio and her nieces and nephews. "I know we didn't do anything in Philadelphia last week," I frowned, "but we could have. And I'm not a home-wrecker."

"Not a home-wrecker, but a party crasher," she smirked.

"Yeah," I laughed. "I guess so."

I felt a hand brush against my thigh under the water. I took the glancing touch as inadvertent until that same hand cupped my pussy over my bikini bottoms.

I sucked in a sharp breath at the assertive touch.

My eyes darted everywhere but Anissa's face as a calm, solid finger lazily stroked my clit through the material of the yellow bikini bottoms. Her nieces and nephews splashed and screamed in the shallow end of the chlorinated pool. Her brother, Sam, continued to work at the stainless-steel gas grill, although I couldn't imagine them needing to make more food. Anissa's sister-in-law and the other woman reclined nearby on lounge chairs. Her mother and father played a card game beneath the shaded shelter of an oversized umbrella.

Anissa's face didn't let on what she was doing to me beneath the water's surface. I tried to do the same, but it was understandably much harder for me to accomplish.

"Are you feeling okay?" she mused musically. "You're looking a little flushed."

"F-Fine," I choked out as she firmly pressed against my slit. Only the bikini's stretchy material kept her from fingering me in front of her family. "It's probably just from the sun."

"Maybe you should get out of the water," she suggested. "You don't want to burn."

I felt the stretch of a second finger knocking at my entrance. A desperate whimper bubbled up my throat. But as much as I wanted her to, she never slipped those fingers underneath the Lycra material between my thighs.

Her voice dropped to a velvet purr. "Still second-guessing coming over?"

I swallowed thickly. "No."

"Good," she responded. I felt mesmerized as she swabbed her tongue across her lower lip. "Because you're 'it' now."

Her hand abruptly left between my thighs and she sprang away, disturbing the water around us. I briefly sputtered on a wall of chlorinated water that tried to drown me in her haste to swim away. But despite the pool water in my lungs and up my nose, the unsatisfied ache between my legs persisted.

Anissa tread water a few feet away. "What are you waiting for, Alice?" she challenged.

"Yeah, Alice!" one of her older nephews parroted.

"Yeah, Alice!" her other nieces and nephews chimed in.

I ducked underwater to momentarily collect myself. I resurfaced a few seconds later, eyes closed.

"Marco!" I yelled out.

## CHAPTER EIGHT

The pool party ended after fingers and toes were sufficiently pruney. Tiny bodies were wrapped in oversized pool towels, lips blue and teeth chattering, but overall exhausted and satisfied with the day's events. The adults exchanged their goodbyes in the front foyer with murmured observations on how well the kids would sleep that night.

Dusk arrived, filling the sky with a pink and purple kaleidoscope display. I picked up a used paper plate from the patio table and stacked it on top of another dirty plate. I collected the red plastic cups strewn around the pool. Anissa didn't have a garbage bag out by the pool, but I started to condense the mess to make the post-party clean up a little easier.

I looked towards the house when I heard the glass sliding door open. Anissa stepped outside. She was still in her bathing suit, although she'd put on her coverup again, leaving her torso covered, but below her thighs she remained bare.

"You don't have to do that," she admonished. "It can wait until morning."

"I don't mind," I said in earnest.

"You're nicer than my own family," she remarked. "They take off as soon as the food's been eaten."

We cleaned up the pool area just enough to dispose of used plates, paper napkins, and plastic cutlery. Leftover food went into plastic storage containers and were stacked in the refrigerator.

Her family was long gone, and I was still uninvited. It had been a nice afternoon, which had turned into a nice evening. I didn't want to wear out my welcome or make her feel like she needed to entertain me. She probably wanted to relax and binge on HGTV like I did most free evenings.

We stood in her kitchen, on either side of the granite island.

"I'm glad you decided to stalk me today," she said.

"I'm not a stalker!" I squeaked. "I'm just very dedicated to customer service."

"All in the name of duty, I see." Her eyes seemed to twinkle even in the dim lighting. "That's the only reason you came out here?"

I pushed out an annoyed breath. "You know you're gorgeous. Don't try to pretend you're not."

Anissa pursed her lips. "Would you like to borrow some pajamas?"

My breath hitched. "Are you asking me to stay the night?"

"I can't expect you to drive home; you've been drinking," she said reasonably.

In truth, I'd only had a single beer the entire afternoon and evening.

"I could call a Lyft," I reflexively defended.

Her eyebrow arched. "So you *don't* want to stay the night?" she questioned.

"I-I do," I admitted. "But not because I'm drunk, and not because I'm some charity case."

"I'm glad to hear it. I wouldn't want to think I was taking advantage of you later."

My throat felt suddenly dry.

"I need a shower," she casually announced. "I need to rinse the chlorine off my body. Do you want one, too?"

My brain was still struggling from her previous line of questioning. I could only nod in response.

Anissa began to climb the stairs to the second floor, and I followed a few steps behind. Her coverup fell to mid-thigh, but the bottom hem crept up higher on her tan legs as she steadily climbed the staircase. I was enjoying the view, but more than that, I needed time and space to let my brain catch up to my body.

Was she planning on us showering together? Were we going to take turns? She'd made me wear a tiny bikini in front of her family, but I didn't know if I was ready to be naked in a shower with her. We hadn't even kissed.

The silent march to the second floor was over too soon.

"Guest bathroom is right in there." Anissa gestured towards an open door. "Towels and toiletries are already in there, so use whatever you need."

She'd been so bold before in her earlier pursuit of me, the change of venue was a surprise. "O-okay. Thanks."

"See you in a bit," she said before padding off in the direction of her bedroom.

The warm jet of water tried to jolt me awake from my surreal dream. I was naked, in the guest bedroom of a woman whom I hardly knew. And yet, I'd met her family. I'd told her details about my life that people whom I had dated over multiple months had never known.

I exhaled deeply. What was I doing here? This had all started as an inter-company competition, but there were no bingo squares for what I was currently doing.

I stood directly under the spray of the showerhead and let the hot water stream down my face. There were few things I enjoyed more than a rainfall showerhead, but I couldn't entirely abandon myself to the feeling. My brain was too busy to let myself relax.

What was I doing in this woman's shower? I was sure I was overstaying my welcome. But had I really forced myself into the situation or had her invitation been genuine? And how many near-strangers had used this shower before? If I dug a little deeper in the cabinets and drawers of the guest bathroom, what would I find? A smorgasbord of single-use toothpaste, toothbrushes, and other travel-sized toiletries? I felt out of my element, but maybe this was common in her world. Her bourbon-inspired sex solicitation in a hotel outside of Philadelphia suggested that very thing.

I hid in the shower for as long as I dared. My fingers were only slightly wrinkled, but if I lingered too much longer Anissa might think I'd drowned in her shower.

I groaned when another realization came to me. I'd pulled a towel from the linen closet, but besides the itty-bitty bikini, I didn't actually have clothes to change into. The outfit I'd so painstakingly picked out to wear that day was still in Anissa's bedroom. I didn't really relish the thought of putting the damp two-piece back on, but the alternative was wandering around in only a bath towel or hiding out until Anissa came looking for me.

I turned off the water and pulled back the curtain. My shower had been hot and the mirror over the vanity was steamed over. A t-shirt and sleep shorts were waiting for me on top of the pedestal sink. Anissa had brought me pajamas. I breathed a sigh of relief at the normalcy of the outfit. She could have set anything out for me—a silk teddy; a giant nightgown. Maybe the bikini had been punishment for rejecting her in Philadelphia and all was forgiven now.

I toweled myself off and pulled on the clothes Anissa had laid out for me. Not having a hairbrush, I ran my fingers through my damp hair. I normally didn't wear much makeup, but I still felt a little naked without at least my mascara and foundation.

I padded out of the second bathroom and into an empty hallway. I stood for a moment, just listening to the silence. There were no more joyous, carefree shrieks coming from the backyard. No monotone baseball announcer calling balls and strikes on the radio. A strange feeling settled into the pit of my stomach. I was completely alone with Anissa.

The door to her bedroom was open; I hazarded a quick glance inside, but saw no sign of my hostess.

My feet were silent on the carpeted stairs as I descended to the first floor.

"Anissa?" I called.

"Back here," I heard her velvety tone.

Floorboards creaked beneath my feet as I made my way back to the kitchen and family room combo. Anissa stood behind the kitchen island like a bartender waiting on my drink order. That decision had already been made for me, however. Two stemless wine glasses sat on the granite countertop. They'd both been filled halfway with white wine.

I'd seen her in professional attire, I'd seen her in a bathing suit, and I'd seen her in pajamas. Of the three options, I discovered I preferred the latter. Could a t-shirt be considered sexy? If so, she'd somehow managed to do it. The scoop necked t-shirt left her clavicle exposed. The thin material clung to the generous swell of soft breasts. Her naked shoulders suggested she wasn't wearing a bra. The shorts she wore fit more loosely than when she'd worn my pajama bottoms, but they still left plenty of tan leg on display.

There was something unquestionably appealing about a beautiful woman stripped down to the basics—no makeup, no fancy clothes or jewelry, her hair pulled back in a haphazard ponytail. I would Netflix and chill with this woman any day.

"Thanks for the pajamas," I said.

"You're very welcome," she replied. "I would have waited until you were done with your shower, but I realized too late that I hadn't actually gotten you any clothes to change into."

"You were so quiet, I didn't even know you came in."

"I didn't peek," she promised.

"Are you sure about that?"

I saw the blush form first on her neck. I wanted to keep making her blush.

"I hope the wine wasn't presumptuous," she remarked.

"It wouldn't be the first time," I observed coyly.

"Touché."

"Your house is really amazing," I repeated my earlier appraisal. "How long have you lived here?"

"In Dearborn—all my life," she told me. "In this house—about three years. I had a condo downtown before, but logistically it didn't make a lot of sense to live so far from the airport. I'm only about fifteen minutes away now."

"I've got you beat," I said. "I live in Romulus."

Anissa laughed. "Geez. You're not kidding. You might as well live *in* the airport."

"It's convenient," I shrugged. "I'm on call a lot, so it's helpful to be able to get to the airport if I'm called in unexpectedly."

"Could they still call you in tonight?" she asked.

"Last flight out leaves for Madison at 10:45p.m."

Anissa glanced at the digital clock on her gas range. "Two more hours until you're in the clear."

"I don't have to go in if they call me," I noted. "There's a whole group of flight attendants with less seniority who are permanently on reserve. They'll even fly someone in from a different airport if they can't find someone close to Detroit to take the flight."

Anissa smiled around the rim of her wine glass. "So you're not going to run out on me tonight?"

Her question and the low burn of her voice produced an involuntary reaction in me.

"I wasn't planning on it."

I was thankful I had the oversized wine glass to clasp between my hands. Without the task, I worried my hands might shake.

I toyed with the rim of my wine glass. "I still can't believe you live here all by yourself."

"I promise I'm not hiding a secret family in the attic."

"I know. It's just so much space." My apartment was a shoebox compared to her square footage.

"I'm gone too much for a pet," she told me. "I thought about getting a roommate, just so I wouldn't come home to an empty house, but I realized I'm not very good at sharing."

"You really buy the seat next to you on all your flights?" I asked. "How does your boss allow that? I thought you had layovers because your company was so stingy."

"It's free," she said. "I do so much flying, the airline gave me a companion pass. And since I don't have an actual companion, I use it to keep the seat next to me open. You meet a lot of weirdos while traveling. I like to have a barrier between the weirdos and myself."

"Too bad it does nothing to protect you from weirdo flight attendants," I nervously joked.

Anissa cleared her throat. "I would like to address the elephant in the room." She set her wine glass on the kitchen island. "I would like to have sex with you tonight."

"R-really?" I managed to choke out.

"Really," she confirmed with a nod. "But not if it's going to make you anxious until we actually do it. I'd like to enjoy some time with you before we actually *enjoy* ourselves," she emphasized. "Will you calm down if you know that, yes, we are having sex—but not *right now*?"

I paused to consider her question. "I think—yeah. That actually might work." It was actually a brilliant proposal. I wet my dry lips. "There's just one thing I need to do first."

She arched an eyebrow, but I didn't elaborate or expand on my explanation. The quizzical expression on her face remained even as I rounded the kitchen island. I leaned closer, eliminating the space left between us. I took a quick breath; she smelled like the same soap that had been in her guest bathroom—light and flowery.

I licked my lips once more before pressing my mouth against hers. My body seized the moment our lips connected. Anissa made a quick sound of surprise before I felt her kissing me back. Any kind of fantasies or daydreams I'd had about what her mouth might feel like paled in comparison to the real thing.

Her lips were soft, yet firm. I loved the gentle press of the side of her nose against mine and the scent of her skin. I could taste the slightest hint of the white wine we'd been drinking. I was tempted to deepen the kiss or at least to brush my fingers against her chiseled cheekbones, but I didn't think I'd be able to stop at a simple kiss if I'd done that.

Anissa's eyes were still closed when I finally pulled away. Her tongue flickered between her slightly parted lips as if still tasting me there.

She seemed to have gotten choked up. I heard her quiet cough as she inspected the floor. "Glad we got that out of the way," she mumbled.

I chuckled. "Such a chore, right?"

Anissa looked up again, this time looking more sure of herself, more aggressive. "I think I need a little more."

My eyebrows arched in amusement. "Is that so?"

She stepped into my personal space and her hands fell to my hips. "Just a little more," she murmured. The low drag of her voice affected me more than I wanted to admit.

"I think I can handle that," I decided.

I leaned forward and cupped either side of her face. I brushed the pads of my thumbs across her thick, pliant lips. Her golden eyes fluttered shut. I could feel her uneven breath on my fingers. I leaned closer still, drawing our faces near until only a breath separated us. Her fingers tightened against my hips in anticipation.

It was she who eventually erased the final distance between our mouths. I heard a small grunt of surprise; it took a moment before I realized that I had been the origin of the sound.

She ran her tongue along the front of my teeth. I parted my lips and accepted her tongue into my mouth. She made a quiet, pleased sound that I'd been so accommodating. My arms circled her narrow waist, and I bent her backwards just slightly. My hands dropped to her round backside—which I'd ogled more times than I was proud of—and squeezed.

I pulled back, a little breathless. I didn't get very far before Anissa was grabbing the back of my head and pulling me back in. "Just a little more," came her plea.

Our mouths reconnected. I'd only intended on a single kiss, but the spark between us was building to a bona fide inferno.

I dropped kisses on her strong jawline and up to her ear. She tasted clean from her recent shower; a few scattered drops of water stubbornly clung to her skin. Her fingers remained firmly cupped behind my neck. They didn't guide my movements, but assured I wouldn't travel too far away. I kissed down the perfumed column of her arching neck and licked at the hollow of her throat.

Her greedy fingers gripped me tighter and her breathy command was music to my ears: "More."

I slid her t-shirt off one shoulder and peppered the top of her bronzed skin with butterfly-light kisses. I sucked her skin into my mouth and bit lightly, not hard enough to leave a mark. Her contented sighs grew to full-throated moans. The noises vibrated up her neck, rumbling against my lips and tongue.

Anissa repeated one word over and over: "More."

I'd left her mouth neglected and idle for too long. I pressed hungry kisses to her lips, slightly agape with uneven breath. I kissed her, far more aggressively than before. Our mouths crushed together and our tongues battled for dominance. I leaned my body into hers until she took a few stumbling steps backwards. Her backside connected with the kitchen counter, pressing her between my body and the granite island. I wove my fingers with hers and pinned them to the countertop. I licked and sucked at her exposed skin.

Her lower body began to move, hips rolling open and legs parting. She rubbed against me, seeking some kind of friction. I dropped one of her hands and used my free arm to grab onto her leg. I raised her lower leg and she wrapped it around me, pulling us even closer.

"More?" I breathed against her throat.

"More," she panted back.

Her brief, confirming word was all the encouragement I needed.

My hand clamped around her exposed thigh. I slid my hand up her toned upper leg and slipped my fingers beneath the leg opening. I couldn't help my own groan when I didn't feel the anticipated brush of cotton, silk, or lace—only more skin. She wore no underwear beneath her shorts.

Her skin grew hotter and smoother and wetter the farther my fingers reached. I brushed against the connecting skin between her upper thigh and pussy lips, eliciting a sharp breath from her throat. I ran the tip of my index and middle finger the length of her outer lips, but avoided her slit. I stroked the shaved skin just about her hooded clit and barely bumped into the sensitive nub.

I had limited movement beneath her sleep shorts, a fact that seemed to frustrate her sooner than me. My hand was still up her pants when she began to wiggle the elastic waistband past her hips. I pulled away, but only long enough for her to rid herself of the shorts. Once past her hips, they dropped silently to the kitchen floor, rendering her naked from the waist down.

Anissa grabbed my right hand and brought it up to her mouth. She sucked my index and middle finger into her mouth and rolled her tongue around the two digits. She withdrew my fingers with a satisfying pop and dragged my hand down the length of her body, between her t-shirted breasts and down the center of her abdomen.

Her lower lip tucked beneath her top row of teeth and she rose up slightly on her toes as she guided my hand towards her pussy. I could only watch in equal measure of astonishment and arousal as she maneuvered my two fingers. She stroked my fingers over her clit, again and again. I kept my fingers rigid while she masturbated against my hand. Her inner thighs and pussy were already slick with her juices.

I was completely mesmerized until I heard her second word of the young evening: "Inside."

I still wasn't in control of my hand. She positioned my fingertips against her entrance and canted her hips forward until I penetrated her. I watched, wide eyed, as her pussy lips parted and then swallowed my fingers. I bit down so hard on my lower lip, I thought I might draw blood. Anissa only dropped my hand when I was one knuckle deep. I flexed my wrist and dipped inside another inch.

My fingers were enveloped in her soft, liquid heat. I pulled my two fingers out, just barely, before plunging back in. I kept my fingers still, but flexed my wrist periodically so she would feel me. My unoccupied hand slipped beneath her t-shirt, and I began to roll her tightening nipples between my fingers.

The kitchen wasn't the ideal location for what I wanted to do to her—although the imagery of clearing away everything that cluttered the granite island with one aggressive sweep of my hand did send a tickle down my spine and cause my thighs to clench. I didn't want to risk another journey to the second floor where I worried the distance would cause us to reconsider or at least make me lose my momentum.

Only a few steps separated the kitchen from the sunken living room. A large L-shaped sectional set the perimeter of the living room in the open floor plan. The couch—like the rest of her house—was too much for one person. The multi-piece sectional was book-ended on one side with a wide chaise lounge, large enough for the two of us.

I retreated from between her thighs and instead took hold of the back of Anissa's thighs, just below her squeezable backside. Engaging my core and leg muscles, I lifted her off the ground. Anissa's surprised noise pulled another smile to my lips. I was strong—disproportionately so for my size and frame. Years of dead-lifting strangers' luggage into overhead compartments had given me unexpected upper-arm strength.

Her legs almost reflexively wrapped around my middle. I had never done this before, but she seemed to trust me. I shifted my grasp to cup the most perfect ass—firm yet soft. Round and completely touchable. Her thighs tightened at my sides while I walked us over to the upholstered sofa. She only unclenched when I lowered her down on the couch cushions.

Anissa was only in her scoop-necked t-shirt, while I was still fully dressed. I quickly shed my own t-shirt and removed the bra I'd been self-consciously wearing. I shivered when my still-damp hair touched the tips of my shoulders. Anissa lay on the chaise lounge and watched it all with slightly lidded eyes.

I climbed onto the couch and hovered over her body, holding myself up on my arms. Pendant lights in the kitchen provided just enough illumination. I could see everything, yet it was dim enough to not feel like we were beneath a spotlight. I swept my eyes over her half-clothed body. A giddy feeling came over me like a sugar or an adrenaline rush. Wine typically made me sleepy, but drinking in Anissa's body had the opposite effect.

"How do you want to cum?" My voice came out a strangled rasp that surprised my ears. "Do you want me to worship your body—tease and touch every naked inch of you—bring you to the edge until you're begging me to take mercy on you and push you over? Or, do you want to cum now?" I offered. "Hard and fast so your orgasm hits like a tidal wave? Hard and fast so you're still feeling me tomorrow?"

I heard her audibly swallow. "B-both of those sound pretty good."

I couldn't help my private grin. Typically I was the one stammering and unsure. It felt good to have flipped the script on her, if only momentarily.

I started with her abdomen. I lifted the bottom hem of her t-shirt just high enough to reveal the flat plane of her stomach. I pressed my nose against her and inhaled the scent of her skin. Chlorine from the pool lingered, but the same soap that I'd used in the guest bathroom similarly perfumed her.

I couldn't help myself. I dug my fingers into her hips and licked hard against her stomach. I heard the hitch of her breath and felt her buck into me.

I pulled her shirt up higher to reveal her bra-less breasts. Dusky-rose colored nipples capped her tanned breasts. I quickly latched my lips around her nipple and sucked hard. Anissa audibly hissed and sharply gasped when my lips turned to teeth. I nipped at the sensitive flesh and lightly tugged on her distended nipple.

I turned my attention to her other breast. I swiped my tongue across her puckered nipple before sucking her breast into my mouth. I sucked hard and flicked my tongue against her nipple while she squirmed beneath me. Her hips canted up, seeking out more contact.

I abandoned her breasts and shoved her t-shirt higher still. I licked against her collarbone and up the side of her neck. I would have gladly licked every inch of her lush body if she would have allowed it.

I found an irresistible space in the crook of her neck to suckle and nuzzle. The scent of her herbal shampoo flooded my senses. I scraped my canines across her pulse point. I had no intention of leaving behind a hickey though; I couldn't bear the thought of blemishing her flawless skin.

I rested more of my body weight on her and wedged one leg between her thighs. Her hands immediately grabbed my backside and she pressed herself up against my naked upper thigh. She gasped at the solid contact and ground harder into my leg. I could feel her slick heat on my thigh. Taking my time was apparently not in her plans.

I separated my lower body from hers just enough to slip my hand between us. My fingers fumbled against her clit momentarily while I blindly sought the origin of her arousal. Her hips continued to move, bucking into me and wiggling from side to side, making my job more difficult.

I finally found her liquid center and slid one finger, and then two, inside. She wrapped her right leg around my midsection, opening herself to me even more. My fingers plunged deeper, causing us both to groan.

Anissa clawed at my naked back while I settled into a comfortable pace between her parted thighs. "Oh shit. Oh God," she moaned. "Fuck, that's so good."

Her fingers curled around my rounded shoulders and she chewed on my lower earlobe. "Alice. I want to feel you."

"You-you are." I gasped when she bit down.

"No. From the inside."

My eyes shut tight. "Fuck."

"Hurry," she pled.

She moved frantically, desperately, to get out from under me. She clawed at my shorts—the only piece of clothing that remained. My hands were somehow more steady than hers as I was able to pull the elastic-waisted cotton shorts past my hips, thighs, and legs.

Anissa pressed a solid hand into my sternum and pushed me back onto the couch. The air threatened to leave my lungs as tumbled onto the leather cushions and woven throw pillows.

"Oh, Alice—why didn't you tell me?"

My head snapped up from the upholstered pillows. "Tell you what?"

The small, pleased smile on her face was undeniable. "That you have a perfect pussy."

My words caught in my throat. "I-I do?"

I heard her affirming hum as she settled on her stomach between my parted thighs. "Perfect shape, perfect proportions, perfect coloring."

"C-coloring?" I stammered again.

Her tongue sliding the length of my shaved slit had my head falling back onto the pillow and my eyes screwing shut.

"God, and perfect taste," I heard her throaty praise.

My fingers clenched the top of the couch material as I surrendered myself to the sensations between my legs. Her appraising mewls continued from the lower half of the chaise. My thighs twitched and quivered, beyond my control, as each careful lick and nip sent electric shocks up my body.

Short, manicured nails dug into the tender flesh of my inner thighs. "Don't cum too soon," she warned me. "I'm enjoying myself."

My head sank deeper into the couch cushions. "Easy for you to say," I wheezed.

## CHAPTER NINE

I woke up to a hand between my thighs. A thumb was softly manipulating my swollen clit, flipping it back and forth. Up and down. Side to side. My eyes were still closed, but I next felt fingers ghosting around my naked right nipple, coaxing it from sleep.

We'd fallen asleep on the chaise lounge in Anissa's living room the night before. Neither of us had wanted to move after sex; her second floor bedroom had been too far away. We'd been too tired to get dressed again, too. The pajamas she'd picked out for me were scattered across the living room floor. Only a crocheted afghan covered our naked bodies.

Her hands continued to explore. She flicked my nipple with the tip of her finger. I felt the edge of her nail rake across the sensitive skin. Beneath the heavy afghan, she lightly scratched her fingernails across my abdomen. I kept my eyes closed, curious how far she'd go if she thought I was still sleeping.

I felt the slight pinch of my nipple between her thumb and a second finger. Her second hand traveled lower beneath the blanket; a single digit traveled the length of my slit. I exhaled in my pretend sleep, and subtly parted my thighs.

"Good morning," Anissa whispered into my ear, just before she sank a single finger into my pussy.

"Oh, fuck," I groaned.

"I'm sorry," she apologized, not really meaning it. "I couldn't help myself. You looked so pretty and peaceful lying there."

My fake sleep abandoned, I let my hips fall all the way open, and she slid a second finger into me. I could practically feel the contour of her double fingers—every joint, every knuckle. The sudden intrusion drew a hiss from my lips, but I didn't make her stop.

"Fuck, that's good," I sighed.

Anissa corkscrewed her fingers into my pussy while she kissed my neck. Her kisses were delicate and light. Her lips were wet and her breath was warm on my skin. Her fingers twisted inside of me, a strange but pleasantly full feeling. She settled into a slow, yet steady rhythm, twisting her fingers in and out of my drenched sex. She ran the pad of her thumb against my swollen clit each time she bottomed out.

The sound of her heavy breathing in my ear turned me on nearly as much as the movement between my thighs. She groaned deliciously when I clenched my pussy muscles around her fingers. Her breath hitched in my ear when she heard and felt how wet she had made me. She had topped me, yet it was strangely empowering to hear how much she enjoyed fucking me.

The slow, torturous pace of her fingers eventually frustrated me. My hips arched off the couch to take control of her pace, but she pressed me back into the cushions. I unabashedly whimpered at her denial. She had only to pinch my clit between two fingers to make me see stars.

My head snapped up from the couch. "Shit," I wheezed. "Just like that."

The torturous pressure on my clit continued. Anissa curled her fingers inside of me while my fingers clawed at the leather upholstery. The pressure was almost unbearable; I thought I might explode.

"Are you gonna cum?" she asked me.

"Fuck," I gasped. "I want to. So bad."

She pinched my clit harder, and a strangled sound I didn't recognize bubbled up my throat.

The twisting fingers inside me stilled so she could concentrate on my clit. She rolled the engorged and sensitive nub in small concentric circles. Her wet mouth clamped onto my earlobe. When she drew her hand up from between my thighs and slid slippery fingers—wet from my own juices—across my nipples, the torture was nearly complete.

"Rub your clit," she rasped into my ear.

Another strangled noise bubbled past my lips.

The fingers lodged between my sticky thighs began to thrust again in earnest.

"Rub your clit, Alice," she demanded again.

I tightly closed my eyes. I moved my right hand under the blanket that covered our bodies. I'd never masturbated in front of a partner before. I didn't even have the benefit of nighttime darkness to cloak me—only a knitted blanket.

Anissa's mouth fell to my neck where she continued to lick and kiss my skin. Her twisted fingers continued to corkscrew in and out of my sex, sloppy and wet. The penetration itself wasn't going to be enough, and I thought she somehow knew that. If I wanted to cum, I was going to have to—literally—take matters into my own hands.

I pressed the tip of my middle finger against my hooded clit. I'd done the action enough in the privacy of my one-bedroom apartment that I knew actually how much pressure I needed and where to apply it. But this was new territory. I'd never had another naked body pressed against mine while I mashed my clit under my fingertips. I'd never had another person feverishly fingering me, bumping into my hand, while I tried to get myself off.

Anissa licked the side of my neck and buried her face against me. "Fuck that's hot," she breathed.

Her own body had begun to jerk erratically on the couch beside me. It didn't take me long to realize that she was fingering me along with herself.

"Cum with me, Alice. Please," she gasped in a desperate plea.

Her hand between my legs had lost its rhythm and any former elegance as she raced towards her own orgasm.

My stomach muscles tightened.

"Anissa," I panted. "I'm going to ...."

"Yes, yes, yes, yes," her voice chanted in my ear.

My throat tightened. My thighs twitched. My pussy clenched.

"Oh, God," came my breathy prayer.

I sank back into the couch cushions and released a long breath. My heart pulsed everywhere. I could feel its echo in my chest, in my throat, in my hands, in the arches of my feet.

"Woah," I breathed out. "That was ..."

"I know," Anissa echoed. "I bet you're kicking yourself for booting me from your hotel room." Her tone was smug. This was a self-aware woman who was confident—maybe even arrogant—about the things she did well.

"I didn't …" I didn't finish my protest. I didn't have the energy for a stalwart defense. Not while my thighs were still twitching, at least.

I didn't know the hour, but it was bright in her living room. I was sticky with sweat under the knitted afghan. The air conditioner was still running, but my naked skin stuck to the leather of the couch. I squeaked with every move and the stubborn leather material restricted my movement with halting starts and stops. I didn't gracefully slide across the couch cushions; I skid. Under normal circumstances I would have probably felt self-conscious, but these were anything but normal circumstances.

Anissa laid on her stomach beside me. The blanket covered the lower half of her body, which left her long, tan back exposed for me to admire. Her hair-tie had loosened in the night and long locks of black hair framed her heart-shaped face.

"Good morning," I quietly greeted, long overdue.

She traced lazy figures across the top of my hand with her fingertips. She played with the blonde, baby fine hairs on my arm. "You surprised me," she said. "Not many people do that."

My heart was still pounding, but I somehow found the strength to prop myself up on my elbow. "How so?"

"For one, showing up here yesterday with that flimsy excuse," she reminded me. "But the sex. It surprised me."

I could feel myself reddening all over. "A good or bad surprise?"

"Definitely good," she affirmed. "You're like a skittish little kitten out in the world, but a lioness in bed. Your confidence last night surprised me."

"I wouldn't call it confidence," I refused. "But maybe I was feeling particularly inspired."

She pursed her bee-stung lips. "Inspired?"

"I've never had sex with someone so beautiful."

I didn't know from where this honesty and transparency had come. Staring into her golden eyes was like a truth serum.

She didn't directly respond to my praise. She didn't deny her beauty or my devaluing of previous sexual partners. Instead, she regarded me in somber silence.

"Do you have to run off?" she finally asked.

I didn't have a practical reason to stay. Because it was a Golden Day, I didn't have to report to the airport or even be on call. If someone called in sick, the airline would call in someone on reserve, even if it meant flying them in from a different city.

Days off like this were few since I tried to pick up as many extra shifts as my company allowed. It was typically when I ran errands or cleaned Honey's tank since I had little energy for either of those tasks after a long day of airport travel. But Anissa looked so hopeful and so beautiful that I couldn't say no. I needed to spend more time with her.

"No. I can stay," I decided.

A slow smile spread across her beautiful features. "How do you like your eggs?"

+ + +

Anissa claimed she had an important errand to run and asked me to come along rather than wait for her at her house. It was a rare scheduled day off for me, and I could think of much more interesting—and naked—things we could be doing to pass the time, but I also didn't want to seem like an ungrateful or lazy houseguest if she already had had plans I was interrupting, so I agreed to tag along.

We sped along the interstate highway in her charcoal grey SUV toward a destination unknown. The day was bright and cloudless, and she'd opened the sunroof. The wind made it too loud for any kind of sustained conversation, much like the constant roar of an airplane's engines. I didn't mind the extra noise; if anything, it was a comfort. I ran my hands along the leather interior and chrome finishes that wrapped the passenger seat. I shouldn't have been surprised that Anissa drove a luxury vehicle considering her oversized home, tailored wardrobe, and First-Class flier status.

I tugged at my low ponytail while I looked out the window. My new surroundings weren't the only thing putting me on edge. I hadn't planned on spending the night, so I hadn't had clean clothes to change into. Anissa and I were about the same size, however, so she'd let me borrow a v-neck t-shirt and skinny jeans. A spare toothbrush and a travel-sized toothpaste had been waiting for me on the guest bathroom vanity after I'd emerged from my morning shower. It was a thoughtful touch, but another detail that had me wondering how often Anissa entertained overnight guests.

After about a half an hour's drive, we pulled off the highway at an exit. I didn't recognize the town or city. We seemed to be in the middle of nowhere. "I hope you don't mind going to the airport on your day off," Anissa remarked.

She hadn't been forthcoming about where we were going, but I also hadn't asked. When I took in our surroundings, I realized we hadn't arrived at Detroit Metropolitan Wayne County Airport, however. Anissa turned on her blinker and pulled into the drive of a small executive airport.

Anissa parked her SUV close to a corrugated metal airplane hangar. It was Sunday, and the parking lot was relatively empty.

"What's your errand?" I couldn't help asking. I couldn't fathom what kind of chore she had to do at a private airport.

"That was just an excuse to get you out of the house," she revealed, turning off the car. She unbuckled her seatbelt and turned around to reach into the backseat. "I want to show you something." Her voice was slightly muffled as she rummaged around.

"What?"

She re-emerged from the backseat, holding onto a clipboard. "I could tell you," she said, smiling, "but it's better if I show you."

Curiosity compelled me to follow her out of the car and towards the metal airplane hangar.

Anissa walked with the confidence of someone who knew exactly where she was going or as if she belonged. It was a gait similar to that of my colleagues and me when we traveled to our morning gate assignments in our airline's terminal. She strode directly into the open hangar doorway, no hesitation, while I lingered a step behind and took stock of my surroundings.

The air smelled like a combination of gasoline and crude oil. Several small aircraft, none larger than puddle jumpers—all presumably private planes—occupied the hangar. Most were covered under protective tarps.

Anissa walked up to one of the uncovered planes and stopped a few steps away. The plane was painted a pearly white color with deep blue accent stripes that ran the length of the aircraft's body.

"Ta da!"

I stopped next to her, still not quite understanding what we were doing there. My eyebrows knit together. "You wanted to show me a plane?"

"I wanted to show you *this* plane specifically," she corrected.

"Wait," I said, slowly starting to put the pieces together. "You have your own plane?"

"I share it with my brother, Sam. You met him yesterday at the barbeque. It actually wasn't very expensive," she qualified. "After the market tanked in 2008, all kinds of people started ditching their toys. Boats, RVs, planes. Sam and I got a really good deal on it."

"But you get motion sickness," I felt compelled to point out.

"It's the strangest thing," she mused. "I don't have any symptoms if I'm the one in control."

Because of my profession, I knew a little about light aircraft. The Cessna 172 Skyhawk was one of the most popular personal planes in the world. I also knew they weren't exactly cheap. I was curious how much of a deal Sam and Anissa had actually gotten. Plus, there were hangar costs to consider. Tie-down gear. Annual inspections. Insurance. Fuel. The dollar signs quickly accumulated in my mind.

"You wanna go up?" Anissa asked, interrupting my crude calculations.

I turned to her. "Really?"

"It's the whole reason I brought you out here," she admitted with a small shrug. "Hey, Jimmy," she called out to a passing man in a baseball cap and coveralls. "Could you or one of the other guys tug my plane outside when you get the chance? I already submitted my flight plan, so we should be all set."

The man—Jimmy—waved his acquiescence.

Anissa and I walked back outside and waited a few minutes while Jimmy and another man pulled Anissa's plane out of the hangar. I folded my arms across my chest and leaned against the corrugated metal siding and silently watched while two men tugged the small plane into position.

"You look nervous," Anissa observed.

"I've never been in a plane that small," I was embarrassed to admit.

"You've never been in a personal plane before? I find that hard to believe." Her lips pursed into a pleased smile. "No handsome young pilot has offered to show you his cockpit?"

I wrinkled my nose at her word choice. "Firstly, that's gross. And secondly, we call it a flight deck now."

"How progressive of you," she teased. "Don't worry; I'm good at this. I got my pilot's license pretty quickly—not as quickly as you became a flight attendant," she qualified, "but when I wasn't flying commercially for work, I was in this plane with my instructor, and then eventually doing solo flights."

"It's really impressive," I said, meaning it.

Anissa shrugged off the compliment. "The plane does all the hard work." She handed me the clipboard she'd brought from her car. "Time to earn your keep, co-pilot."

I let out a nervous breath, but I was determined not to disappoint. "What do we do first?" I asked.

"Preflight checks start before we even get to the plane. Is it sitting level or is it leaning to one side? Is there any obvious damage? Then, we get in the plane."

"We don't have to, like, check out the prop or look at the engine?" I wondered aloud.

Anissa's eyes crinkled at the corners. "You're really cute—taking this so seriously."

"I'd like to not crash," I said.

"Get in the cockpit, Alice," she deadpanned.

"Flight deck," I corrected.

I gingerly climbed into the passenger hatch while Anissa perched in the captain's seat. When I closed the door behind me, the airplane walls seemed to constrict. I was used to the confined quarters of commercial flying, but even that couldn't prepare me for the narrow space within Anissa's plane. The interior smelled like new leather and plastic. It made me wonder how much use the plane's previous owners had gotten out of the aircraft.

"So, the first thing I do is make sure we're legal," Anissa began. "I've got to double check I have all my FAA required documents like my registration, air worthiness certificate, manuals and weight and balance information. Once we're legal, I remove the control lock."

She popped off a metal contraption from the yoke that looked suspiciously like a bent wire clothes hanger.

"I make sure all my gauges are at zero before I hit the master switch." She clicked a large orangish-red button to her left and the whole plane began to whine. My pulse involuntarily quickened; it didn't sound very encouraging. "I check the fuel gauge and make sure I've got enough gas."

"How far can this go on one tank?" I asked.

"It depends on who or what I'm carrying. You're just a little skinny thing," she smiled, "so we'd probably make it over 600 miles."

"Gotta check my flaps next." She flipped another switch in the center of the control panel. She seemed to be talking to herself instead of me, but I didn't dare interrupt. I didn't want her to lose her place or forget a crucial step. "Make sure my flaps go down, good. And then master switch off."

The humming sound stopped when she flipped the orange-red button again.

"Okay, *now* Ms. Worrier, now we're going to pre-flight the exterior of the plane." She opened the hatch on her side of the plane and climbed back out, so I did the same.

I stood beside Anissa while we regarded her aircraft. I observed her out of the corner of my eye. She looked casually stunning in her white t-shirt and ripped boyfriend jeans, but there was a lightness to her body and a nearly tangible energy vibrating from her form. If I'd ever wondered, this was definitely her happy place.

"You're going to be my hands," she told me. "I want you to run your hands along the body and the tail and make sure the rivets are in place and that there's no cracks or other damage."

I did as she instructed; I flattened my hands on the exterior of the plane and ran my palms along the white, shiny surface. It felt a little awkward, like I was feeling up her plane.

"Like this?" I asked.

"You're doing wonderfully," she approved.

I glanced over my shoulder to see her watching me, although the mirrored lenses of her aviator glasses obscured half of her face.

"The tail is called the empennage," she continued. "You want to make sure all of those pieces like the rudder, elevator, and tail flaps can move freely and aren't going to fall off mid-flight."

"You really know how to make a girl feel secure," I murmured while I wiggled the tail flaps up and down and moved the rudder side to side.

"Good! Time for the wings!" she chirped.

We walked together around the rear of the plane to the right wing.

"Same thing here," she instructed.

"Make sure the flaps move but they won't fall off?" I guessed.

She grinned broadly. "See? You're practically a pilot."

Under her careful tutelage, I checked the flap and aileron, the lights and wingtip, and the leading edge.

"Now climb up that step ladder and check out the top of the wing."

I eyeballed the short ladder which was positioned close to the plane. "You're really putting me to work."

Hands wrapped around my waist and Anissa spun me around to face her. Her nose slid along mine and she brushed her lips against my surprised mouth.

"It's gonna be *so* worth it," she murmured against me. "I promise."

I felt a little wobbly from her proximity. "O-okay."

Her youthful grin returned and a firm palm found my right buttock. "Now, get up that ladder!"

I was thankful I hadn't worn impractical shoes the day before in an effort to impress her. My canvas slip-ons tread easily up the three-step ladder and I stared across the expanse of the Cessna's long, elevated wing.

"Check the fuel level while you're up there," Anissa called to me. "It's that orange cap. It's just like the fuel cap on your car."

I looked down on her from my raised position. "Didn't we just look at the fuel gauge in the cockpit?" I pointed out.

"I thought it was the flight deck," she teased.

"Whatever."

"We did. But you should always visually check, too, in case the internal gauge is malfunctioning. I'd hate to run out of fuel up there because of your laziness."

"Okay! I get it!" I unscrewed the red cap, which was just like the gas cap on my car, and looked inside the opening. "We've got gasoline, Captain," I confirmed.

"Ooh—Captain. No one's ever called me that before. I think I like it," she mused.

I hopped down the ladder rungs to solid earth. "You don't want to be like the pilots I work with. They're notoriously cocky."

"Perfect. So am I."

I rolled my eyes. "What's next on your list?"

It took a few more minutes to inspect the tires, oil levels, fuel trainer, propeller and spinner, air intakes, struts, and other mechanisms. After Anissa convinced me it was safe to fly, I climbed back into the co-pilot seat.

I buckled myself in and accepted the headset she handed me. While I double-checked on the security of my safety harness and made the headset fit snugly on my head, I heard Anissa mumbling to herself while she went through her start-up instructions. Her thoroughness put me at ease even though I was admittedly still nervous about going up in a small aircraft.

Anissa inserted a metal key into the ignition and yelled out the opened window on her side of the plane. "Clear front!"

The propeller began to spin and the engine audibly sputtered.

"Come on," she urged the engine. Her voice was right in my ears because of the headset.

The engine finally roared to life, loud despite the headset that covered my ears.

Anissa turned to me. "Are you ready for this?"

Her smile was disarming. I couldn't image anyone refusing her. How the hell had *I* refused her?

I nodded and placed my nervous hands in my lap, worried I might inadvertently touch something I wasn't supposed to. "Ready."

The plane slowly rolled forward and Anissa guided the plane in the direction of the runway. We bumped along the paved surface; the blacktop looked freshly laid, but I felt every small dip and bump. The propeller spun lazily against the horizon. I could see the individual blades, so I knew it couldn't be moving that fast.

"Why is the propeller spinning so slowly?" It felt like I was shouting. The volume of the engine and the headset were a little disorienting.

"Because we're not flying yet," came her common sense response.

I tried to breathe normally. I could do this. I'd been on hundreds, maybe even thousands, of planes before. Sure, they'd been big enough to carry two hundred people instead of two, but flying was flying, right? Or at least that's what I tried to convince myself.

We paused at the end of the long runway and Anissa turned the plane around. The engine grew louder and the prop began to spin faster.

"Is that better?" she asked.

I swallowed hard and stared straight ahead, but I managed to nod.

"Don't worry, Alice," came her reassuring words. "I'm good at this."

She fiddled purposely with a few more knobs and switches on the control panel. When she pulled on the throttle, the engine roared impossibly loud. We finally began to move forward again, first at a slow creep and then with incremental bursts of speed.

A quiet—or at least I hoped it was quiet—gasp escaped my mouth when the front of the plane lifted off the ground. The rear wheels followed suit and the ground fell away. As we made our initial ascent, the plane tilted to one side and then the other before finally leveling out.

I exhaled noisily and the sound of my breath echoed in my ears.

"We made it!" Anissa cheered. She removed her hands from the yoke and shook them around. "Look, ma! No hands!"

I slapped her shoulder. "Stop messing around!" I hissed.

Her head tucked into her raised shoulders and she had enough sense to look sorry. "Okay, I'm sorry. I'll behave."

I peered out my window and looked straight down. We weren't so high that I couldn't make out highways and the shape of various buildings and parks. "How high up are we?"

Anissa pointed at one of the circular gauges. "10,000 feet. But don't even think about joining the Mile High Club. I've got too much work to do over here."

I snapped my eyes in her direction. There was no way Anissa could have known about the bingo card and its challenges. I tried to laugh at what I was sure she'd meant as a joke, but it sounded more like a choking noise.

"So, uh, where are we going?" I asked.

"I'm on the lam." She contorted her voice into a strange, old-timey accent. "We're making a run for the Canadian border."

I stared at the instrument panel, but it was all Greek to me. I thought I might have recognized a wind speed gauge and maybe a speedometer, but nothing looked obviously like a compass to tell me where we were going. The giant blue lake beneath us, however, said due north.

I was confident she was only teasing me, and yet, I really didn't know this woman. I'd had sex with her, sure, but what did I really know about Anissa Khoury?

I sat a little easier in my seat when I remembered that Kent technically knew where I was—not specifically in a Cessna 172S somewhere above Lake Huron—but he'd been the one to procure Anissa's home address for me. When I didn't show up for work the next day and they discovered my empty apartment, the next place they'd look would be Anissa's house.

"Are you okay over there?" Anissa's voice in my ears snapped me out of the *Dateline* episode I was silently scripting.

I forced a grin in her general direction. "Everything's great."

"I'm not stealing you away from something, am I?"

*Stealing. She was stealing me.*

I barked out a too-loud laugh. "No. This is great. Thanks for taking me up."

I nearly jumped out of my jump-seat when a hand touched my knee. Anissa flashed me another encouraging smile. Her twin dimples were almost enough to pacify my nerves.

"Do you want to give it a try?" she offered.

"Flying?" I held up my hands in surrender. "I've never done this before," I needlessly reminded her.

Her smile was patient and placating. "I promise I won't let you crash the plane."

I hesitatingly placed my hands on the black yoke in front of me. "What do I do?"

"Just point the nose where you want to go."

I grabbed more firmly onto the yoke and the plane tilted to one side, not dramatically, but enough to make me audibly squeak. I immediately let go.

"Small corrections," Anissa gently instructed as she leveled the plane back out. "Wanna try again?" she offered.

I swallowed and wiped my palms on the top of my thighs. I flexed my fingers once before I set my hands again on the yoke and let my fingers curl around its edges. I didn't move. I didn't do anything for fear of making a mistake; I held my arms and hands rigidly static.

"Exciting, right?"

"Terrifying," I corrected.

Anissa laughed. "It's okay. I'll take it from here. I've made you work enough for one day."

I gladly released the yoke and returned my attention to the surrounding scenery beyond my window. From this height and angle, the terrain below better resembled the Caribbean than the state of Michigan. The bright sun made Lake Huron sparkle. Small islands and shallows looked like the coral reefs of an exotic land.

"It's beautiful," I thought aloud.

"I was worried you might get bored," she admitted. "Don't you see this every day at work?"

"Not really. We're so much higher in the air then," I explained. Plus I'm working—not exactly window gazing. And I can see the whole horizon here." I waved my arm across the expansive view for affect. "You get to see all of this in panorama, not through a tiny porthole."

Anissa rewarded my exuberance with a dimpled grin.

"Why did you decide you wanted to fly?" I asked. "You're in airplanes all the time, too."

"It was mostly my brother, Sam. He wanted a plane for God knows why, but he needed someone to split the costs with. My sister Aleyna and her husband weren't interested, so I felt an obligation to help him out. I figured if I was going to own half a plane, I might as well learn how to fly it. Now, I think I'm up here more than him. I travel so much for my job," she continued, "but I don't actually get to enjoy the ride. Up here, even though we're moving, I actually feel like time slows down." She paused and chuckled. "And now I'm rambling."

"I like it," I jumped in. "I like learning all of these things about you."

"I like telling you," she smiled in return.

"Good," I said with finality. "I'm glad we got that out of the way. But really—*where* are you taking me?"

A coy smile spread across Anissa's features. "The nineteenth century."

## CHAPTER TEN

The little plane touched down smoothly on the paved runway. I considered it a small victory that I didn't make any embarrassing noises when Anissa applied the brakes. My body leaned forward and my safety harness dug into my chest. The plane's engine roared and the prop continued to spin while we taxied toward the hangar.

Anissa had continued to play coy instead of telling me where she was taking us. I peered through the front windshield to gain my bearings. A sign hung from the open doorway of the metal hangar.

"Mackinac Island Municipal Airport," I read aloud.

"Ever been?" Anissa asked.

I nodded. "Once. But it's been a while."

My parents had brought my sister and me to the northern island on vacation when I was little, but I hadn't been back since. Being an island, the only way of accessing the popular tourist destination was by small plane or ferryboat. Ferry service ended in winter when Lake Huron froze over, but braver souls could reach the nine-miles-around island by snowmobile.

Mackinac Island State Park covered eighty percent of the island. The remaining twenty percent was a small residential area in the center of the island, the airport into which we'd flown, and a picturesque Victorian Era-inspired downtown that hugged one side of the island's coastal shore.

Towering above it all, built into the limestone bluffs, was Fort Mackinac, an actual fortified military outpost built by the British during the American Revolutionary War. I could remember visiting the living history museum with my family, gawking at the costumed interpreters in their military uniforms, and covering my ears when they shot their guns and cannon.

Anissa cut the engine and hit a few more buttons and levers on the instrument panel. When she removed her headgear, I took that as a sign to do the same. She unbuckled her safety harness and jumped out onto the pavement and I followed along.

Anissa stood tall and stretched her arms above her head. She took a long breath and loudly exhaled. "I totally love it here," she approved. "It's one of my favorite places. It's a total escape from the hustle and bustle of my regular life."

"How many other girls have you brought up here?" I questioned.

I didn't feel like part of a routine, but this was the exact kind of showy thing you did to impress someone.

She winced at my question. "Would you believe me if I said you were the only one?"

I smirked. "Nope."

"Well, a girl can try."

I cocked an eyebrow and waited for a real answer.

"Okay, fine," she relented. She shoved big yellow blocks behind the plane's wheels so it wouldn't roll away. "You're number three."

My posture softened. Three. That didn't seem so bad.

"All the other girls I invited refused to go up in my tiny plane."

My mouth fell open in silent shock and protest.

Anissa held up her hands like a shield. "I'm kidding! I'm kidding!" she squeaked.

I tried to shove her, playfully, but her arms wrapped around my waist and she pulled me tight to her. My posture remained defensive as I turned away from her like a petulant child.

Her lips went to my cheek. "I'm sorry," she murmured against my skin. "I shouldn't joke about that."

"Typical pilot," I scoffed.

I wasn't really angry with her. I wasn't even wounded. But it felt like the appropriate response to a situation in which I'd never found myself before.

The weight of her hands at my hips and the soft nuzzling of her nose against my cheek had my resistance swiftly crumbling.

"I'll buy you ice cream," she sing-songed.

"You don't fight fair," I grumbled.

"You have to forgive me. I'm your only way off this island."

I couldn't help my bratty response to her cheeky statement. "You assume you're the only person I know with a personal plane."

She pulled back slightly, with her arms still around me. Her eyebrows rose up quizzically. "Oh, really … and who are all these people?"

"Friends," I huffed.

"Oh, I see." She snuggled close again. "And do these friends *fuck* as good as me?" she husked into my ear.

My eyes shuttered at her question and my body tingled all over. "How about that ice cream?"

I was amazed my voice didn't crack.

"You're real cute, Alice." Anissa kissed me firmly on the cheek and her hands dropped from my waist. I instantly missed her embrace.

I let out a shaky breath and stared up at the clear, blue sky. *What are you doing, Alice?*

The day was warm, but a cool breeze coming off Lake Huron kept the mounting heat at bay. Anissa and I meandered down the island's main street at a leisurely pace, our mouths busy with making sure the ice cream piled on top of our respective waffle cones didn't end up dripping down our elbows. I'd chosen mint chip while she had selected the eponymous Mackinac Island fudge ice cream.

The major defining feature of the island was its total absence of cars. When horseless carriages were first introduced at the turn of the century, the island's residents made the decision to ban all motor vehicles. Most people got around the island by foot, bicycle, or horse taxi. These weren't the kitschy horse-drawn carriages from New York's Central Park, however. These were massive, working horses.

Tourists flocked to the Upper Peninsula's island from all over the world, drawn to the area for its unspoiled natural beauty, its history, and of course—Mackinac Island fudge. The confectionary shops downtown pumped the scent of freshly-made chocolate treats into the street, making it nearly impossible to leave without at least indulging in a free sample or two.

We stopped in front of one of the many candy shops that lined the main street to watch a worker making fudge. A uniformed employee poured a steady stream of liquid chocolate from what appeared to be an oversized copper caldron onto a marble slab the size of a modest kitchen table. His hands worked quickly and deftly as he used a paddled stick to push the cooling chocolate liquid across the marble slab.

"That would be quite the job," Anissa remarked.

"I'd gain 100 pounds if I worked here," I laughed.

"Do you want some fudge?" she offered. "We came all this way."

"No thanks," I refused. "This ice cream is all the sweet I need today."

Anissa stuck out her full, lower lip. "Not even room for me?" she faux pouted.

I rolled my eyes, but couldn't deny how much I liked seeing this sillier side of her. She was definitely different—lighter, more carefree—away from the airport. But then again, I probably was, too.

"How's your ice cream?" she asked as we continued to walk down the concrete sidewalk.

"Dreamy," I hummed my approval. "Yours?"

"Amazing. You should have a bite," she urged. "You can't come to Mackinac Island and not have any fudge."

"I suppose I can't fault that logic," I relented.

She held out her cone toward me and I leaned closer. My tongue darted out to quickly lick at the ribbon of fudge closest to my mouth.

"Oh yeah, baby," she growled throatily. "Get in there."

I half laughed, half choked on the ice cream and jerked my head back. I hadn't gotten any fudge, but I had succeeded in smashing the end of my nose into her ice cream cone. My hand moved to wipe away the vanilla ice cream that had gotten on my nose, but she stopped me.

"Don't worry; I've got you."

I stood still, expecting her to wipe away the errant ice cream with her napkin. Instead, her own tongue darted out to collect the small dab of vanilla ice cream.

My initial response was to laugh and maybe to be a little grossed out that she'd licked the end of my nose, but self-consciousness quickly set in. We were in Northern Michigan, no longer the Greater Detroit area, which meant that people tended to be more conservative. I quickly scanned the immediate area to gauge other peoples' reactions, but no one appeared to be paying us any attention. No one seemed concerned about two girls and their ice cream cones.

Anissa and I continued on our walk. When we came to the end of the downtown stretch, we kept walking. We strolled past a city park and the city marina, filled with expensive boats. Normally I would have wondered what kind of person was rich enough to have a giant boat moored at Mackinac Island, but the woman with whom I was spending the day had her own airplane.

Away from the bustling downtown area, the crowds thinned out and our surroundings became more peaceful. I felt my blood pressure lower without the constant din of traffic, the squeal of tires, the revving of engines, and general road rage. I was so relaxed, I apparently hadn't noticed that some of my mint chip ice cream had dripped down the side of my waffle cone and had crept onto my knuckles.

"God, I'm a mess," I laughed at myself.

"Let me help you."

Before I could insist that I didn't need her kind of help, Anissa grabbed the hand that held my ice cream cone and licked across my knuckles and up my cone to clean up the dripping, sticky residue. The lick to the tip of my nose had been playful; this was different. Her tongue was wide and warm and efficient, and I felt its reverberations everywhere.

"Delicious," she slyly grinned. She knew exactly what she was doing to me.

I let out a shuddered breath. "You're evil."

"I'm helpful!" she protested, voice raising.

"Uh huh."

I wiped at my face with the thin, paper napkin one last time and tossed the rest of my leaking waffle cone into a nearby trashcan.

"Oof," I groaned, "that was good, but I have to stop."

"Full already?" she posed.

"No. But I don't want to get fat."

She shook her head and scoffed. "You're crazy. You're like the opposite of fat."

"I know," I conceded, "but if I gain weight, I have to buy a new uniform, and those things cost $500 a pop."

Anissa's jaw slackened. "That's robbery."

"Or, good incentive not to gain weight," I reasoned.

We'd come to a natural stop in front of a little white house. I probably wouldn't have noticed the building if not for the monarch butterfly flag that hung near its entrance.

I read the signage out front: "Oh, how cute. Mackinac Island Butterfly House."

"More like House of Horrors," Anissa proclaimed.

"What?"

Anissa licked her lips. "I'm terrified of butterflies."

"You're such a liar," I scoffed. "No one's afraid of butterflies."

"*I* am! Have you seen those things?" she countered. "Why do they need such big, floppy wings? And they fly all crazy. I'm convinced they purposefully divebomb me so they can flop their wings in my face."

A mischievous grin settled on my features. "So we're going in, right?"

"Did you miss what I just said?"

I grabbed onto her hand, suddenly feeling giddy. I blamed it on the sugar rush from the ice cream. "Oh, come on. It can't be that bad. I'll protect you from the big bad butterflies," I promised.

Anissa dug in her heels to prevent me from pulling her any closer to the butterfly house. "You think it's funny, but I'm serious. I'm terrified of butterflies."

"Did something happen to you as a child to cause such trauma?" Anissa's face looked too serious, but I couldn't help the smile still on my lips.

"No. I've just always been afraid. If I see one, I run away."

"Are you afraid of birds, too?" I asked.

"They're not my favorite."

I shook my head.

"What?" she huffed.

"I don't know what to do with this information," I said with a smile. "I thought you were this cool, bad ass chick, but now I find out butterflies make you pee your pants."

Anissa covered her face with her hands. "This is humiliating. I never should have said anything."

I grabbed her hands and pulled them down. "I'm sorry. I shouldn't tease," I apologized in earnest. "You just seem so cool and put together compared to me. It's a little relieving to discover you're not perfect."

The word seemed to trigger something in her. She stood a little straighter, a little stiffer. "Oh, I'll go in that butterfly house," she proclaimed. "I'll show those butterflies who's boss."

Her antics pulled a laugh from my throat. "We really don't have to. I don't want you to be uncomfortable."

"It's all fair. I trapped you on a tiny airplane. I can handle a few stupid butterflies."

"Stop," I softly admonished. "Let me have this."

"What do you mean?"

"You've got a massive house, a fancy job, and an MBA. You *own an airplane*," I listed off. "I'm not afraid of butterflies. Let me beat you at something."

"I didn't realize it was a competition," she frowned.

"It's not," I assured her. "But you have to admit—you're kind of intimidating."

She pointed a finger at herself. "Me?"

"Yes, you," I laughed. "You have all of this confidence. All of this swagger. And I'm such a haphazard, awkward mess."

"Can you stay the night?" she blurted out.

The unexpected request had me stammering. "I-I don't want to overstay my welcome."

"I wouldn't have asked if I didn't want you to stay. It's not a pity ask."

Honey would be fine another day on her own, but I thought about the long Monday I would be creating for myself. I would have to go back to my apartment in the morning before I was expected at the airport, not just for a shower, but I also needed my uniform. My blazer was dry-clean only, but I'd still have to iron and starch my blouse and pencil skirt. I would have to squeeze a grocery trip into my workweek, too, since my Golden Days were usually spent running errands. I had every reason to go directly home whenever we flew back to Detroit and only one reason to spend another night with Anissa.

My voice was unsteady; my reply nearly caught in my throat. "Yeah, I can stay."

+ + +

I sank into the thick pillowtop mattress. The material puffed up around me like I'd submerged myself in marshmallows.

"Your bed is ridiculously comfortable," I groaned in approval. "How do you ever get up in the morning?"

Anissa reclined only a few feet away from me in her bed, but even that distance felt too far. After flying back from Mackinac Island, we'd showered off the day and had shared a quick dinner of leftover burgers and brats from the night before. Her thick hair was still damp from the shower. She'd pulled it away from her face in a tight bun, like a ballet dancer. She looked magnificent without makeup.

I made another groaning noise. "I'm *so* not looking forward to work tomorrow."

The day had felt like a vacation from my real life, and I really didn't want to go back.

"My job would be great if I didn't have to deal with passengers. I get it. People get stressed when they travel. But we end up becoming their punching bags, and that's not fair. They throw up in little paper bags and just hand it to us." It was a practiced rant—one I'd often complained to my friends about. "And when they're not puking, they're ignoring us and forget to say please or thank you. It's just 'give me a Coke' or bitching that our flight ran out of complimentary Chez-its."

"Have you ever thought about becoming a pilot?" Anissa posed.

I shook my head. "It's a totally different job. It's like being a doctor versus a nurse. I take care of people. I keep them comfortable. I'm not a bus driver."

"You're doing a very good job keeping me comfortable," she smiled in approval.

"Did you always want to be an HR consultant?" I laughed at my words. "Okay. Dumb question."

"I may have been a precocious child, but even I have limits," Anissa grinned. "No. I probably wanted to be a veterinarian or a pop star."

"You sing?"

"Only in the shower."

"I think I'd like to witness that," I murmured. I ran my hand along her torso, feeling the delicate ribs beneath her skin. I traced my fingers in a light path against faint tan lines. I could see the high-cut outline of the bathing suit she'd been wearing by the pool the previous day.

"Are you Out to your family?" I asked.

My question was generic and full of assumptions. Maybe she didn't identify in any particular way. Maybe she simply enjoyed having sex with whomever was a convenient body.

"I told them when I was in high school," she confirmed

"Were they okay with it?" I asked.

I was probably asking too personal of questions, but I felt safer about it considering we'd had sex in multiple rooms in her house.

"Not at first, no. My parents are pretty traditional, but not as bad as if they'd grown up in Lebanon. They thought I was too young to be having sex, period, let alone know that I was exclusively attracted to girls."

Well—that answered my next intrusive question.

"What about you?" she asked.

"I was a late bloomer. I didn't realize I was gay until I got to college." I chuckled at the realization. "I guess accumulating all of that student debt wasn't for nothing."

She propped herself up and leaned her weight on one elbow. "You really think you wouldn't have figured it out without having gone to college?"

I shrugged beneath the weight of her blankets. "I grew up in a pretty small, conservative town. No one told me that being gay was an option. College made me realize there was a world beyond my little hometown."

She squinted as she looked at me. "You're telling me you never had a crush on one of your girl friends in high school or pined over some Hollywood starlet from the safety of a dark movie theater?"

"Looking back, it should have been obvious," I agreed. "But hindsight is twenty-twenty and all that. I thought every girl had those kinds of thoughts."

"You thought every girl wanted to go down on Kate Winslet in *Titanic*?" Anissa laughed, but not unkindly.

I could feel myself blush at the suggestion. "I didn't have those kinds of thoughts. I was raised super religious. Good Catholic girls weren't supposed to think about sex until after they got married."

"Bullshit. You thought about sex."

"I swear I didn't!" My voice raised an octave as I tried to defend myself. "I *admired* other girls, but I didn't think about having *sex* with them."

"Geez, you're like a nun."

"Whatever. You were the one calling out to God last night, not me," I shot back.

"I was only teasing, Alice." Her generous mouth flipped into a frown. "I'm sorry if I offended you."

I didn't want to be so thin-skinned, but my naivety could be embarrassing. I envied people who had been able to give a name to their sexuality earlier in life.

"When we were stranded in Philadelphia, did you know I was gay?" I asked.

"I had my suspicions," she confirmed. "You were very chivalrous. And not just the pajama thing. Queer girls tend to hold doors."

"You didn't chalk it up to good customer service?"

"You went a little above and beyond—kind of like you bringing my iPad all the way out here."

"Dearborn's not so far away," I grumbled, turning away.

Anissa refused to let me retreat. She captured the end of my chin between her thumb and forefinger and turned my face toward her own.

"I think you're very sweet, Alice." She lightly pressed her lips against my stubborn mouth. "And genuine." Her mouth traveled across the sweep of my cheek. "And kind." She pressed another kiss at the apex of my cheekbone. "And very sexy." Her warm breath ruffled the hair near my temple.

"Sexy?"

I'd heard words like pretty or cute to describe me, but never sexy. Pleasant. Pleasing. Could fit into small spaces.

I tried to protest the descriptor. "I'm-I'm not the one. Y-y-you."

Anissa flicked the tip of her tongue along the outer shell of my ear. It was hard to formulate thoughts and even harder to finish a complete sentence with her ragged breath in my ear.

She gripped me hard at my hipbones and pressed the length of her body against me. "You're sexy, Alice."

She ran her hands around my hips and to my backside. "Tight little body."

"We have to watch our weight at work."

"Smooth, delicious tasting skin." She licked up the side of my neck in one, long dramatic drag of her tongue.

"I-I used the soap in your bathroom," I sputtered.

She buried her face into my hair and inhaled. "Silky, soft hair."

"It's your conditioner."

Her face remained pressed against the side of my head. I couldn't see her face, but I could feel her body shake with what I interpreted as silent laughter.

"Shut up and accept the compliments, Alice."

"Okay," I breathed.

## CHAPTER ELEVEN

It was still dark outside when the alarm on my cellphone chimed. I'd set the alarm for an early hour knowing I'd need time to drive back to my apartment and get ready for the day before going to the airport. I probably should have spent the previous night at my apartment, but I hadn't wanted to leave. Losing a few hours of sleep seemed like a small sacrifice in exchange for another night with Anissa.

I turned off the alarm and buried my face into a pillow. "Don't wanna," I mumbled.

I felt Anissa reach for me across the expanse of the mattress. Her hand slipped under my t-shirt and curled around the elastic waistband of the borrowed shorts I wore. "Where are you flying to today?" she asked.

"What day is it?" I was only partially kidding. The last two days had been like a time warp where only Anissa and I existed.

"It's Monday."

"Monday, Monday," I sighed. "Today I'm boomeranging to Seattle and back. How about you?"

"No flying for me today, but I have some distance meetings and online trainings to facilitate. But at least I get to do all of that from home."

"Lucky."

"Do you want to shower here?" she asked.

"No. I'll do all that stuff back home." I glanced at the clock on my phone once more and sighed again. "I should probably get going before traffic gets bad."

Anissa sat quietly in bed while I changed out of the pajamas she'd let me borrow. Even in the dark, I could feel her eyes on me as I pulled on my clothes from the Saturday pool party.

"I guess that's everything," I announced.

I was a little disappointed that she hadn't tried to get me to linger in bed longer or hadn't tried to convince me to play hooky with her. I would have resisted and still have gone to work, but it would have been nice. Instead, she solemnly nodded and got out of bed herself.

Her silence continued as she padded down the stairs and led the way to the front door. The sudden lack of dialogue concerned me, but it wasn't yet dawn, and she might not have been a morning person.

Anissa flipped on the front porch light and stepped outside with me. She immediately began to run her palms over her bare arms. There was a slight chill in the air outside, and a light dew had settled across the front yard. The neighborhood was silent, still sleeping.

"Thank you for bringing me my tablet," she said, breaking the morning's silence.

"You're welcome," I routinely replied. "When can I see you again?"

Her lips drew into a smile. "I'll see you on Wednesday, won't I?"

"Yeah," I confirmed. "But can I see you *away* from the airport?"

Her teasing smile lost some of its brilliance. "I travel a lot. And my schedule isn't very flexible."

"Neither is mine," I pointed out. "But we made the past two days work, didn't we?"

I heard her quiet sigh. "I'm not very good at relationships, Alice. I'm used to having my own space and not having to think about anyone but myself. I'm pretty set in my ways."

The corner of my mouth twitched. "You could have just said no."

"I'm sorry."

I held up my hands to stop a longer, more drawn-out apology. "It's cool. I get it. We had fun, but now that fun is over."

"Alice," she sighed.

I turned around abruptly on my heels, nearly tripping down the front concrete stoop in my haste to leave. I held my hand in the air in parting, but I didn't look back.

"Alice!" she called out my name again.

I ignored her. Saying my name loudly wasn't going to be enough to get me to stay a little longer.

I hadn't been expecting anything when I'd first dropped by her house to return her tablet. I hadn't even expected anything from her when I'd stayed the night for the first time. But I'd given her one of my Golden Days. I'd invested *time*, which to me was more valuable than money, and that was saying something. I didn't have much money, but I had even less time. I hadn't been asking for forever; I hadn't even asked for a commitment. But she could have had the decency to go on a proper date with me.

I started up my car and stared straight ahead. I rolled my shoulders and tried to ignore the sting of rejection. I was used to goodbyes, I told myself. I said it about six hundred times a day when passengers deplaned.

I forced myself not to look back at Anissa's house. It would hurt too much to know she'd gone back inside before I'd even left. And it would hurt too much to see her still standing on the front stoop.

It hurt too much, period.

+ + +

I wasn't looking forward to the following Wednesday's flight. I even considered trying to get someone to switch with me, but I couldn't avoid Anissa forever. There was a Wednesday every week. My bruised ego would simply have to get over it.

I readied beverage service while the passengers in First Class boarded the plane to Philadelphia. Typically I started handing out water and taking drink orders from the back of my section and worked my way toward the flight deck, but I decided to serve the front of the plane first. I needed to rid myself of the anxious knot in my stomach. I needed to rip off the metaphorical Band-Aid.

I kept my eyes low, practically glued to the ugly blue carpet that lined the plane's center aisle, as I passed out cups of water and took drink orders from the front of the plane.

Like usual, Anissa sat in seat 3B. Not typical, however, were the noise-canceling headphones she wore. Her head was lowered, eyes focused on the screen of her tablet—the tablet I had hand-delivered to her house only a few days earlier. The headphones and her body language indicated she was just as eager to avoid me as I was her. She had already lowered her seat tray, so all I had to do was drop off her cranberry, splash of seltzer and I wouldn't have to think about her again until we were up in the air and delivering the second beverage and snack service.

I lingered, unacknowledged, by her seat, clutching the cranberry, seltzer, and ice in its flimsy plastic cup. Gemma had already achieved for me the bingo square for dumping a drink on a passenger, but nothing was really keeping me from following through on the original task I'd intended at the start of the month. I imagined myself pouring the full drink over the top of her head like the ALS Ice Bucket Challenge. I envisioned in my mind's eye the mixed look of surprise and horror on her beautiful face as the liquid poured off her dark, glossy hair and saturated her freshly pressed blouse and spilled onto her wrinkle-free linen pants.

My hand slightly shook as I bent at the waist and carefully—painstakingly so—set her beverage of choice on her tray table, next to her tan hand. I expected her golden eyes to lift to mine or to even hear a quiet word of thanks. But instead, she continued to ignore my presence.

I finished delivering water to the other First Class passengers and returned to the front galley while the rest of the plane boarded. Although my focus should have been on the newly-arriving passengers, my attention continually strayed to the woman in 3B. My position in the front galley gave me an unobstructed view of the third row and the woman seated in the aisle. Anissa never once looked up, although her fingers lightly gripped the filled plastic cup I had left on her seat tray.

I began to angrily fill the drink order for the other passengers in my section. Ice cubes noisily struck the sides of each glass as I practically threw ice into the plastic cups. I chewed on the insides of my cheeks and my nostrils flared.

Anissa continued to ignore me while I served drinks to the rest of my section. Her eyes remained glued to her tablet when the cabin doors closed and the safety video played. The longer I stared without her looking up from her tablet, the more frustrated I grew. She could at least acknowledge me. We were consenting adults who had spent an intimate weekend together. I deserved more. I deserved eye contact at the very least.

Anissa's blatant dismissal had made me feel cheap and disposable—like complimentary airline earbuds. They sufficed if you'd forgotten your own, but you realistically didn't keep them around for more than the duration of your flight. You threw them away after one use or left them behind in the seatback pocket. I had been like a perk for a valued customer.

The plane began to taxi towards the runway, and I began my final walkthrough down the plane's center aisle. My eyes swept from seat to seat, checking to make sure that seatbelts were securely fastened and that seats were in their upright position. I paused towards the back of Business Class when I noticed a middle-aged woman with her cellphone pressed against her ear.

I spoke loud enough to be heard over the increasing volume of the airplane's engines: "Ma'am, the cabin door has closed and we're preparing for takeoff. I need you to end your call and turn your phone to airplane mode."

The woman waved me off, confirming she'd heard my request, but she continued to talk on her phone.

"Yes, I'll see you when I land in three hours," she told the person on the other end of the call, "if the plane even makes it there at all."

The woman paused and lowered her voice, but not so much that I couldn't hear her next words: "There's an *Arab* in First Class."

She said the word as if it felt funny on her tongue—like she had never said the word aloud before. "I know! You'd think the government would have banned them from flying by now," she clucked. "After what they did, they should feel lucky we even let them stay in our country."

The plane bumped along in preparation of takeoff. I held the top of a headrest to keep my balance and ground down on the back of my molars. "Ma'am," I said more sternly. "It's time to end your call."

She waved her hand at me again and continued to ignore my instructions. "At least she's not wearing one of those headscarves," she spoke into the phone. "They make me so uncomfortable."

The annoyance I'd experienced before quickly flipped to a boiling rage. I reached for the woman's cellphone and aggressively yanked it out of her hand. My fingers mashed against the screen to end the call and I converted the device to airplane mode.

The seated woman stared up at me, dumbstruck. I set a saccharine smile to my lips and held the silenced phone out to her.

She grabbed one end of her phone, but I maintained a firm grip at its other end.

"The passenger about whom you're speaking so disparagingly is an American, just like you and me," I snapped. "Her grandparents immigrated from Lebanon in the 1910s. When did *your* family get here?"

I abruptly released my hold on the phone and the inertia caused the seated woman to jerk back in her seat as she regained possession of her cellphone.

I leaned over the still-startled woman and showed her my teeth. "Make sure your seatbelt is securely fastened, ma'am. We'll be taking off shortly."

I turned on my heel and marched down the rest of the center aisle. I didn't wait for the woman's reaction or the reaction of any of the other passengers within earshot. My heart was lodged in my throat and my legs felt unstable as I wobbled towards the back of the plane. I had to grip the tops of passengers' seats to keep myself steady.

I'd never been rude to a passenger before. Regardless of the blatant disrespect or disregard I might encounter, my job was to keep our passengers safe and comfortable. Nothing in my job description called for a social justice warrior.

My heart remained in my throat as I took the empty jump-seat between Gemma and Kent. It choked me and constrained my breathing. My adrenaline was beginning to wane, leaving me to suffer the cold sweat collecting under my arms and in the center of my back.

My friends were on their own phones—which also weren't in airplane mode—while the engines roared in the seconds before takeoff. Neither confronted me about my passenger interaction, which made me believe they'd missed it entirely.

"Will you take over First Class during beverage service?" I asked Kent.

Gemma looked up from her phone. "But what about 3B?" she asked, in reference to my bingo card.

"There's really nothing I can get this time around," I excused. "Maybe next flight I'll be luckier."

Kent hummed his agreement and returned his attention to his phone. He didn't follow up on Gemma's question about why I was forfeiting First Class, and for that I was grateful. I could only imagine the disapproving looks I'd get from Gemma if she knew I'd practically assaulted a passenger. There wasn't a bingo square for that.

Neither Kent nor Gemma seemed aware of my behavior, but my blood pressure remained elevated as I expected the passenger from First Class to march into the rear galley at any moment. The remainder of the flight was uneventful, however. Kent took over beverage and snack service in Business Class while I hid in Economy with Gemma to avoid the woman I'd berated.

At the conclusion of the flight, I stayed in the rear galley to record whatever supplies the next flight crew would need to replenish. It was standard procedure, but I volunteered for the tedious task rather than having to stand at the front of the plane and say goodbye to the passengers as they departed. The number of passengers I wanted to avoid had risen to two.

Kent, Gemma, and I were the last ones off the plane. They chatted and teased and joked like usual, but I was noticeably more subdued. My anxiety had nearly leveled off, but I still worried in the back of my mind that the woman from Business Class might report the incident to my airline. I half expected a gate agent to be waiting for me at the end of the jet bridge.

There was someone waiting for me, but it wasn't another airline employee.

It was Anissa.

My steps halted when I saw her. She held her cellphone in one hand and the handle of a roller bag in the other. Kent and Gemma noticed how I'd paused. They looked to me for an explanation, but I wasn't ready for that.

"I'll catch up with you," I told my friends.

I knew they would expect a full report from me later.

I sucked in a breath while I waited for my friends to leave. I didn't know why I felt nervous—even guilty; I hadn't done anything wrong. I didn't even really know what to say.

"Hey," I settled on.

Anissa dropped her eyes to her phone and swiped her fingertips across the screen. "Excuse me, Miss. Could you help me with something?"

I didn't know what game she was playing, but I found myself going along with it: "Of course," I said cautiously. "How can I be of assistance?"

Her eyebrows pinched together as she continued to scrutinize the cellphone screen. "I'm trying to find a feedback form for your airline, but I can't seem to find it online."

"Was something dissatisfactory about your recent flight?"

She looked up from her phone. "Just the opposite. I wanted to commend the service of a flight attendant who stood up to a bigoted passenger in my defense."

I swallowed hard. I'd thought her noise-canceling headphones would have canceled out that interaction. "You heard that."

A small smile played on her generous lips. "You weren't exactly whispering."

I rested my hand on the wall of the jet bridge. My stomach felt slightly nauseous, like I was experiencing vertigo, and I didn't trust my legs. "I-I don't know what came over me. She just ... she made me *so mad*," I said, replaying the interaction in my mind. "I'm never like that with passengers."

Anissa gently touched my forearm. Her hand was solid and reassuring. "Thank you," she said softly. "Not many people would do that. It really meant a lot."

"It's not a big deal," I dismissed.

"It is," she insisted. "Let me buy you dinner. On purpose this time."

"You think you can fit me into your schedule?" Ice crept into my tone, but I couldn't help myself. Her recent rejection still stung.

Anissa frowned. "I probably deserved that."

"You do." I wasn't going to pull any punches.

"How much time until your next flight?" she asked.

"I have to be at my gate in two hours."

Her lips pursed in thought. "That should be just enough time."

I was almost too stubborn to vocalize my curiosity, but I asked anyway. "For what?"

Anissa and I walked down the terminal, not speaking, with our wheeled luggage rolling behind us. She passed up the typical food court options without notice. The various terminals were anchored by sit-down restaurants, but nothing very fancy. I knew from experience that the food in those places was typically flavorless and overpriced. Most travelers didn't have time for such meals unless their flights had been seriously delayed.

I wanted to break the uncomfortable silence with idle chit-chat—commenting on her extra carry-on luggage perhaps—but Anissa walked with purpose and it was all I could do to keep up.

When Anissa finally stopped walking it wasn't in front of a fast food kiosk or even in front of any of the anchor restaurants; she'd stopped in front of one of the in-airport hotels.

"I thought you were buying me dinner," I questioned.

She turned to me, features impassive. "Trust me, okay?"

I hovered in the background while Anissa spoke to the man working the hotel's reception desk. I watched them exchange a few words before she produced a credit card and he handed her a plastic room key. She still didn't explain herself as she gathered her work bag and her wheeled luggage. She rolled over to a bank of elevators and I followed.

The glass elevator ride provided a birds-eye view of the terminal. It was still early in the afternoon and we were the only ones in the elevator. We might have been the only people in the airport hotel. In the exposed glass box, I couldn't help but feel like everyone's eyes were on us.

The elevator paused at the next floor and the doors open. Anissa walked into the hallway, and I continued to dutifully follow behind. She fumbled slightly in balancing her workbag and wheeled luggage while she used the plastic card to unlock the hotel door. It was clear that she was still getting used to the carry-on luggage; it hadn't become an extension of her body yet, like my own.

She pushed the door open and stepped into the room, awkwardly dragging her luggage behind her. The black carry-on bag had turned on its side and the wheels no longer served their intended function.

I bent down and picked up the bottom of her bag, and together we carried the luggage across the threshold.

"Thanks," she said, looking a little flustered.

The hotel room was small, but efficient. A queen-sized bed, a bathroom, and a TV inside of a wardrobe. Airport hotels were for people with long layovers or canceled flights. Maybe a random hook-up. You wouldn't make this an extended stay.

"You do this often?" I eyeballed the room and then Anissa.

She flopped down on the queen-sized bed like a preteen at a slumber party. "Sometimes. Like, if I need a nap between flights. I've never been able to fall asleep at the gate."

A knock at the door behind me pulled my attention away from the woman and the bed. Anissa hopped to her feet and went to the door while I continued to stand in the center of the room. There was no place to sit except for the bed.

Anissa came away from the door holding a large silver serving tray from room service. I could see a carafe of orange juice, two glasses, two tiny bottles of champagne, and two plates covered with silver covering dishes.

She set the tray on the bed and removed both plate covers with a flourish. "Ta-da!"

Pancakes, stacked three cakes high, steamed underneath. Each plate had its own tidy pile of bacon.

"Breakfast in bed?" I remarked, still keeping my distance. "Cute."

Anissa snatched a piece of thick-cut bacon from one of the plates and took a bite. "Are you going to join me?"

"I'm not sure I should get in a bed with you," I said in earnest.

She held up her right hand as if taking an oath. "I solemnly swear I am not trying to seduce you."

I rubbed the back of my neck. "I don't know about that. Pancakes are my weakness."

Anissa patted an empty space on the mattress, close to her. "We'll stay on top of the covers. Clothes will stay on," she vowed. "I know you have a flight to catch soon."

I sat down on the edge of the bed instead of next to her, not entirely giving in. I didn't want to get too comfortable, but I also knew I needed to eat before my next flight. Low-blood sugar at 35,000 feet was not a good look.

Anissa grabbed one of the miniature champagne bottles and released its cork. The bottle made a loud popping noise, but no liquid shot out. She emptied the bottle's contents into one of the glasses and poured a splash of orange juice on top. She tried to hand me the hotel-room mimosa, but I waved it off.

"No thanks," I refused. "I'm on the clock."

Anissa stuck out her lower lip. She looked like she wanted to protest, but decided against it.

I took one of the plates and slowly began to eat. Anissa was quiet as well as she cut up her stack of pancakes into small, precise bite-sized pieces.

I couldn't stay silent for long. "What is all of this?"

"An apology."

"What do you need to apologize for?" I asked, playing dumb.

She frowned. "You know what, Alice."

"Is this because I said something to that woman on the plane?"

"Not entirely. Although that was pretty bad ass," she approved. "But I've felt guilty about how we left things pretty much the minute you left my house."

"I don't think '*we*' is the right pronoun," I cut in. "*You* basically made all the decisions for both of us."

"Can you let me get my apology out?" she huffed.

I pressed my lips together to keep from saying anything else.

"So here's the thing—I'm terrible at relationships," she scowled. "I'm more of a situation-ship kind of girl."

"Situation-ship?" I echoed. "I haven't heard that one before."

"Situation-ship: a relationship without labels. Friends, but a little more."

I curled my lip. "Oh. You mean like friends with benefits. Fuck buddies."

She shrugged. "Whatever you want to call it. I travel too much, and when I'm not traveling I'm on-call and have to get to an airport at a moment's notice if someone calls in sick. My schedule changes all the time. I'm probably going to miss your birthday and every other holiday of importance."

"That sounds like the exact speech I give to women who get too clingy," I deadpanned.

"I don't think you're clingy!" she insisted. "I just want to be realistic about expectations."

"I wasn't asking for a ring, Anissa," I said, shaking my head. "But I have fun when I'm around you. And I hope you have fun, too."

She dropped her head in an uncharacteristic show of bashfulness. Her long hair fell in front of her eyes. "I have fun with you."

"Good," I smiled. Her affirmation bolstered my confidence. "Now that we've established that we're both a lot of fun, I have a serious question for you."

She looked up at me, her hair falling back into place.

I took a breath. "Do you like baseball?"

## CHAPTER TWELVE

I was trying not to overthink my outfit. We were going to a baseball game, not a fancy restaurant. We would be sitting in the sun all game, and not in the air conditioned comfort of a darkened movie theater. I'd chosen high-waisted skinny jeans instead of shorts so the backs of my thighs wouldn't stick to the narrow, plastic seats. I only had one shirt with the team's logo on it, so that had made that decision for me. I'd gotten the shirt as a free giveaway the last time I'd been to Comerica Park. Free ballpark shirts were typically extra large, so I'd rolled up the sleeves and had cinched the extra torso material into a knot that showed off a sliver of my pale midsection. I'd left my hair down, flat-ironed to submission. A well-loved and well-worn Tiger's baseball cap would keep my hair in place and the sun off my face.

I frowned at my full-length reflection. This was as good as it was going to get.

My body was filled with a different kind of trepidation when I parked my car in front of Anissa's home. Dearborn was positioned halfway between Romulus, where I lived, and downtown Detroit, so I'd offered to pick her up and drive us to the ballpark. The first time I'd dropped by her house I'd been walking in blind with no real expectations. But now, weeks later, we were at a completely different place. For one, we'd had sex. And sex tended to complicate everything.

I still couldn't understand why she'd chosen me. I wasn't anything special—nothing to write home about. It made me worry that maybe I was convenient. She'd admitted to not having time to date and being bad at relationships, and I'd practically fallen into her bed, complete with gift wrapping. I'd been the only one around in Philadelphia when she'd propositioned me, and I'd shown up on her Dearborn doorstep not much later. I worried that once the convenience of our situation ran its course, so would her interest in me.

I was only halfway up her walkway when her front door opened. I immediately second-guessed my extra-large, free t-shirt when she stepped into the sun, looking perfect. She wore a fitted Detroit Tigers home jersey, the material blindingly white as if she'd never even thought about spilling mustard down the front. The jersey was unbuttoned just enough to show off her chiseled collarbone. A tiny gold cross on a thin chain rested near the hollow of her throat. Her makeup was light, and her hair curved around her face and shoulders in generous curls. Skinny jeans and white Keds with no socks finished off the outfit.

A femme-presenting woman wearing sports team gear made me clench all over. My body didn't stop seizing when she skipped down her walkway and greeted me with a kiss.

The kiss was brief—little more than a quick peck—but it was welcomed.

She pulled back and smiled, showing off her deep dimples. "Hey."

"Hey yourself," I returned.

She tugged at the front brim of my hat, pulling it lower on my forehead. "This is cute."

I tugged my hat back into place. "You are," I juvenilely retorted.

I wasn't expecting the second kiss. Her hands fell to my hips and her lips softened against mine. I made a surprised noise into her pliable mouth when her hands traveled to my backside and squeezed. The kiss made me think about the two game tickets in my car's center cup holders. We technically wouldn't be missing out if we never made it to the game. The tickets had been free—a company perk. My airline had season tickets to Detroit's major sports teams, and we could put in requests to get free tickets every once in a while. I wondered how much convincing it would take for her to turn around and go back into the house and upstairs to her bedroom.

When she deepened the kiss, her tongue probing my mouth, my thoughts took a left turn. I thought about how out in the open we were, practically making out in her front yard, the full sun shining down on us like a spotlight. The side yards were small in her subdivision and the houses were close together. Her neighbors would only have to look out a window to see us. I wondered how close her family lived; she had said they lived in her neighborhood. She was Out to her family, but were they supportive? How did she identify? She'd had sex with women before, that much was obvious, but did she actually date them? What had been her longest relationship? And why had it ended?

"I'm glad we're doing this."

My brain had started to spiral out with so many questions that I hadn't realized she'd ended the kiss.

I licked my lips, tasting her minty toothpaste on them. "Me too," I agreed.

We started to walk down the sidewalk to where my car was parked. Anissa seemed to bounce on the balls of her feet, light and carefree, while my stomach continued to churn with unsettled nerves. I became suspicious when she started to lag behind, just a few steps. Maybe she'd forgotten something back in the house.

I looked back to her. "What is it?"

Her head tilted to one side. "Your ass looks particularly delicious in those jeans," she remarked.

The open compliment made me strangely uneasy, but I didn't know why. Maybe it was because I had no idea where we stood. Was she ogling me as a friend-with-benefits or was this an actual date? Was she going to situation-ship me like everyone else?

My nerves still hadn't settled between the drive from Anissa's house to the downtown stadium. I felt only mildly better after she let me buy her a hot dog and a beer from the concession stand.

We balanced overpriced draft beers and steamed hot dogs wrapped in wax paper as we climbed up the stadium steps. My company's seats were actually really nice. We were in the lower bowl, along the third base line, and on an aisle so beer runs and bathroom breaks wouldn't disturb the entire row.

I really enjoyed going to baseball games. The crack of the bat. The scent of grilled meat and roasted peanuts. Vendors hoofing up the steep stadium stairs, barking their wares. Kids with baseball mitts and sticky cotton candy fingers. Millennials taking selfies and paying more attention to their phones than to the game.

Comerica Park was a newer stadium, but that didn't mean extra leg room. Wasted space was lost money. The irony wasn't lost on me. I spent my workdays wedged into tight, confined spaces; I was spending my day off doing the same thing. The narrow seating arrangements meant that Anissa and I were practically pressed together in our assigned seats. Every time I took a bite of my hot dog or reached for the beer in the cup holder in front of me, my arm brushed against her shoulder or bumped into her thigh.

The afternoon sun was hot and our seats' positions provided no shelter from its unforgiving rays. I could feel the sweat start to trickle down the small of my back in my extra-large t-shirt. Anissa looked undisturbed and unaffected by the heat while I wilted under the extreme conditions.

I tried to tease away my insecurities. "You look like a professional in that jersey. Sure you're not actually on the team?"

"I could probably field better than half the infield," she said, frowning slightly. "When's the last time we went through a complete game without an error?"

She spoke like she knew the sport, more than the casual fan.

"Do you go to a lot of games?" I asked.

She shook her head. "I haven't been to too many recently—not since the team went all-in on the rebuild. I don't know how you go from winning the American League pennant in 2012 to rebuilding. Avila made a huge mistake when he didn't give up Fulmer for Javier Baez or Alex Bregman. It could be worst though," she mused aloud. "I remember when we broke an MLB record in 2003 for losing 119 games in a single season. Those aren't the kinds of records you want your team making."

My eyes widened with each new statistic and observation. "You're beautiful *and* you know about baseball? Where have you been hiding all my life?"

My outburst of exuberance had me back-peddling. "I mean, uh, it's cool you're into sports or whatever."

She smiled at me, earnest and indulgent. "I like you, too, Alice."

I rubbed the back of my neck. "Oh, okay. Cool. I mean, uh, that's good."

She squeezed the top of my knee affectionately, and I felt its aftershocks traverse the rest of my body.

I did a mental victory dance when she kept her hand resting on my thigh during the game, removing it only to clap when our team did something good—which wasn't too often. Anissa didn't talk much during the game, which I actually appreciated. I tended to get annoyed by fans who chatted about banal topics during a game instead of actually watching the contest. If I had wanted constant conversation, I would have gone to a coffeeshop or a bar.

The weight of her hand felt good on my knee. Solid. Reassuring. My extra-large t-shirt might have been an unwise fashion choice, but I was thankful for my decision to wear jeans to the game. Without the denim barrier between her palm and my knee, I would have sweat all over her hand.

As the game neared the seventh inning stretch, I noticed our empty cups.

"Do you want a refill?" I offered. "Or something else to eat?"

Anissa's eyes turned from the playing field to me. "You don't have to wait on me, you know," she noted. "You do enough of that in the air."

"I like it when it's you," I said in earnest.

Her lips twisted in contemplation. "Okay. But maybe a bottled water this time? I don't think there's any more room in my stomach after that giant beer," she said, motioning to our giant, empty cups.

I nodded. "One bottled water, coming right up."

Before I could stand up, her hand fell again to my knee and the other to the side of my face. She drew me in for a soft, unexpected kiss that had my toes curling in my sandals.

"Hurry back," she quietly murmured, pulling away. Her hand went to my hair and she brushed at some of the fly-a-ways that had worked their way out of my ball cap. "I don't want you missing the game."

It was too easy to get lost in the golden depths of her pooling eyes; I nearly forgot where we were and what I was supposed to be doing. Each kiss, each touch, had me yearning for more.

"I'll be right back," I managed to choke out.

I hustled to the closest concession stand with refrains of "Take Me Out the Ballpark" ringing in my ears. I outwardly groaned when I saw the length of the food and drink lines. Flat-screen TVs positioned around the area were live-broadcasting the game, but I wasn't worried about missing a home run. I wanted to get back to my seat so I didn't miss out on Anissa. I licked my lips as my thoughts drifted back to her and her baseball jersey. A beautiful, brainy woman who wasn't afraid of public displays of affection, and it was I who was the recipient of that affection.

The concession line moved too slowly, but I didn't have much choice but to endure. My feet shuffled on concrete as we inched forward. I felt like I spent my life waiting. Waiting for a flight to arrive. Waiting for late passengers to get to the gate so the plane could leave. Waiting for the final person to deplane so we could clean the plane and go home.

After what felt like an eternity, I was finally able to purchase two bottles of water. Truthfully, I probably would have gotten myself another beer, but Anissa and I had consumed alcohol each time we'd hung out outside of work. Flight crews had reputations for being big drinkers—specific regulations had been put in place to make sure we didn't drink too close to our next flight because it was such an entrenched problem—and I didn't want her to think I fit that stereotype so early into a relationship.

*Relationship.* The word made me simultaneously giddy and light-headed. Was this a relationship? Or, was I someone she hung out with and sometimes had sex with? I envied my eleven-year-old self when passing notes containing the question 'Will you be my girlfriend, circle yes or no' could clear up any ambiguity.

I returned to our section, a bottled water in each hand. I surveyed the area where we'd been sitting, but I didn't see Anissa. Our empty plastic beer cups were still in their respective cupholders and the wax wrapping from our hot dogs were crumpled up evidence beneath the stadium seating. I even double-checked my paper ticket to make sure I hadn't gone to the wrong section, but Anissa had definitely disappeared.

I sat back in my seat and tried to ignore the empty place beside me. I couldn't focus on the game's action, however, without wondering where she'd disappeared to. The concession line had moved slowly, but I hadn't been gone for that long. I couldn't imagine her getting worried and coming to look for me.

When the eighth inning started and she still hadn't returned, I wrote her a quick text: *Where did you go?*

Her answer arrived a few moments later: *Bathroom.*

I frowned at my phone and the one-word response. Something felt off. I was no expert on how Anissa texted, but the terse reply seemed out of character. Instead of remaining in my seat and waiting for her return, I left in search of the closest women's bathroom.

My footsteps squeaked and my voice echoed hollowly in the windowless, concrete-dominated space. "Anissa?"

I felt borderline ridiculous calling out her name in a public bathroom. But it was mid-inning, so the women's bathroom was relatively empty. Only a few of the stall doors were closed and no one was at the wall of sinks.

I heard her slightly muffled voice come from one of the closed stalls: "Over here."

I didn't know which stall was hers until I recognized her white shoes underneath the door.

"Is everything okay?" I asked, the closed door between us. I lowered my voice. "Did that hot dog make your stomach angry?"

"My stomach's fine."

I stood outside of the bathroom stall, not really knowing what to do or what to say. Finally, Anissa spoke again.

"After you went to get water, someone said something to me. Something not nice."

My throat tightened. "Because we kissed?"

"No," I heard her sigh. "Because I'm brown."

My stomach dropped. "What did they say?"

The locking mechanism of the bathroom door made a sound before the stall door swung open. Anissa stepped out, and I grabbed her hand. I searched her face for answers. The glow, the joy, the lightness of the day had been erased from her features. I could see how her normally erect shoulders slumped forward with the weight of the confrontation. The area around her eyes was puffy, and the whites of her eyes were spider-webbed red from obvious crying.

I pulled her into a tight embrace, unconcerned with the other baseball fans who milled in and out of the women's bathroom. I ran my hand down the back of her head while my other hand rubbed circles in the center of her back. Her arms wrapped tight around my ribcage, almost aggressively so. I could feel the anger and frustration radiating from her slight form.

"What happened?" I quietly asked.

She stayed in my solid embrace for a long moment before pulling away. She retreated back to her former bathroom stall and pulled several squares of toilet paper free to dab at her eyes and to blow her nose. I remained silent and patient until she was ready to answer my question.

"I wasn't even doing anything," she sniffled. "I was looking at my phone and then I heard them. Some woman in the row behind me made a comment about how many *foreigners* were at the game that day—how not even baseball—America's national pastime—was safe from immigrants. I tried to ignore her—I really did," she insisted. "We were having such a nice day. But I couldn't help pointing out to her that over a quarter of major league players were born someplace else. That if she really wanted to get technical about it, football was the most American sport, not baseball."

I sucked in a sharp breath.

"She apparently didn't like me correcting her. She got right up in my face and told me to go back to where I came from."

My mouth fell open. "Are you kidding me?"

Anissa shook her head bitterly. "It's just so hard, you know? And I try to rise above it, try to take the high road, but there's only so much a person can take."

"Should we report her or something?" I worried my lower lip. "That's definitely harassment, and I'm sure major league baseball doesn't want to condone that kind of behavior. There's got to be a security guard we can tell or a number we can text. You said she was sitting close to our seats?"

Anissa held up a hand. "It's okay, Alice," she tried to appease me. "We don't have to make a big deal about it. I'm only sorry I let her get the best of me."

"No, it *is* a big deal," I emphasized. "No one has the right to talk to you or treat you like that." I started to rant. "That woman can't get away with this. I want her picture up at every baseball stadium." I swung my arms, and my body vibrated with agitation. "I want her banned from sports forever; I want—."

My next thought was abruptly cut off by Anissa's lips on mine. Her kiss efficiently silenced my indignation. Her fingers curled around my ears and brushed at the nape of my neck. The intensity and feeling and sweetness behind the embrace melted away my rage, and I momentarily forgot we were kissing in a public bathroom at a baseball game.

Anissa eventually broke off the kiss, but her hands remained on either side of my face. Her caramel-colored eyes scanned my features, looking for what, I couldn't tell. A small, sad smile played at her lips. "Let's get out of here, okay?"

I swallowed down my leftover rage. "Okay."

Her hands left my face, but her right hand took up residency in mine. In the background, I noted a cheer erupting from the stands—our team must have finally done something good—but the score of the baseball game was the farthest thing from my mind.

We walked out of the stadium together, hand in hand. As we crossed a busy intersection to return to the underground parking lot, Anissa slipped her arm around my waist and rested her head on my shoulder. I should have been jubilant about the open intimacy, but Anissa hadn't spoken a word since we'd left the women's bathroom.

I didn't know if I'd done the right thing in leaving the game. A part of me worried that I'd too readily run from confrontation. I should have insisted on challenging the woman whose hate speech had made Anissa cry in a public bathroom. That would have been the right thing—the brave thing—to do.

I could only imagine what it must be like to be a person of color in this country. I was gay, but I was also femme and could pass for straight. I had the privilege of choosing who to Come Out to and when to be openly affectionate in public. It certainly wasn't easy being queer in America, but Anissa would have experienced triple jeopardy as a queer woman of color as well as guilt by association for being tenuously connected to the Middle East.

It was just layer after layer of discrimination and oppression. My heart ached for her.

Anissa only untangled herself from my side when we reached my parked car. We had to detach to get into the car, but I didn't like it. I wanted to scoop her up and put her in my protective pocket, away from all the hate and ugliness. But it wasn't my job to save her. She'd been doing a fine job long before I came along.

Anissa broke the silence once we were outside of my car. "Do you mind if we go back to your place?"

"Your house is closer," I pointed out.

"I know. But I'd like to see where you live."

"It's nothing special," I resisted.

"Is there a reason I shouldn't see where you live?" she questioned. "Do you have a secret, double life I don't know about?"

"Just poverty," I tried to joke.

Anissa didn't laugh or even smile, but I didn't blame her. It wasn't very funny.

"I'll take you to my place," I gave in.

As I steered my car in the direction of my apartment, Anissa continued to sit in silence. She leaned her head against the passenger side window and stared outside. The final inning of the baseball game played quietly in the background on my car radio.

"I'm sorry," I heard her quiet murmur.

"For what?" I glanced briefly in her direction. Her eyes were closed and her head was still against the window.

"We were having such a nice day."

"You didn't do anything wrong," I tried to insist.

She sighed, but didn't make additional comment.

"Does that happen a lot?" I knew she probably just wanted to put the day's events in the rearview mirror, but I couldn't help asking.

Anissa regarded me with a frown. "I don't know what a lot is. Everyday? No. Once a month? Probably." She sat up straighter and ran her fingers through her hair. Her thick, careful curls had somewhat wilted under the summer heat. "In my neighborhood, everyone looks like me. I don't have to worry about taking up too much space or standing out. But then I leave that bubble and I'm not protected anymore."

She sighed and chewed on her lower lip. "It's hard because I travel so much. Airports bring out the worst in people, plus I'm not always traveling to big cities. Try looking like me in the deep, rural South. It's worse in the summer, too." She held out her sun-kissed arms for inspection. "I get more tan, which makes me look more ethnic, more 'Other,' I suppose."

"It's not fair," I spoke aloud. It was a massive understatement, but I didn't know what else to say.

"No," she sighed again. "It's not."

We drove the rest of the way in silence.

# CHAPTER THIRTEEN

I had to insert my front entrance key at just the right angle and wiggle the door handle with just the right amount of pressure to get my apartment door to unlock. Most days I didn't mind the song-and-dance, secret handshake details of opening my door, but with someone else waiting in the hallway with me, my anxiety only heightened.

I was a little embarrassed to show Anissa where I lived. It wasn't a dump, but it also wasn't a grown-up space like her suburban McMansion. In fact, most of my neighbors were senior citizens on fixed incomes or college students, also with limited budgets. I didn't know many people in my building because of the constant turnover of the demographic.

Anissa silently entered behind me. I closed and locked my apartment door and watched her survey the room. I knew what she was thinking; it was the very reason I never brought people over—not even Kent or Gemma. This wasn't a home. It was a storage container. The separate bedroom and kitchenette were the only things elevating my apartment from a college dorm room.

I didn't have a TV. I didn't pay for cable, so there was really no need for that purchase either. Nights at home were spent streaming TV shows and movies on my laptop on the subscription services I shared with other friends.

I didn't have a dining table. I did have two stools at my kitchen island, but I ate most of my meals standing up. It was a bad habit picked up from work. On a plane, I tended to hide in the galley and shovel food in my face out of passenger view and in between services. I'd started to do the same, sad thing at home, facing the kitchen wall and devouring my food in no time.

I reflexively opened the refrigerator door even though I knew what I'd find. Not much of anything. I hadn't been grocery shopping in a shockingly long time, even for me.

"Can I get you something?" I routinely offered.

Anissa came up behind me and peered over my shoulder into the refrigerator. Her hands fell to my waist in an innocent, but intimate gesture. "What do you have?"

"A tub of butter and a bottle of ketchup."

She pressed her lips close to my ear. "How about we order a pizza?"

I shut the refrigerator door. "You're a goddess."

"You're pretty free and loose with those comments," she smirked.

"Maybe I think you're totally deserving of them," I proposed.

Anissa pulled out her phone to search for a pizza delivery number while I tried to low-key pick up my apartment. I hadn't really thought about what we might do after the game, but I also hadn't anticipated us coming back to my place. Her house was significantly closer to the stadium, and it was an actual house, not a 700-square foot apartment.

"Detroit-style pepperoni sound good?" She held her hand over the bottom of the phone.

I gave her a thumbs-up sign of approval.

I walked over to Honey's aquarium while Anissa finished the phone call. I tapped against the glass, causing Honey to slide off of her floating island and crash into the water. My turtle and I shared the same level of physical coordination.

"Pizza will be here in half an hour," Anissa announced. She ended her phone call and slipped the device into the back pocket of her jeans.

She walked toward me; the wooden floor creaked under her feet. "What's in your aquarium?" she asked.

"Honey."

"Honey?"

"She's my pet turtle," I explained.

Anissa stood beside me and hunched over to get a better look. "I've never met anyone with a pet turtle before."

"Well, now you have," I remarked.

Anissa continued to stand in the bent over position while we watched Honey together. "It's very peaceful watching her swim."

"Mmhm," I agreed. Without proper television to entertain me, I sometimes poured myself a glass of wine, put on some ambient music, and watched Honey float around in her tank.

"Why did you name her Honey?" Anissa asked.

"It's really dorky," I resisted.

"Tell me," she insisted.

"It's dumb."

Anissa straightened. "I've had a terrible day, Alice," she reminded me. "I need this."

I frowned. I'd nearly forgotten the reason we'd left the game early; it made me feel terrible. Anissa didn't have that luxury. "I'm so sorry about that. I wish I'd been able to do something."

"Stop deflecting," she chastised. "I want to hear your turtle's origin story."

"I got Honey when I went to college. I lived alone in an off-campus apartment my sophomore year, and it got lonely coming home from classes to an empty place. So I got a turtle and named her Honey."

"That explains the turtle, but not the name," Anissa pointed out.

"Fine." I winced as if in pain. "I liked saying 'Honey, I'm home.'"

"You're right," Anissa deadpanned. "That's pretty dorky."

"Have you lived here long?" she asked.

"Since I started at the airline," I confirmed. "So, wow, close to eight years. Time sure flies."

She hummed, but didn't share what she might be thinking.

"You can say it."

"What?"

"My apartment is terrible."

"It's fine, Alice," she resisted.

"You don't have to lie. I know it's pretty bad."

"Maybe not bad," she decided, "but boring."

My jaw dropped a little. "*Boring?*"

"Where are your photographs? Wall art? Books?" she listed off. "There's nothing personal in here, nothing that's you. Besides, Honey, of course."

"My bedroom's better."

She laughed at that.

"What?" I demanded. I couldn't help stomping my foot a little.

"Is this all a ploy to get me to your bedroom, Kaminski? Pretty smooth."

"I don't spend a lot of time out here except to eat. Everything is in my room."

"Well now that you've built it up, I've got to see this impressive bedroom of yours."

"It's not impressive," I denied, "it's just not boring."

"I'll be the judge of that." She grabbed my hand and tugged me in the direction of my bedroom. The apartment floor plan wasn't complicated, so I wasn't surprised she knew where to find my room.

My bed wasn't made, but it also wasn't a complete disaster zone—contained chaos. I did a quick scan to make sure there was nothing embarrassing out in the open before I sat down on the edge of my queen-sized mattress. I leaned back on the bed while Anissa made her rounds. She didn't go so far as to open up the drawers of my wardrobe, but she took her time, touching knick-knacks and stopping to peer at the people in framed photographs.

"Not bad," she remarked.

"Not boring?" I challenged.

She grinned broadly. "The jury's still out on that one."

She picked up one particularly crowded imagine. "Is this your family?"

I nodded. "Un huh.

She returned the framed photograph to its place on my dresser. "Are you guys close?"

"Not live-in-the-same-neighborhood, have weekend barbeques close. My parents retired to Florida, but my sister and her husband live a little north of me in Bloomfield Hills. She's a mom—two kids. I try to go to ballet recitals and swim meets when I can, but it's not as often as I'd like."

"Cute," she mused. "I like being the Cool Aunt. I don't know if I'd want kids of my own. Honestly, I'm probably too selfish to be a mom. I'm pretty set in my ways to prioritize anyone over myself even if they popped out of my own body."

"That's quite the visual," I chuckled.

"You're welcome," she smiled. She scanned the bedroom once more. "It's a nice room," she decided.

"I'm glad it meets your approval."

I reached for her wrist and she accepted the nonverbal cue to climb onto the bed next to me. We laid on the mattress, bodies parallel to each other, and stared at the ceiling. I folded my hands under my head like a pillow. We were both quiet, listening to the sounds of traffic and sirens outside.

"How many others have you let into your sanctuary?" she wondered aloud.

"Nobody," came my honest reply.

Anissa rolled onto her side and arched a dark eyebrow at me. "Not even Lara?"

I couldn't help my smirk at her tiny admission of jealousy. "No. Not even Lara. I really don't have people over."

"How come I got to?" she questioned.

"Because you asked."

Her eyes slightly narrowed as she regarded me. "Are you always so straightforward with everyone? I feel like you've never lied a day in your life."

"I've lied to you," I said evenly.

Her voice pitched up. "Oh, really?"

She pulled away, putting distance between us, and I instantly missed the press of her body against mine.

"That night in Philadelphia," I started. "When we were stranded, and you wanted to, uh…"

"Fuck," she finished the sentence for me.

I could feel my cheeks grow warm at the expletive. "Yeah. I, uh, I wasn't really on my period."

Her lips thinned in a smug smile. "I didn't think so. But it was a clever cover story." She made an amused humming sound. "I thought you were this shy, awkward, little thing—but then you showed up at my house unannounced, and I had to reassess my assumptions about you."

"Oh, you're not wrong. I'm pretty shy, and I'm most definitely awkward," I said with feeling.

"You practically threw a glass of water down your shirt the first time we met," she laughed. "I have no idea how you managed that. The plane hadn't even taken off yet!"

I chewed on my lower lip. I was tempted to tell her about the bingo card, but I wasn't sure what she'd think about it. Were we creative to pass our time that way, or was the contest immature and cruel? I couldn't make up my mind.

"Although if it was a ploy to get my attention," Anissa continued, "then you succeeded. Nothing like a wet t-shirt contest to get a girl interested."

"Yeah, you figured me out," I snorted. "That was my master plan all along."

Anissa wiggled back to her original position and even a little closer so our shoulders knocked together. Her body naturally curled against mine. It felt so right, it made my chest seize.

"Did I just find your vibrator?"

I blinked, not understanding. "Huh?"

"I think someone's texting you," she noted. "I feel you buzzing."

"Oh. Right. Sorry."

I had silenced my phone earlier, but the vibrating function was still active. I pulled my phone from my front right jean pocket. A series of text messages, all from the same person, filled my phone's screen.

*June has a piano recital tomorrow if you're able to make it.*

The following texts provided the time and location of the performance along with her typical passive aggressive guilt trip.

I felt Anissa press closer. "Another girlfriend texting you?"

Her use of the word 'another' was unexpected. Did that mean she considered herself my girlfriend?

"No. It's my sister, Dawn," I said, holding out my phone as proof. "My niece has a piano recital tomorrow."

"Cute. Are we going?"

I looked up sharply from my phone. "You really want to go to a seven-year-old's piano recital? It's going to be, like, 'Hot Cross Buns' on repeat."

Anissa pursed her lips. "No. But I want to spend more time with you. And you shouldn't have to decide between spending time with your family or spending time with the person you're dating."

My throat involuntarily tightened. "I didn't realize we were at that point."

"What point would that be?"

I wrinkled my nose. "You're going to make me say it?"

A ghost of a smile reached her lips. "I don't know what you're referring to."

"Don't be coy," I complained. "Like, is this a real relationship? Are we exclusive?" I nearly choked on the question.

"I hardly have time to date you," she breezed, maddeningly casual. "How could I possibly juggle multiple girls?"

"That's not a real answer," I sourly protested.

Instead of giving me the direct answer I desired, Anissa grabbed my hand and toyed with my fingers, mine pale in comparison to her golden skin tone. Our fingers clasped together like pieces of a jigsaw puzzle. She turned our enjoined hands over so mine was on top. She stroked her fingertips over the top of my hand in quiet contemplation. Her touch was light and soothing. I felt rough and unpolished.

"I really need a manicure," I complained. I started to wiggle my hand free from hers, but she only tightened her grip.

"I like your hands," she said simply. "I like what they do to me."

Our heads were already close; I didn't have to lean in too far to bring our mouths together. Our lips barely touched at first, brushing slowly and tentatively against each other. Her tongue peeked out between her parted lips and slid across my bottom lip. I sucked on the tip of her tongue and pulled it more fully into my mouth.

I felt the bite of her hipbones when she rolled on top of me. I sank my hands into her thick, luscious hair as the kiss deepened and intensified. She held me by the front belt loops of my jeans and periodically tugged up. I groaned into her open mouth each time the inseam of my jeans dug into me, pressing the denim material tight against my clit.

She dropped hot, wet kisses to the side of my neck and her solid knee found its way between my jean-clad thighs. I groaned again, this time in frustration. The pencil skirts I wore as part of my work uniform were more constricting than jeans, but they at least had easier access.

She tugged at the dumb knot I'd tied at the center of my stomach to retrofit my extra-large, giveaway t-shirt until it unraveled. The way she was moving her hips and pressing her upper knee between my thighs would have me unraveling as well. The extra loose t-shirt, unlike my skinny jeans, gave her license to roam. Her hands moved beneath the excessive material as she continued to lick and suck on my exposed neck. I desperately wanted her mouth tasting more intimate areas.

She slid her palms up my stomach until they rested on the padded cups of my bra. I arched my back, thrusting my breasts into her hands. Her fingertips curled around the tops of the demi-cups and I hissed at the feeling of her warm fingers brushing against my more sensitive flesh.

I heard a quiet, constant chime coming from somewhere in my room. I paused my movements to listen to the noise. It took a moment before I recognized the sound as Anissa's cellphone ringing in her back pocket.

She heard it, too. "That's probably the pizza," she mumbled into my neck.

I huffed in protest at the bad timing. I was hungry, but I really didn't want to stop kissing her.

Anissa removed her hands from my t-shirt and fished her phone out of the back pocket of her skin-tight jeans. "Hello," she answered the call.

I was tempted to distract her from the phone call with my mouth and hands, but I remained motionless beneath her in case the caller wasn't actually the pizza place.

She grinned down at me, her dimples making another appearance. Her hair fell around both of our faces, hiding us as if in our own secret lair. "Yep, you found the place," she confirmed with the caller. "I'll be right down."

She ended the call and peppered a quick kiss to my mouth and then the tip of my nose. "Pizza's here," she chirped.

She rolled off of me and bounced to her feet.

I sat up, albeit reluctantly. "How much is it?"

"Don't worry about it." She waved her hand. "I've got it."

"It's my apartment," I frowned. "I should buy."

"That's not a real rule," she refused. "Besides, you bought hot dogs and beer at the baseball game. That's got to be like half of your paycheck." She frowned suddenly. "Because stadium food is really expensive," she clarified, in case I'd taken her words the wrong way. "Not because you don't make money."

"I want to pay," I insisted. My tone was nearly a whine.

Anissa regarded her reflection in the mirror above my dresser and smoothed her hair. I'd disturbed a few of her thick curls. "Too bad," she sing-songed. She bounced back onto the bed, long enough for a loud, wet kiss to my mouth. "I'll be right back. Don't go anywhere."

We ate the pizza in my living room straight out of the box, eschewing plates and forks or any other eating utensils. We used my coffee table as a dining table and sat on the floor. I opened a bottle of a California red blend that wasn't too terrible, or else Anissa was too polite to make me feel insecure about my wine choice.

The pizza was delicious. I never could understand in those national debates about whose pizza was best—New York thin crust, Chicago deep dish, etc.—why Detroit was on hardly anyone's radar. The chewy deep dish crust, thick caramelized cheese, and crispy pepperoni was like heaven. I especially liked watching Anissa eating Detroit-style pizza. She took large, enthusiastic bites, sinking her white teeth into the soft, chewy crust. Strings of whole milk mozzarella cheese hung in the balance between her closed lips and the pizza slice. She separated each piece of pepperoni from the top of her pizza square and, holding the crispy, greasy sphere between two fingers, popped it into her mouth. I'd never seen someone get so lost in a meal. Each bite was followed by a quiet murmur of pleasure that made my throat tighten and my thighs clench.

Anissa caught my stare. "What?" she questioned around a mouthful of pizza.

I discovered myself overwhelmed by the moment. This girl might have been the woman of my dreams. I lunged forward and pressed my mouth to hers. Anissa made a surprised noise and jerked her head away.

She held a single finger in the air and swallowed the bite of pizza that I'd interrupted. She licked her lips. "Let's try that again," she husked.

She grabbed a handful of the front of my too-large t-shirt and tugged me towards her. The aggressive motion had us both tumbling off our centers of gravity and onto the area rug. Her fingers left the front of my shirt to tangle in my loose hair. She bit down on my lower lip and pulled. I moaned from both pain and pleasure while she deepened the kiss, sliding her tongue into my mouth. She tasted like oregano and marinara.

Anissa pulled back suddenly. She pressed a single finger to my parted lips to halt my protest. "What's that noise?"

I stilled as well and listened for whatever it was that Anissa had heard. It took a moment until I recognized the blooping sound coming from my aquarium. "It's just Honey," I said. "She's getting a little excited."

"She's not the only one," Anissa quipped. Her legs wrapped around my midsection, and she pulled me back down for another crushing kiss.

## CHAPTER FOURTEEN

I typically fell asleep with the assistance of a white noise machine. The churning of jet engines and the noises of a crowded airport terminal had become the soundtrack of my life, making it a challenge for me to find sleep without something constantly humming in the background. Silence was too loud.

I hadn't remembered or at least hadn't needed to turn on my sleep machine the night before, however, so when I opened my eyes and heard only the sounds of a Sunday morning in Romulus, Michigan, I became slightly disoriented. There was no sweet chirping of birds to be heard; no gentle breeze rustling through the trees; no even the jarring buzz of a lawnmower or leaf blower. Nothing but concrete and pavement surrounded the city blocks around my apartment building. Squealing tires, revving engines, and honking noises filled the morning soundscape.

More concerning, I could have sworn I'd fallen asleep with a beautiful woman, yet the opposite side of my mattress was vacant. I reached across the bed and ran my palm across the cotton sheets. They were still warm.

I pulled on a t-shirt and cotton sleep shorts and adjusted my ponytail before leaving the sanctuary of my bedroom. The scent of warm coffee grounds greeted me as I entered the main living space. My apartment was small, so there were few places Anissa could hide, not that she'd been trying to. She'd pulled one of my kitchen island stools next to Honey's aquarium, giving her a front row view of Honey's morning routine.

She drank, I assumed coffee, out of my favorite ceramic mug. She'd also commandeered my extra-large Detroit Tiger's t-shirt. I had felt like a clown in the oversized t-shirt. Anissa, however, looked like a goddess. Her tan skin contrasted appealingly with the white cotton t-shirt. What was it about beautiful women in oversized shirts that made my legs turn to rubber? Or maybe it was just this beautiful woman in general.

"Morning," I greeted. My voice was still rough from sleep.

"Good morning," she returned. "Coffee?" She offered the drink as if she were the hostess instead of me.

I nodded.

She rose from her chair and padded into the kitchen. "What time is your niece's piano recital?" she asked.

She pulled a second mug from an upper cabinet and poured me a cup of coffee from my coffee maker. I marveled at how easily she'd familiarized herself with my space.

I leaned against the kitchen island and watched her work. "1:00 p.m. But we really don't have to go," I insisted. "I'm sure you didn't imagine spending your Sunday in the suburbs."

She poured the steaming liquid into a cup and scooted it closer to me. "Do you need cream or sugar?" She frowned. "How do I not know how you take your coffee?"

"You know *where* I keep my coffee," I pointed out. "I think you're ahead of the curve."

Satisfied, Anissa sat back down on the stool she'd moved closer to Honey's tank. I brought my coffee cup with me and stood beside her. After a short moment, she rested her weight against me.

"I could watch your turtle all day long," she observed.

I hummed in agreement, enjoying the press of her body against mine. "It's pretty peaceful. Better than a piano recital," I couldn't help add.

Anissa turned to appraise me. "Is there a reason you don't want me to meet your family? Am I a dirty little secret you don't want them finding out about?" Her tone was light and teasing, but I could sense the insecurity and self-doubt embedded in her words.

"I don't really get along with my sister," I admitted. "Everything ends up becoming a competition, and I'm always on the losing end."

"Am I cuter than her husband?"

I didn't quite understand the trajectory of her question. "Oh, for sure—that's not even debatable."

"I don't mind if you want to show me off," she said. "I'm okay with being a trophy."

"You're so much more than a pretty face," I denied.

"I know," she grinned, dimples on full display. "I'm a hot body, too."

+ + +

My sister and her family lived in the northern Detroit suburb of Bloomfield Hills. Medium home values neared the $1 million dollar mark and the public schools consistently received A+ ratings. It was the perfect environment for a show-off like my sister.

My niece's piano recital was being held in her elementary school's gymnasium. A small, elevated stage had been set up at one side of the gym. Rows of metal folding chairs faced the performance space. I looked around the well-lit space, but didn't immediately recognize any familiar faces.

I saw my nephew, Peter, first. He had a shock of red hair, like his father, and he stuck out amongst the sea of blonds and brunettes in the gymnasium. My sister, Dawn, sat in the chair next to him.

I took a quick breath. "It's not too late to change your mind," I told the woman standing beside me. "I hear Bloomfield Hills has a Frank Lloyd Wright house we could visit."

Anissa grabbed my arm and held onto the crook of my elbow. "Come on, Kaminski," she urged. "You shouldn't neglect family."

My feet began moving, first the right and then the left. I couldn't understand the feeling of dread I experienced as we shuffled towards Dawn and Peter. Maybe it was because I could think of a million other things I'd rather be doing on my day off. Or maybe it was because I didn't know how to introduce Anissa to my family. Were we just friends? Was she a girl I was dating? Or was she actually my girlfriend?

I stopped at the end of the row where Dawn and Peter sat. I waved in their direction, until my sister spotted the movement. "Hey," I awkwardly greeted.

It took Dawn a second to recognize me. Her face was initially blank when she looked in my direction.

"Hey. I wasn't expecting you," she said. "I would have saved you a seat." She glanced once in Anissa's direction. "Or two."

"I didn't know it myself," I admitted, "but Anissa," I nodded towards the woman at my right, "said we should come."

I gave myself a mental high-five. I'd introduced Anissa to my sister while simultaneously avoiding defining our relationship.

Dawn's eyes shrewdly narrowed. "You brought flowers?"

I looked down at the assorted mix of flowers in their cellophane wrapping. They had been another of Anissa's thoughtful suggestions on our drive out to the suburbs. "They're for Junie," I said. "Where's David?"

I reflexively looked in the surrounding area, but I didn't see my sister's husband. I liked David fine, but I couldn't recall us ever hanging out or even having a conversation, just the two of us.

"Work," Dawn said. "He got called in for an emergency surgery."

I could have made a snide comment about her husband's job being as inflexible and unpredictable as mine, but I only nodded instead.

The people seated in my sister's row moved down so Anissa and I could sit next to my family. My nephew, Peter, sat between my sister and me. Anissa sat in the seat to my other side. I was thankful for the physical space between Dawn and myself. I felt far more comfortable making small-talk with a five-year-old boy than with her.

"Is your sister any good?" I asked him, gesturing to the piano on the elevated stage.

His freckled nose scrunched. "No."

I knocked my shoulder against his smaller, bonier one. "Be nice."

His face remained comically contorted. "*You* don't have to listen to her practice."

The lights in the gymnasium flickered, indicating the performance was about to start. The conversations around us quieted and the few stragglers who'd remained standing took their seats among the family and friends in the sparse audience.

A small, older woman in a long, flower-patterned skirt and grey sweater took center stage. Her outfit was conservative, but I wondered at its practicality for a warm, summer day. The gymnasium wasn't air conditioned and there were no exterior windows to let in any cooler air. The performances hadn't even begun, yet the air was already sticky. Several people around me used their paper programs as fans.

The woman stepped up to a lone microphone. "Good afternoon, everyone," she spoke to the crowd. "And welcome to our summer recital. Our students have worked hard since their last performance so thank you for coming out to support them."

She continued with some reminders about technology etiquette, which reminded me of the innumerable pre-flight announcements I'd made over the years. I had to hold back an audible snort. This woman was wasting her breath; no one ever remembered to silence their ringers. I should have made a wager on how many times a phone would go off that afternoon.

Over the next hour, a succession of children ranging from kindergarten to pre-teen took the small stage. Most played piano while others played string instruments like the violin or cello. My niece, June, had her moment about forty-five minutes into the program. It was a long enough delay that I'd started to suspect Dawn had tricked me into watching stranger's children poorly play their instruments as some kind of twisted punishment. If not for Anissa's presence beside me, I probably would have dozed off in the overly-warm gym, or worse yet, rudely paid more attention to my phone than to the performers on stage.

I periodically observed Anissa in my peripheral vision. She didn't know any of these kids and yet she'd remained attentive and supportive throughout each painful performance. In fact, I caught her leaning progressively forward in her metal folding chair, as if silently willing the terrified adolescent on stage through each awkward performance. Every wrong note, every off-key exchange, seemed to pull even more empathetic energy from the woman beside me.

When my niece June crossed the stage in her pretty sundress, Dawn scrambled to pull out her phone to record the performance while simultaneously nudging Peter awake. June was small for her age. Even though two years separated she and Peter, she wasn't much bigger than her younger brother. Peter had gotten his father's bright red hair and freckles while June had pale blonde hair and skin so white it was almost light blue. Her pallid skin always looked like she never went outside, contributing even more to her fragile appearance.

June didn't make eye contact with anyone in the audience. She walked directly for the piano and solemnly sat down at the piano bench. My stomach twisted in knots before she struck her first note; I didn't want to see her struggle.

My niece played slowly and carefully. I didn't recognize the song; it wasn't "Hot Cross Buns," but it wasn't overly-complicated either. But she was also only seven years old, I had to remind myself.

I could feel Dawn clenching beside me during June's song. I couldn't imagine the stress of a parent watching their child perform in a public venue. I was nervous enough, and I was only an aunt.

June's song came to an end, thankfully, with no major errors or tears. She turned towards the crowd with a pleased smile on her tiny, pale face. I joined the others in clapping. I wanted to stand and make a scene, but Dawn had remained in her seat, so I took my cue from her. I didn't want to embarrass the poor girl.

When Anissa finished clapping, she set her hands lightly on the top of her thighs. I was keenly aware of the press of her leg against mine. The tip of her pinkie finger just barely touched the outer edge of my leg. Her movements were slow, like an inching caterpillar. She moved her finger discreetly so the short nail scratched against the denim of my jeaned thigh.

The touch was subtle and unassuming, yet its intimacy affected me. It was the secret, stolen touch of a new couple still trying to figure the other person out. She might have wanted to be more overtly physical, more obviously Out, but she was sensitive to the fact that maybe I wasn't comfortable with PDAs around my family.

We only had to suffer through a few more performances until the recital came to a close. Families collected their children and had begun to scatter while we waited on June. My niece skipped across the gymnasium, holding onto her sheet music.

"Great job, Junie!" I congratulated.

"Aunt Alice!" she squealed when she saw me.

Her excitement produced a pang of guilt and regret. I really needed to make a better effort to spend more time with my family.

"These are for you." I handed her the bouquet of flowers. I was suddenly very thankful that Anissa had suggested we pick them up. The gesture made me feel a little less rotten. "You were so good up there!"

June mashed her face into the flowers.

"We were going to grab a late lunch after this, if you're free," Dawn said as she gathered Peter and her purse. "You probably have to get back to the city though."

I couldn't tell if my sister was giving us an excuse for an early exit, or if it was more of her passive-aggressive guilt tripping.

I looked in Anissa's direction, not sure how much more of my family she wanted to endure.

She shrugged. "I can always eat."

"Good," Dawn approved with a rare smile. "Anissa, do you eat pizza?"

"She's American, isn't she?" I snapped.

"I … I was more asking about food allergies," my sister explained. She looked startled by my outburst. "Mom reflexes. You wouldn't believe how complicated pizza parties have gotten. It's all gluten-free crust and vegan cheese these days."

Anissa flashed my sister a brilliant smile as if I hadn't just been rude. "I eat everything."

My sister's eyes squinted in contemplation. Her voice dropped conspiratorially. "What's your opinion on pineapple on pizza?"

Anissa pursed her lips, matching Dawn's level of seriousness. "With Canadian bacon," she slowly drawled, "there's no perfect pairing."

The smile on Dawn's features grew. "Oh, I like this girl."

I closely followed the taillights of Dawn's SUV, not knowing the directions to the restaurant. I'd turned on the car radio for background noise, but that didn't help ease the tension I'd felt since I'd snapped at my sister. We drove through several stoplights before Anissa spoke.

"You've never dated a person of color." It wasn't a question, but rather an observation.

My fingers tightened around the steering wheel. "That was terrible back there. I'm sorry if I made things awkward."

"I know you mean well and you're only looking out for me," Anissa said lightly, "but I've been living in this skin for thirty-four years. I don't need you jumping to my defense every time you think someone is being a bigot."

"At least now I know how old you are," I tried to joke.

Anissa didn't take the bait. Her features remained serious. "You can't freak out like that, Alice. It makes me feel like *you're* the one uncomfortable with the color of my skin."

I let out a deep, uneven breath. "I'm sorry," I apologized again. "My sister puts me on edge. Ever since we got to June's piano recital, I've felt like a rubber band being pulled tighter and tighter. It's like my brain was just waiting for an opportunity to snap on her. I'm sorry I overreacted and I made you uncomfortable. That's literally the last thing I wanted to happen today."

My earnest apology coaxed an encouraging smile onto Anissa's face. She reached across the center console and rested her hand on my knee.

When we arrived at the mom-and-pop Italian restaurant, a hostess led us to a large, circular table in one corner of the restaurant. It was too late for Sunday brunch and too early for dinner, so the restaurant was fairly empty. When I saw the table, I instantly became concerned about seating arrangements. There were five of us for six place settings. Even though I knew she could hold her own, I didn't want Anissa stranded by my sister, knowing Dawn wouldn't be able to resist peppering her with questions. But I also didn't want the empty seat beside her, which might make her feel like she was isolated on an island.

Peter and June claimed two chairs next to each other. My sister clucked her tongue. "Can you handle sitting next to each other? I'd better not have to separate you," she warned.

My niece and nephew ducked their heads as they sat down. "We can. You won't," they collectively mumbled.

Anissa and I similarly grabbed two adjacent chairs.

"I'd better not have to separate you two, either," Dawn said pointedly.

My eyes widened at the suggestion. My sister looked pleased by her clever and quick thinking. I was privately impressed by the uncharacteristically sassy remark, but I didn't want to give her too much credit. Her ego was big enough.

Once seating assignments had been settled, Dawn produced a plastic bag full of crayons from her mom-sized purse and dropped it onto the table. June and Peter reflexively reached for a handful each and began to solemnly draw on the back of their paper placemats.

My eyes darted between my niece and nephew and then back to my sister. "Don't kids always have their faces pressed against some electronic screen?"

"Never at the table," Dawn clipped. "They get an hour of screen time a day."

"Wow. You really are Super Mom, aren't you?" I couldn't help remark.

Dawn's mouth flattened. I felt fingernails bite into the top of my thigh, a silent under-the-table-warning from Anissa to behave.

The restaurant wasn't busy so we didn't have to wait long for our food to be delivered. Our waitress returned with two extra-large pizzas and a bowl of salad. Dawn took charge and began filling plates with slices of cheesy pizza and Italian salad. Cherry tomatoes rolled around on the plates.

"Is this okay?" I asked quietly while Dawn continued to serve the table. "Pizza two nights in a row?"

Anissa leaned her head closer to mine. "I hope you're not preoccupied by the calories," she replied. She spoke more quietly in a low voice meant only for my ears. "But if you are, I can give you a workout later."

Her suggestive words had my cheeks burning. "I'm not worried about that," I corrected. "I just don't want you to be bored with the food."

*Or me and my vanilla family*, I silently added.

"Alice, I eat most of my meals at airport food courts. This is practically gourmet." She popped a crouton from her plated salad into her mouth for affect.

"So Anissa, are you a flight attendant, too?" my sister asked.

*Oh, Lord,* I thought. *Here it comes.*

Despite my cajoling, Anissa didn't spend the night that evening. She didn't have a business trip in the morning, but she was on call. Her work situation was very similar to mine. We had days off that were untouchable by our employer, but other days when we weren't scheduled to travel we still needed to be able to get to the airport in case our services were needed.

She insisted on calling a Lyft, but I insisted more strongly on driving her back to Dearborn. When we arrived, I parked in front of her house and walked her to her front door. The safety precaution was unwarranted; it was a safe neighborhood—much more so than where I lived—but I wanted to delay our saying goodbye for as long as possible.

We stood on the front stoop together, holding hands. We'd spent a lot of time together recently. We'd even had sex. But the moment felt more important and significant than me simply dropping her off after a routine day.

She'd had the foresight to keep on the porch light or maybe it was on a timer. A moth fluttered stubbornly against the glass-enclosed lantern. I could hear its delicate wings tap against the glass. It would never reach the illusive heat source, and even if it did, it would be its own demise. Despite these obstacles, it tried again and again.

Anissa didn't seem to notice the winged insect and I didn't bother pointing it out to her, sure that she would scamper inside before I got a proper goodbye.

The question nearly got caught in my throat, but I needed to ask. "Can I see you again?"

A small smile played at the corner of her mouth. "On Wednesday?"

I couldn't tell if she was teasing me, but my heart dropped nonetheless.

My face must have revealed my disappointment, because before I could mutter another convincing syllable, she was grabbing the sides of my face and kissing me deeply. A surprised noise tumbled up my throat, but she swallowed it down before it could escape.

There was no controlling her pace or pressure. It didn't feel like she was kissing me; it felt like she was kissing *through* me. I held on to the front of her t-shirt—a shirt she'd borrowed from my closet—to keep from tipping over.

She pulled back from the kiss, leaving me panting. She continued to hold onto my face. Her caramel eyes stared hard into mine. "I would love to go out with you again."

She said the words with conviction, like it was essential that I heard and believed her.

"Okay," I happily sighed.

She released her grip on the sides of my face, but I could still feel her fingers like branding irons on my cheeks. "Call me when you're done flying tomorrow."

"I might not be able to wait that long," I blurted out.

I was supposed to be coy. Play it cool. Not let on that I felt too much so soon. But my heart was already hanging on my sleeve, and there was no sense trying to put it away.

## CHAPTER FIFTEEN

The next morning, I stared at my cellphone and chewed on my lower lip. I stood on the moving sidewalk, trying to compose the perfect text message that was both charming and nonchalant, thoughtful without looking like I was trying too hard. But everything I'd come up with so far was coming across as too clingy.

I scrutinized my most recent construction: *Good morning, beautiful.*

It was morning. And Anissa was beautiful. Both statements were facts. But was it too forceful? Too coupley? She'd said she wanted to see me again, not move in together.

I looked up from my phone when I reached the end of the moving sidewalk. Gemma was waiting for me, two cardboard cups of coffee in her expectant hands. I pocketed my phone for the moment without sending the over-analyzed text.

"Good morning!" Gemma beamed. She pressed one of the black coffees into my outstretched hand like a relay team passing their baton to the next runner.

I popped off the plastic cover and inhaled the coffee's rich aroma. "You're an angel," I hummed in approval.

"Late night?" she asked. We started to walk in step with one another in the direction of our Monday morning gates. My flight to Seattle happened to be right next to her gate to San Francisco.

"Actually, I got to bed pretty early," I admitted.

Gemma grinned and gave me a knowing look. "Oh, I bet you did."

Her reaction made me laugh. "Nothing like that. Just a long, busy weekend."

"Oh yeah? What did you do?"

"On Saturday, Anissa and I went to the baseball game and we ate pizza at my apartment afterwards."

"That sounds dreamy," Gemma sighed wistfully. "I wish I was a lesbian."

"It's never too late," I winked. "We're always accepting applications."

"Did you see her yesterday, too?" she asked.

I nodded. "We went to Bloomfield Hills for my niece's piano recital."

"She met your *family*?" Gemma squeaked.

"Just my sister and her brood." I didn't want to make a big deal about it, even though it actually was. Very few women I'd dated had made it that far.

Our bodies instinctively veered towards the women's bathroom closest to our gates. I hated nothing more than having to use the bathroom mid-flight. Not only did I dislike the claustrophobic space, but the moment I locked the bathroom door behind me was inevitably the moment someone pressed the Call button to request my assistance.

"She's met the family, but when do *I* get to meet this amazing woman?" Gemma pressed. "I know you've said I saw her on a jet bridge in Philadelphia, but I don't remember so it doesn't count."

"I don't want to scare her away," I laughed. "I barely got her to agree to go out with me."

"What if you casually pointed her out to me on a flight?" Gemma suggested. "I can play it cool."

I raised an eyebrow. "No offense, but subtlety isn't exactly your strength. Remember that pilot you had a crush on? What was his name?"

"Desmond," she sighed. "Don't remind me. I've never fake laughed at so many dad jokes in my life."

Because of the early hour, the women's bathroom was relatively empty. We entered separate stalls that were close to each other.

"Tell me I need my head examined if I ever suggest dating a pilot again," I heard Gemma's voice.

Gemma was a notorious bathroom talker. She continued her conversations from her stall instead of waiting until we'd finished in the bathroom. I typically only responded to her comments with noncommittal hums.

"I can't believe your luck," she continued from the next stall over. "You get a girlfriend, *and* you're going to win at bingo."

I winced when Gemma said the words aloud. I didn't consider myself superstitious—especially not in comparison with some of the people I'd flown with before—but I didn't want to jinx anything. Despite an almost-conversation about if we were exclusive, Anissa wasn't my girlfriend yet. And I hadn't finished the bingo card yet either.

"I was really skeptical about the game at first, but now that you're so close to winning, I'm actually getting excited," Gemma continued. "Like, I'm probably more excited than you!"

I didn't really participate in the conversation. Not only did I feel weird about hollering my business in a public restroom, but I also hadn't been focused on completing my bingo card as of late. Instead, I'd been counting down to when I could see Anissa next.

Gemma was already standing at the line of sinks when I exited my bathroom stall. "It's perfect. Like, absolutely perfect," she effused. "You could complete the Mile High Club task with Anissa on Wednesday, and I'm sure someone's going to puke before the end of the month. I'm actually surprised it hasn't happened yet."

Gemma grabbed an extra paper towel from the dispenser and had it ready for me. "I wonder how much money you're going to win," she mused. "I've never heard of anyone completing all the challenges before; you're going to be, like, a flight attendant legend."

"Nothing's a done deal," I finally spoke. "I'm not going to count my chickens before they've hatched."

I looked up from washing my hands when a stall door behind me opened. The movement in the mirror's reflection drew my attention, but I instantly froze when I realized I knew the woman who'd been in the bathroom stall. Water continued to rush out of my sink's faucet and swirl down the drain.

My tongue felt heavy in my mouth. "I-I didn't think you were flying today."

I watched the woman's reflection in the mirror as she approached the empty sink beside me to wash her hands.

"A colleague called in sick," she said calmly. Coolly. "I'm going to Denver today."

"Mile High City," I stupidly recited, as if playing a game of word association. "Have you been before?"

"No. You?"

"Only the inside of the airport. It's nice."

She remained silent. Her mirrored reflection belied no emotion.

"Anissa. I …" My explanation died in my throat.

She shook the excess water from her hands back into the sink. "I have a flight to catch," she said. Her tone was tense and dismissive.

She didn't bother drying her hands before exiting the women's bathroom.

I stared after her. I knew I should have run after her, chased her down the entire terminal if it came to that, to try to explain what she'd overheard. But my feet were stuck.

"That was her?" Gemma said in a voice little more than a whisper.

I tried to swallow down the lump that had formed in my throat. I couldn't speak, so I nodded.

My friend looked close to tears. "I ruined it."

"No, you didn't," I said when I was finally able to speak. "I did this all myself."

+ + +

My phone calls went straight to her voicemail. She wasn't responding to my texts. I had her home address, so I could have stood in her front yard with a boom box, *Say Anything* style, but I probably would have had the cops called on me.

I couldn't be angry with Gemma for talking publicly about the bingo card. The only person I could be angry with was myself. This was my fault. I was the one in the wrong. I'd used Anissa to get a few steps closer to the game's winnings. All I could do was apologize for the circumstance under which we'd met. But if I was correctly interpreting her refusal to answer my calls or reply to my text messages, she wasn't accepting my apology.

She couldn't ignore me forever, however. On Wednesdays she flew out of Detroit to Philadelphia, and I would be on that flight.

I stood in the first exit row in First Class, not wanting to appear too eager to pounce on Anissa the moment she stepped onto the plane. I was in the wrong; I could admit that. I'd had plenty of opportunities to come clean about the bingo game, but I'd been equal parts embarrassed and ashamed. The game was only a means to an end—an end to my student debt—and I needed to make clear that what I was feeling for her was real and not part of those juvenile pranks.

I waited with an emotional rock in my stomach as the First Class passengers boarded the plane. I did my best to smile as each passenger passed through the cabin door and found their seat. My stomach flip-flopped each time a dark-haired woman boarded the plane. Anissa was typically one of the first to board, and I became more concerned as the plane filled up and seat 3B remained empty. Had she called in sick to avoid me?

A nondescript man in a dark blue suit boarded the plane and stopped within the first few rows to place a roller bag in the overhead bin Anissa typically used. I slipped out of the exit row and maneuvered my way around other boarding passengers to reach the front of the plane.

"Excuse me, sir," I interrupted. "That area is reserved for passengers seated in our business class cabin."

"This is my seat," he said, motioning to the third aisle.

"Do you mind if I check your ticket?" I found myself asking.

The man fumbled with his briefcase momentarily before producing the electronic boarding pass on his cellphone. My heart dropped when I saw his seat assignment.

3B.

I forced a smile to my lips despite the wave of nausea that rolled over me. "Thank you for your cooperation. Have a nice flight."

I turned and wobbled back to my position in the first exit row and manically grinned at each new passenger that walked by. My instinct was to immediately text Anissa to find out what had happened, but my phone was in my carry-on luggage in the rear of the plane.

The next twenty minutes slowly crawled by. I delivered cups of water to the passengers in my section and took their primary drink orders. I spoke to those seated in the exit aisle to make sure they were ready and willing to assist me in case of an emergency landing. I communicated with the captain on the interphone when he was ready to depart. It was only when I initiated the safety video that I had time to rush down the center aisle to the back of the plane to retrieve my phone.

*Why aren't you on my flight? Did you change your schedule?*

My thumb hovered over the send button while I scrutinized my message. I meant the text as a show of concern, but the words by themselves might have read as demanding or accusatory when Anissa didn't owe me any explanation.

I deleted the two questions in exchange for the more streamlined text I'd been sending ever since the incident.

*I'm sorry.*

+ + +

The overhead light that normally illuminated the hallway outside of my apartment door had burned out a few days earlier and my building's supervisor had yet to fix it. I didn't really need the light though. I'd lived in the building for nearly eight years. I could have probably walked from the parking lot to my front door blindfolded.

I hadn't parked my car in its usual parking space though. I'd left it at the parking lot outside of a wine bar not far from the airport. I hadn't wanted to go home after work that day, so I'd agreed to go out with Gemma. A single, respectable glass of wine and a charcuterie board had quickly descended into a bottle of wine and fast food delivery, but at least I'd had the good sense not to drive myself home.

I quietly cursed when my high heels caught on something in front of my front door, causing my already unsteady feet to stumble. I bent down and grabbed the offending object off the ground. It was dark in the hallway, but it felt like a t-shirt, probably an overboard passenger from one of my neighbor's laundry baskets.

I successfully unlocked my front door and turned on the barely used light in the foyer so I could better see. I frowned when I realized I recognized the t-shirt that had been outside of my door. It didn't belong to one of my neighbors; it belonged to me. The last time I'd seen the shirt, however, it had been on Anissa and we'd been kissing on her front stoop.

I shut my eyes when a fresh wave of remorse washed over me. Anissa had come over, but I'd been out with Gemma. Maybe she was only bringing back my t-shirt so I'd have no reason to reach out to her, but maybe she'd also wanted to talk.

I used the glow of my cellphone to investigate the hallway around my doorway, but nothing else had been left with the t-shirt—no note of explanation. I didn't have any missed calls or unread text messages. I pressed the t-shirt to my nose and unabashedly inhaled. But like the absence of a note or a text, like the flight to Philadelphia that morning, Anissa was no longer there. It smelled like fabric softener. No traces of the woman who had worn it remained, no matter how deeply or how often I pressed my nose against the fabric.

+ + +

Gemma found me the next morning at our usual café table in the Detroit airport. I winced beneath the cover of my sunglasses at the ugly racket the legs of her chair made when she scooted closer to the small table. My blueberry muffin remained intact on its plate on the tabletop; I hadn't trusted my stomach to be able to keep it down.

"Tell me you didn't keep drinking when you got home last night," my friend censured.

I hoped that it was only the inside sunglasses and my slightly disheveled look that gave me away. I hoped I didn't also *smell* like alcohol.

"I might have kept drinking," I admitted.

"I know you know this," Gemma qualified, "but that's not healthy."

I pinched the bridge of my nose. "I know."

I considered telling my friend about the t-shirt that Anissa had brought over to my apartment, but that I'd missed her because I'd been at the wine bar. But I didn't want Gemma to blame herself any more than she already did. Besides, Anissa might not have even knocked. Maybe she'd dumped the shirt at my doorway and I would have never known she'd ever been there.

"You have to be in the air all day," Gemma reminded me. "And of all days to be hungover! All we do is takeoffs and landings today."

"Do you think the puking bingo card square can apply to myself?" I tried to joke.

I didn't need to look at Gemma's face to anticipate her reaction. I could practically hear the disapproval in the cadence of her breath.

"I hope you didn't drunk dial Anissa last night."

Amazingly, I hadn't. I'd woken up in a slight panic that morning after I'd blacked out after a few more strong cocktails, but luckily I found no evidence on my phone of attempted calls or misguided texts that could have made my situation worse.

"I didn't," I told her. "But she's not responding to any of my voicemails or texts anyway. Even if I had drunk dialed her, she never would have answered her phone."

Anissa was too angry to pick up the phone or even to text me back. I could handle getting yelled at—at least she'd be talking to me then—but this silent treatment was killing me.

"So that's it, then?" Gemma posed. "You're just giving up?"

I peered, almost guiltily, over the tops of my sunglasses. "I did come up with an idea last night. But I don't know if it's genius or idiotic."

The strategy had come to me in the middle of my third vodka and seltzer of the night, so it was probably ill-conceived.

"That *is* a thin line," Gemma concurred.

I licked at my lips and leaned forward in my chair. "What if I ask Kent's friend to find out her new flying schedule?" I started. "I could have him schedule me for that flight—either as a flight attendant or a passenger. Anissa always books two seats together, but she only sits in one. I could be in the seat right next to hers. She'll *have* to listen to my apology. She won't be able to leave. There will be no place for her to go."

Gemma gave me a disapproving look. "Is that really how you want to apologize? Corner the poor woman with more deceit?"

"It's not deceit!" I protested. "It's using my resources to my advantage."

"Yeah, to *your* advantage," she pointed out. "What about Anissa's?"

I realized, reluctantly, that Gemma was right. I'd be able to get my apology out if I followed through with my plan, but how receptive would my audience be?

I felt deflated and defeated. "What do you suggest I do?"

A small frown formed on Gemma's features. "What about baggage claim? After her flight she'll be waiting at the carousel for her luggage. Confront her there. She'll still be blindsided by you being there, but at least she won't be captive at 35,000 feet."

I shook my head. It was a smart idea—much better than my own—but it wasn't going to work. "She doesn't check her luggage anymore. She's a carry-on passenger now."

"Then we use what little influence we have to make sure she has to check her baggage."

I cocked a skeptical eyebrow. "We can do that?"

"I'll make sure it happens," Gemma vowed.

I let Gemma's proposal bounce around in my brain. "Baggage claim," I considered aloud. "That might actually work."

# CHAPTER SIXTEEN

I watched the arrival board with an anxious pit in my stomach. Kent's friend had been able to find Anissa's flight number and arrival time. Gemma had used her own connections, *Godfather*-style, to somehow assure that Anissa would be forced to check her baggage on her return trip. My friends had done the heavy lifting; all I had to do was apologize.

Easier said than done.

I knew Gemma had been right about not trapping Anissa in the air with no way to exit unless she grabbed a parachute, but if she didn't give me a chance to talk at the baggage carousel, I feared this might be my final opportunity. I'd been practicing my speech over the past few nights. I'd even had Gemma pretend to be Anissa for me. I felt prepared—rehearsed, but not robotic. I knew what I wanted to say; I only hoped she would humor me long enough for me to apologize and try to explain myself.

I positioned myself near the baggage carousel where her flight's luggage would soon be appearing. A loud buzz alerted everyone in the area that the luggage belt would soon be moving. The crowd became significantly more dense as people jostled for position.

I walked a little closer, but maintained a safe distance. It didn't really matter though. No one noticed a flight attendant in baggage claim. Like in the air, I was simply part of the atmosphere. The flight's passengers all stared at the luggage belt, trying to identify their specific bag in a sea of identical black roller bags.

My eyes continued to scan the area surrounding the slowly moving luggage belt. My gaze paused at each dark-haired woman until I found the person I'd been waiting for. Anissa stood close to the conveyor belt. Like the other nearby passengers, her focus was singularly trained on the moving belt, anticipating when her own suitcase might appear. I watched her from a careful distance. I didn't want her to notice me before she'd retrieved her bag, but I couldn't wait much longer afterwards or she would leave the area before I ever had the chance to talk to her.

Anissa reached for a nondescript, black suitcase and attempted to tug it free from a tangle of duffle bags and backpacks. A man in a Detroit Lions t-shirt and cargo shorts interjected his body to assist her. He looked exactly like the kind of passenger I traditionally targeted for the bingo card game. My stomach tightened at the realization. He was only being helpful, and I'd been taking advantage of that kind of kindness for my own profit.

I continued to watch from a careful distance. Anissa's appreciative smile took over her face. She and the obliging man exchanged a few words before she rolled her luggage a few yards away from the baggage carousel to check her cellphone. It was now or never.

I strode towards Anissa, wiping my sweaty palms on the sides of my uniform skirt. I'd come straight over to baggage claim after my last flight of the day. I didn't feel as freshly pressed as I had at the start of the work day, but at least I hadn't needed to stress out about what to wear. I had enough to overthink already without adding my wardrobe to the pile.

"Hey."

At the sound of my voice, her head snapped up from her phone, and her golden irises trained themselves on me.

"Hey," she flatly returned. Her eyes left me momentarily and inspected the space around us, as if expecting to be ambushed by hidden cameras. "Is this a coincidence or something else?"

"Something else," I readily disclosed. "I had a friend look up your flight."

Her eyebrows rose in a look more displeased than curious. "So you're *actually* stalking me now? I already changed my flight schedule because of you; am I going to have to change airlines, too?"

Her visible frustration caused my carefully rehearsed apology to fly from my brain. Where there once had been carefully crafted syntax was only a blank space.

"I'm an idiot," I blurted out.

"No lies detected so far," she deadpanned.

"I can explain everything."

Her lips thinned and the skin around her eyes tightened. "I'm not sure I'm interested."

"Please, Anissa. Just hear me out."

I watched her glance furtively at our surroundings. No one in baggage claim was interested in our conversation, and as long as we kept ourselves composed and spoke at a reasonable volume, it would stay that way. My skin itched at the alternative. She was the last person to want to draw attention to herself.

She didn't reject my plea, so I took that as a sign to continue. "There's a secret competition among the flight attendants at my airline. We get a bingo card with challenges to be completed within the month. Most of them are pretty dumb, like talk with a fake accent during your flight. Some of them are a little risqué," I admitted, "but most are totally harmless."

She wet her lips. "How many squares did you complete using me?"

I flinched at her word choice. I understood from where her anger stemmed. She felt used. She felt like a means to an end instead of me genuinely having feelings for her.

"One," I answered truthfully. "Get a passenger to buy you dinner; you inadvertently did that one at the airport in Philadelphia. Flight Gods and all that. I could have done another one, but I changed my mind at the last minute."

Anissa's nostrils flared in anger. "Have sex with a passenger when your flights are canceled?"

My eyes widened. "No! Spill a drink on a passenger! That flight when I spilled water on myself. You were supposed to be the target, but I changed my mind."

"Why?" she demanded to know.

"You said thank you."

I realized how stupid the words sounded, but they were the truth.

"It's a totally dumb and immature game," I said. "I only started playing because I thought if I won, it could put a dent in my student debt. No one's ever filled their entire bingo card before so the pot of money keeps growing."

"How much?" she questioned.

"No one knows the exact figure," I disclosed. "Maybe upwards of ten thousand dollars."

"I suppose I should be impressed that you used me for a good amount of money," she sniffed, "and not just a few hundred dollars."

"I wasn't using you!" my voice strained. "Okay, maybe in the beginning I was when I didn't know you—when you were just another passenger," I qualified. "But all of that changed."

"When? When did things 'change' for you, Alice?" she demanded. "Was it before or after we had sex? Did you bring my tablet to my house because of your game or because you really liked me? When you met my family, was that all part of your little game, too?"

"The bingo card was the last thing on my mind when I came out to Dearborn. I swear," I tried to convince her. "In fact, it was *because of* the bingo card that I realized I really liked you. There were no bingo squares I could have crossed out when I was there with you that weekend. But I stayed anyway."

"Lucky me," she sneered.

"I'm so sorry, Anissa," I said in earnest. "I hate that I hurt you. I can only imagine what you must have thought you overheard in the bathroom."

Anissa's jaw visibly tightened. "All of your flight attendant friends know about me, then?"

"Shit," I muttered, realizing I'd made another mistake. "Listen, it's totally not like that. I wasn't bragging or showing off or even suggesting you were going to help me win the game. My friends only know about you because I've been super psyched to be spending time with you."

She closed her eyes and shook her head. "I was already straying from my routine to date you, Alice. I think this is all the proof I need that I should stick to what's been working for me."

"Was it really working?" I challenged.

"Of course," she said stiffly.

I could sense our conversation was coming to its end. I'd given her my apology and explanation, yet the walls between us had not been moved.

"I think I could make you happy," I asserted.

Her hazel eyes narrowed. "My schedule doesn't have time for that."

+++

The week had started with Anissa shutting me down at baggage claim, and on Wednesday's flight a brand-new stranger had been sitting in seat 3B, which only added to the sting of rejection. Gemma had spent all of our Thursday flights trying to come up with new schemes for me to win Anissa back, but eventually even my bighearted friend had given up.

By the time Friday came around, I was overly anxious for the weekend to begin. I was technically on call the following day, but I fully expected to spend my Sunday emptying my liquor cabinet. Only a trip to Philadelphia, Boston, and then back to Detroit stood between me and the weekend. I was cautiously optimistic that the workday would pass by quickly with no incidents and no drama, but nothing could ever be that easy for me.

I froze when I walked onto my Friday morning flight. My colleague Derek stood in the front galley and Lara Peterson was sitting, high-heeled shoes already off, in one of the First Class seats. I'd expected to be working that day with Derek and Cheri; I hadn't expected to see Lara again, especially so soon.

I'd never been very good at masking my emotions. When Lara looked up from her pre-flight checklist, she caught the look of surprise written across my face.

"Cheri asked to switch with me. Her kid got sick," she explained, almost apologetically. "I swear it wasn't me this time."

I nodded; I could only take her word for it. I passed both Derek and Lara and rolled my luggage to the rear of the plane for storage in its designated area.

Lara hopped up from her seat and practically skipped down the center aisle. "Looks like clear skies across the East Coast today," she said conversationally. "No chance of us getting stranded in Philadelphia again."

I smiled tightly while I stored my luggage. "That's good."

"I heard a good joke the other day. What do you call when you're sick of being in the airport?" She didn't wait for my response before delivering the punchline: "Terminal illness," she grinned.

I could only muster a weak laugh. "Good one."

The smile and lightness dropped from Lara's features, but she kept her eyes trained on me. "Hey, Derek," she called over her shoulder. "Do you want to be purser today?"

At the front of the plane, my other colleague's features lit up at the offer. "For real?"

Lara's stare never left my face. "Sure. It looks like a relatively empty flight this morning. You might as well get in some practice."

Most pursers I knew—with the exception of Kent—clung desperately to their seniority benefits. I'd never heard of anyone voluntarily giving up First Class privileges.

"Thanks!" Derek chirped in earnest. "I'm gonna rehearse right now. I've been practicing a funny version at home."

I couldn't keep my curiosity contained for long. "That was nice of you," I remarked.

"I don't really feel like dealing with Business Class today," she explained. "Besides," she said, her penetrating eyes intense and unblinking, "it'll give us a chance to work together like old times."

*Like old times.* I could practically feel my blood pressure spike. When Lara and I had worked Economy together, months ago, I'd had my hand up her navy blue pencil skirt at every opportunity.

"Sure, I managed to choke out. "Old times."

Beverage service went by quickly with Lara and I standing to the front and back of the beverage cart. We'd worked together for a solid month before, and we fell into a familiar rhythm working multiple rows at a time. We worked well together, but I still felt on edge around her.

After we served sodas and snacks in Economy, I stood in the rear galley, attempting to slide the beverage cart back into its storage container.

"Hey," Lara called to me.

I ignored her for the moment in favor of my task. The stupid latch refused to reconnect. I repeatedly slammed the metal cart into the compartment where it typically remained when not in use, but it wasn't cooperating with me.

"Alice. Can you stop for a second?"

I was exhausted. The past two weeks had been a nonstop rollercoaster of emotions. And now this piece of junk refused to go back to where it belonged. "What?" I practically bit out.

Lara held up her hands like a shield. "I want to help."

I gestured to the beverage cart and the storage cubby it refused to latch into. "Go ahead. Maybe you'll have better luck than me."

"I don't mean that," she corrected. "I saw Gemma on Tuesday on a layover in Dallas."

"Oh yeah?"

Gemma hadn't said anything about running into Lara. It seemed the kind of thing she would have at least mentioned, especially because we'd spent all day Thursday together.

"She told me you were super close to winning the bingo contest, but that you needed a little help with finishing the card."

I stared at her, silent and dumbstruck. *Was she suggesting ...*

"Beverage service is over, and the bathroom back here is empty."

Yep.

"I ..." I had no words. No thoughts. Only a red warning flash the same color as her vibrant lipstick.

Lara frowned. "Am I too late?"

I cleared the lump in my throat. "No, there's still a few more days until the month is over."

"No. I meant am I too late for *us*?" Lara worried her lower lip. "Did I miss my opportunity?"

"Lara, I ..."

I liked Lara. We got along, and I thought she was wildly attractive. And I wanted to be in a relationship, but I didn't want to date just anybody. I wanted Anissa Khoury.

+ + +

I hadn't bothered to tell Dawn I was coming; I hadn't made the decision until earlier that morning while drinking coffee at my kitchen island. Technically, I was on call on Saturdays. But Anissa's words about not neglecting family and not letting myself become a prisoner to my job ran through my brain.

A goofy smile tickled the corners of my mouth as I observed my family, unnoticed. Dawn and June sat next to each other in the sparsely populated bleacher seating of the elementary gymnasium where I'd watched June play piano only two weeks earlier. Dawn's texts had said that Peter was testing for his first taekwondo belt that day. I welcomed the mid-day distraction that would keep me from drinking and feeling sorry for myself.

I grabbed my phone from my purse and shot off a text to my sister.

*New haircut?*

Dawn hadn't actually done anything different to her hair since the last time I'd seen her, but I couldn't resist creeping her out, just a little. I watched her rummage in her purse for her phone. When she read my text message, I saw the confusion settle on her features.

I bounded up the risers with a bounce in my step. "Hey."

Dawn looked up from her phone and folded her arms across her chest. Instead of looking pleased to see me, she actually looked annoyed. "Two visits in a month? That's got to be a record."

I tried to ignore her sour attitude. I wasn't there for her, after all. I was there to support Peter.

"Hey, Junie," I greeted my niece.

"Hey, Aunt Alice," she returned.

I noticed another absence in the bleacher seating. "Where's your dad?"

Her small shoulders shrugged. "He had to work."

I looked briefly in my sister's direction. She stared straight ahead, her jaw set at a hard angle. I wondered if David's repeated absence was the reason for her bad mood.

I plopped down on the bleachers seating next to June. She sat in between Dawn and me. "Has your brother been practicing breaking boards at home?" I asked.

In truth, I had no idea what went on at one of these things or if five-year-old ninjas were supposed to be able to do that.

June giggled at the suggestion. "No."

"That would be a pretty cool skill to have," I continued, teasingly. "We could send him outside in winter to chop all the firewood. He wouldn't even need an axe."

June laughed again, louder this time, earning a quick glare from her mom as a warning to settle down. I was a riot to seven year olds.

"Uh oh," I faux whispered, loud enough so Dawn could still hear me. "We'd better behave or your mom's gonna yell at us."

I quickly sat up straight, which was uncomfortable to sustain in the bleacher seating. I kept my back erect and stared straight ahead.

My niece copied my posture, but I could feel her smaller body shaking next to me as she tried to contain her giggles.

"Don't laugh," I warned her out of the side of my mouth. "The Fun Police will get you. Don't do it, Junie. Hold it in. You'd better behave."

June snorted and covered her mouth with her hands.

I heard my sister's loud sigh. "You're like a human Pixy Stix, Alice."

I grinned broadly. I felt lighter and less depressed about my situation with Anissa after only a few moments of being silly with my niece. "Regretting inviting me yet, sis?"

My family and I walked outside into the Saturday afternoon sunshine. I'd happened to park in the same area as Dawn, so we walked to our vehicles together. I gave June and Peter giant hugs and helped my sister buckle them into their respective booster seats.

"Where's your friend today?" Dawn asked when the kids were both strapped into the backseat.

I frowned at her question for multiple reasons. First, because she hadn't bothered to ask before. It also annoyed me that she hadn't used Anissa's name. Dawn hadn't forgotten her name; it hadn't even been two weeks. Instead, it was another of her passive aggressive moves like when people uncomfortable with your sexuality insist on calling your same-sex partner or spouse a 'friend.' But I was more upset because I was the reason Anissa wasn't there.

"It's a long story," I said.

"It's okay. It's private," Dawn said in a rush. "You don't have to tell me."

"I *want* to tell you. It just really is a long story," I said in earnest. "Besides," I frowned, "I'm kind of the villain in this story."

I could practically see the gears churning in my sister's brain. I knew she wanted to say more or had questions to ask or at least had an opinion she wanted to share. But she surprised me with the words she finally settled on: "How about a hug?"

Tears immediately welled in my eyes. I couldn't get out the words, so I responded with a watery nod.

My sister's arms surrounded me, and I leaned into the embrace. People continued to pour out of the school gymnasium into the parking lot, but for a rare moment I didn't care who might be staring at us. I needed that hug.

When we pulled apart, I noticed the tears in my sister's eyes as well.

"Are *you* okay?" I ventured to ask.

"I'm getting a divorce."

"You're what?" I exclaimed.

She wiped at her eyes with the back of her hands. "Nothing's official yet. I haven't said anything to David, and I definitely haven't said anything to the kids, but I think it's only a matter of time."

"What happened?"

"Nothing—not like one isolated incident, at least," she said. "But he's never around anymore, and I didn't sign up to be a single parent."

"Work or something else?" I was afraid to ask.

"He says work, but who can tell anymore," she shrugged. "His phone rings or he gets a text and then he's out the door with barely a goodbye. That's probably why I've been so hard on you lately. You not being available and putting your job before your family—." She held up her hand, anticipating my protest. I decided to let her finish her thought before defending myself. "I wasn't really mad at you; I was frustrated with David."

I nodded in understanding. "Have you talked to him about it?"

"He'd have to be home long enough for that to happen," she complained.

"Talk to him," I insisted. "Even if you have to stalk him at the hospital."

Tracking Anissa down at baggage claim hadn't worked out in my favor, but we also didn't have the relationship history that Dawn and David had.

Dawn nodded, looking serious instead of dismissive. "I should get these two back home. Peter's taekwondo uniform gets a little ripe after these things."

"What kind of competition do the kids have next week?" I asked. "Youth soccer? Hip-hop dance troupe? Competitive hot dog eating?"

Dawn laughed. "It's actually a rare, activity-free weekend for us."

"Maybe I could come over to your house next Sunday," I proposed. "Play some boardgames with you and the kids?"

Dawn's normally pinched features softened. "That sounds perfect." She touched a comforting hand against my forearm. "And if Anissa decides to forgive you between now and then, tell her I'm making a pineapple pizza just for her."

Her suggestion and offer nearly had me crying in the parking lot for a second time. I swallowed back the overwhelming emotions.

"I will."

I returned home later that evening to Honey and an empty apartment. I was no longer on call, and I had the next day off, which meant I could drink as many cocktails, glasses of wine, or bottles of beer as I could handle, but I settled on a seltzer water instead. I made myself a quick dinner and spent the rest of the night lying in bed.

I flipped through the photos and videos I'd recorded on my phone of the day's activities. Multiple selfies with June, each of us making funny faces; videos of Peter walking through a few of his poses, punches, and kicks; and images of the moment Peter's taekwondo instructor handed him the coveted yellow belt.

I tried not to overthink my impulse to share Peter's accomplishments with Anissa. I was proud of him and wanted to share his accomplishment with someone. I sent her a short video of Peter attempting to kick through a thin, wooden board.

I could have left it at that, but I kept going: *I saw Peter get his yellow belt today,* I texted her. *You were right – I should make more of an effort to see them.*

I stared at my phone's screen and chewed on my lower lip. I didn't have alcohol to blame for my next actions. I typed out one, final text: *I miss you.*

I continued to stare at my phone and silently willed for something to happen.

My chest tightened and I sat up in bed when three little dots appeared on my text thread. After so much dismissal and rejection and avoidance, something was finally happening. Anissa was writing me back.

I sat in bed, clutching my phone, my heart in my throat, as I waited. What was she going to write back? Had she accepted my apology? Did she miss me, too?

My mind leapt ahead to the following day. Maybe she wasn't working, and we could spend the day together. Maybe we could take a picnic lunch to a local park. Maybe we could go on another trip up north. Maybe her nieces and nephews wanted a pool party and we could spend time with her family.

I began to visualize what I wanted to say and do the first time I saw her. The apology I had wanted to give at baggage claim reformulated in my brain. I would keep apologizing as long as it took for her to trust me again.

But then, the message box with its three little dots disappeared.

## CHAPTER SEVENTEEN

Gemma leaned against the beverage cart in the back of the plane and shifted her weight from one foot to the other as the cupboards and cubbies around us rattled and shook. Our flight that afternoon was unusually bumpy. Rough air had its advantages though, as beverage service was typically suspended for the duration.

"We make excuses all the time with this job. How we're forced to put our life on hold because of our schedules. I'd been resisting it for too long," she said, "but as soon as I saw his handsome face on the website, I knew I had to have him."

She swiped her fingers across her phone and tilted the screen so I could see the picture for myself.

"He's very cute," I approved. "But are you sure you're ready to deal with all that hair?"

Gemma pulled her phone back and gazed fondly at the screen. "Wouldn't you put up with a lot more to have this guy waiting for you when you got home?"

"Does he cook dinner?" I laughed. "If so, maybe I'll get a dog, too."

"The shelter said I can pick him up on Saturday if you want to tag along?" she offered.

It hadn't escaped my notice that ever since Gemma had over-shared about the bingo game in the Detroit airport bathroom, my friend blamed herself for what had happened with Anissa and had been desperate to make it up to me. First, there was Lara and the Mile High Club. More recently, Gemma had been inviting me to all of her non-work activities. Yoga classes. A rock climbing gym. A manicure and pedicure. A dim sum cooking class. It was like she'd purchased a Groupon for how to apologize to a friend.

I pressed my hand against the galley wall to steady myself when the plane shuddered from another rough pocket of air. "Thanks for the invite, but I promised Dawn we'd hang out on Saturday."

The month had passed and with it came a whole new flying schedule. I hadn't bid on any lines with overnight stays in different cities, and I was going to try to take less on-call days so I could be a more steady presence in my niece and nephew's lives. And if Dawn actually went through with her divorce, I wanted to be there for her. For all the heartache that had come with meeting Anissa, at least it had helped me recognize the importance of family. Even though I returned nightly to an empty apartment—with the exception of my turtle, Honey—I wasn't really alone.

"Fun! What's the family activity this week?" Gemma asked.

"We're taking June and Peter to the zoo."

My friend practically clapped with excitement. "Oh, I love the Detroit zoo! It has all my favorites. The penguins and polar bears. The big cats. The primate pavilion," she listed off. "Make sure you go to the butterfly garden, too. Your niece and nephew will love it."

The muscles in my mouth twitched. Just the innocent mentioning of a butterfly house pulled too fresh and raw emotions to the surface. But Gemma had no way of knowing that, and I wasn't going to tell her. She'd already beat herself up about my curtailed relationship too much.

"Look alive, ladies." Kent rushed into the already cramped space of the rear galley. "Someone in First Class got sick."

Even though it was a new month and a new schedule, we'd been able to secure another day of the week of flying together.

I waved off my friend. "Why are you telling us? That's your section, buddy."

Kent made a frustrated noise. "Don't you have a bingo square or something?"

I shook my head. "I'm done with that. It screwed up everything."

"I *really* think you should help them out," Kent said through clenched teeth.

I narrowed my eyes shrewdly. "You're just passing off one of your pukey passengers on me. They must really be a mess."

Kent sighed loudly. "You're ruining everything," he complained. "She asked specifically for you."

The pronoun reveal had me standing up straighter. "Who?"

"She's in 4C." Kent didn't answer my question; he plopped an extra barf bag and a package of wet naps into my hand.

My legs felt unsteady as I walked down the airplane's center aisle from the rear of the plane. Even without the rough air, my body would have wobbled. My throat tightened in anticipation with each unsure step.

I stopped just short of the fourth row. The woman in 4C had her head in her hands. My eyes started at her canvas slip-ons and her slender ankle. Her skinny jeans left a few inches of tanned ankle bare. I traveled up the denim calf and thigh. My gaze stopped at her hands and the multiple rings and metal bracelets. Her black, glossy hair was down, but she'd tucked it behind her ears—probably to keep her hair out of the way while she got sick.

I cleared my throat. What was I supposed to say?

The woman in 4C slowly turned her head toward me. Her caramel-colored eyes were bloodshot and her mascara had begun to travel down her cheeks. Her skin was considerably paler than its normal golden bronze hue. She was still beautiful though.

"Your Dramamine didn't work?"

Anissa groaned a non-answer and pressed her forehead against the seatback in front of her.

"This isn't your normal seat," I couldn't help observing.

"I'm lucky I got a seat at all," she mumbled. "I had to finagle my way onto this flight. All of your other flights out of Detroit were booked this week."

I had a myriad of questions for her, but it was obvious that her air sickness wasn't an act. I gently placed my hand on her arm. "I'll get you a cool washcloth for the back of your neck and see if I can find some Vernors to settle your stomach."

Anissa grabbed my wrist before I could walk away. "Now you just have the Mile High Club to complete, right?" Her tone held no malice.

I blinked, letting her question roam around in my brain. "Did you … did you make yourself sick on purpose?"

"I didn't make myself puke," she corrected. "I just didn't do anything to make sure it wouldn't happen."

"You didn't take your Dramamine," I spoke aloud as the puzzle pieces came together.

She shook her head.

I made a snap decision. "Come with me." I reached into her lap and unfastened Anissa's safety belt.

The passenger in seat 4D, who had been useless up to this point, finally noticed his seatmate's distress. He, too, unfastened his seatbelt and together we gently raised Anissa out of her seat. Luckily she had upgraded to the First Class cabin. I could only imagine the disaster she would have orchestrated if she'd been in a middle seat in Economy.

The Flight Gods were displeased that day, and the plane continued to hit pockets of rough air as I assisted Anissa's shuffling walk to the front galley. I pulled down the seat on one of the flight crew jump-seats and eased Anissa back down in the leather chair.

I pressed a new paper vomit bag into her hands and dug around in the beverage cart until I found the familiar ginger ale aluminum can. I dumped its contents into a plastic cup and delivered it to Anissa.

"Small sips," I encouraged.

Anissa wrapped both hands around the glass to keep it steady while the plane continued to shake. I watched her gingerly bring the plastic cup to her pursed lips.

I chewed on my lower lip. "So, is this a coincidence or something else?"

Anissa shook her head. "Something else." Her voice sounded as rough as the mid-flight turbulence.

I waited for more, but she didn't elaborate.

"Does this mean you're not mad at me anymore?" I ventured to ask.

She took another measured sip of the ginger ale. "I'm still mad," she qualified. "But I'd hate to see all your hard work go to waste. Besides, how else could I be sure you didn't sleep with someone else next month? Oh, God," she mumbled just before another wave of nausea hit.

She handed off the ginger ale and opened the new barf bag just in time. I kneeled beside her and rubbed small circles across her back while she continued to puke into the little white bag.

"I hope you remember this sacrifice," she mumbled into the bag.

I helped pull back her hair to keep it out of her face. She sounded so miserable, I tried not to laugh. "You're quite the martyr."

"Just give me a second, and I'll be ready for the Mile High Club."

I smiled wistfully at her singular determination. I didn't have the heart to tell her that the month was already over. I'd let my bingo card go unfinished, and I hadn't re-entered the contest for the current month.

I pressed my lips against her sweaty temple. "Don't worry. There's no rush."

# EPILOGUE

Her hands were on me the moment the flimsy bathroom door shut behind us. She tugged at the front of my uniform shirt until the bottom hem yanked free from my pencil skirt. I helped her efforts by unbuttoning the top few buttons of my blouse. There wasn't time to unbutton the rest. Her greedy hand dove into my cleavage and her fingers slid between my naked breast and the cup lining of my beige bra.

I wasn't checking off a bingo square. I'd given up the game. In fact, I'd let the previous month lapse without collecting any winnings. It had become a point of contention between us. Anissa didn't understand me forfeiting the contest money I'd legitimately earned, but my conscience wouldn't allow me to financially benefit from meeting and dating her.

Our work schedules changed every month, which could make it incredibly frustrating if we'd been dating someone with a more traditional job. But since both of our schedules were ever-changing, we actually could coordinate those schedules to match up. I didn't bid on lines that had me working most of her flights—that would have been too distracting—but I could find layovers and multi-day trips that had us in the same cities at the same time. It was far from perfect, but neither were we.

I let my head fall back as nimble fingers twisted my pebbled nipple. Anissa seized the opportunity to press her mouth against the side of my neck. She sucked on the skin while she continued to maul my breast beneath my bra.

"No hickies," I protested weakly, although I really didn't care what she did to me as long as she didn't stop.

She bit down harder in defiance of my words, and licked against the tender spot. "Isn't that what scarves are for?" came her cheeky reply.

I was ready to turn the tables on her, but a knock on the bathroom door made me pause.

"Hey guys?" I heard my friend Gemma's voice through the cheaply constructed door. "We're going to being landing soon."

"Thanks, Gemma," I called back. "I-I'm just helping a passenger with something. We'll be right out."

"O-okay," Gemma returned. I could hear the anxiety in her tone.

"Not very convincing," Anissa breathed against my neck.

"I hate to disappoint you, babe," I retorted, "but we're not fooling anyone."

"Good."

Anissa grabbed the bottom hem of my skirt and pulled the material up my hips. I was thankful for the stretch material that, among other things, allowed for more movement.

Anissa paused long enough to admire her work. Without having to look in a mirror, I knew I was a disheveled mess. My skirt was hiked up over my hips. My normally pale skin would be flushed with arousal. My shirt was untucked and unbuttoned obscenely low. My right breast spilled over the top of my bra. And hidden beneath my nylons, my underwear was a sodden mess.

"The nylons are sexy, but they get in the way," she told me.

"They're company policy," I retorted. "You wouldn't want me getting in trouble, would you?"

She cocked her head to the side. "What's your company's policy about having sex with a customer mid-flight?"

"At least I'm not fraternizing with co-workers anymore," came my cheeky reply.

Anissa pressed her canines against my neck and nipped at my pale skin. "You'd better not," she growled.

Her hands tight at my hips and her possessive growl made me shiver.

Anissa jerked away when the whole plane seemed to shudder. A loud thunking noise reminded me of how close we were to landing.

"Landing gear," I thought aloud.

"Guess I'd better make this quick," Anissa rasped.

She thrust a solid hand down the front of my nylons and her fingers worked past the top of my underwear to my naked sex. I heard her quiet groan when she discovered the liquid that had accumulated between my thighs.

"Fuck, you're wet," she hissed.

I leaned into her arm. "It's all for you."

Her free arm wrapped tight around my waist. My backside pressed hard against the bathroom sink. I tried to spread my legs for her, but between the tight confines of the airplane bathroom and my sheer nylons, there was little else I could do.

Her fingers moved quickly inside me. It was inelegant and rough; her knuckles dug into my pelvic bone, but her curling fingers had located the extra sensitive anterior location in my sex. I knew her wrist must have felt like it was breaking, but she didn't let on or complain.

A nimble thumb swiped against my clit and didn't stop. Anissa covered my mouth with her own to muffle the noise of my obvious pleasure. The constant churning of the plane's turbofan engines were no match for the sounds I wanted to let loose.

I tried to be quiet. I tried to not slam my palms against the narrow sink area. Over two hundred passengers and two of my friends were on the other side of the flimsy plastic door. But if anything, that singular realization prompted me to orgasm more quickly rather than turn me off.

Anissa's fingers stilled inside me as my muscles spasmed around her. She continued to stroke my clit, but only until I could take no more.

Our foreheads lightly touched together. I was sure mine was a sweaty mess, but I was too exhausted to care.

"You're amazing," I breathed out.

"Glad I convinced you to have sex in a port-a-potty?"

Her question pulled a quiet laugh from my lips. "I can't feel my legs."

"I was about to say the same thing about my right hand," she chuckled.

I brought her aforementioned hand up to my mouth and kissed it. Her warm, hazel eyes widened as I drew her index and middle finger into my mouth. I lightly sucked on her fingers, tasting myself on her digits.

Anissa bit down on her lower lip. "*Fuck*. Are you sure we have to go back out there so soon?"

"I'm on the clock, and you have to return to your seat, Ms. Khoury."

"Always such a rule follower," she sighed. "Okay. So, how do we do this? Does one of us go out there and then the other person waits for a while before leaving?"

I pulled my skirt down and wiggled it back into place. "You act as if I'm the expert at this."

Anissa wrapped her fingers around my biceps and drew me in close. Her lips brushed against mine. "Are you still having lunch with me on our layover?"

"Only if you let me pay."

Anissa laughed and playfully pushed me, although in our tight confines, there wasn't really anyplace for me to go. "Not a chance. I've got those Flight Gods to appease."

I stuck out my lower lip. "What about appeasing me?"

Anissa wiggled close again, close enough to kiss the tip of my nose. "I thought I'd just done that."

After a final lingering kiss, I exited the bathroom first. I figured a flight attendant would draw less attention than a beautiful passenger. I calmly strode down the center aisle. We were in our final descent, yet I had to remind a few passengers to return their seats to the upright position or to stow their laptops.

The pounding of my heart had nearly returned to normal by the time I slipped into my jump-seat at the front of the plane. Kent and Gemma were already fastened into their respective seats.

Kent curled his lip at my arrival. "Still think it's romantic, Gemma?"

My friend sighed dreamily. "Yep."

"Fix your lipstick, Alice," Kent scowled. "You're a mess."

I wiped the pad of my thumb across my bottom lip. A bright pink color stained the skin. "It's not mine," I couldn't help brag.

From my jump-seat I had an unobstructed view of the First Class cabin. Anissa had returned to her seat and was trying to look as nonchalant as possible. Her hair was a little disheveled, but only just so. Her lipstick had been kissed off her mouth, but I doubted anyone but me would have noticed.

I stared in her direction until she spotted me. When I caught her eye, she pursed her lips and blew me a kiss. While still strapped to my jump-seat, I pretended to flail my arms in the air to capture the airborne kiss, like a baseball player catching a foul-tipped ball.

"Lesbians," I heard Kent mutter in disgust.

I wasn't going to apologize for being happy. I ignored Kent's jab and shared a happy, dopey smile with the woman in 3B.

## ABOUT THE AUTHOR

Eliza Lentzski is the author of lesbian fiction, romance, and erotica including the best-selling *Winter Jacket* and *Don't Call Me Hero* series. She publishes urban fantasy and paranormal romance under the penname E.L. Blaisdell. Although a historian by day, Eliza is passionate about fiction. She was born and raised in the upper Midwest, which is often the setting for her novels. She currently lives in Boston with her wife and their cat, Charley.

Follow her on Twitter and Instagram, @ElizaLentzski, and Like her on Facebook (http://www.facebook.com/elizalentzski) for updates and exclusive previews of future original releases.

http://www.elizalentzski.com

Printed in Great Britain
by Amazon